Books by Patricia Zelver
The Honey Bunch
The Happy Family

THE HAPPY FAMILY

THE HAPPY FAMILY

BY PATRICIA ZELVER

AN ATLANTIC MONTHLY PRESS BOOK
LITTLE, BROWN AND COMPANY
BOSTON · TORONTO

COPYRIGHT © 1972 BY PATRICIA ZELVER

ALL RIGHTS RESERVED. NO PART OF THIS BOOK MAY BE REPRODUCED IN ANY FORM OR BY ANY ELECTRONIC OR MECHANICAL MEANS INCLUDING INFORMATION STORAGE AND RETRIEVAL SYSTEMS WITHOUT PERMISSION IN WRITING FROM THE PUBLISHER, EXCEPT BY A REVIEWER WHO MAY QUOTE BRIEF PASSAGES IN A REVIEW.

LIBRARY OF CONGRESS CATALOG CARD NO. 75-175481

T03/72

FIRST EDITION

Lines from "White Rabbit": © 1966 by Copperpenny Music Pub. Co., Inc., and Irving Music, Inc. (BMI). Words and music by Grace Slick

ATLANTIC–LITTLE, BROWN BOOKS
ARE PUBLISHED BY
LITTLE, BROWN AND COMPANY
IN ASSOCIATION WITH
THE ATLANTIC MONTHLY PRESS

*Published simultaneously in Canada
by Little, Brown & Company (Canada) Limited*

PRINTED IN THE UNITED STATES OF AMERICA

For Al

THE HAPPY FAMILY

PART ONE

1

IT was the last day of exams, then the Christmas holidays would start. Always a melancholy time, Professor Eldridge thought, as he sat at his desk making out grades. His teaching assistant had come down with the flu and was not here to advise him on who deserved what. He himself, noted for his witty, learned lectures, scarcely knew his undergraduate students. He did not want to know them; they were a scruffy lot nowadays. Moreover, he needed to reserve his time and energy and emotions for his book, *Poet and Pulpit: A Study of Crosscurrents in American Colonial Literature*.

The carillon rang the time. Three o'clock. Then it began a medley of Christmas carols. He gazed out of the window, through Romanesque arches decorated with arabesques, at the deserted Inner Quad. Islands of stiff palms encircled by beds of bright calendulas; farther on, the cloistered arcades, the sloping red tile roofs, the gilded mosaics of the chapel glittering in the December sunshine.

The weather, which encouraged hedonism, kept him from his work. But the weather was also deceptive, mercurial. It changed from day to day, rather than from season to season. One never knew what to expect; one wore the wrong clothes. Some bug was always going around. Right now he felt a chill; he had probably caught the T.A.'s virus. As soon as he got home he would have a strong drink, a hot bath, and go to bed.

There was a knock on the door. He quickly bent his head over the papers; muttered, "Come in, please." His voice was weary, protectively pompous.

A girl marched into the room. Eldridge glanced up, made a half movement of standing, gestured her to a chair. He recognized the face but could not place the name. His eyes turned back to the papers; he heard her sit down. Without looking up he said, "May I do something for you, Miss — Miss — ?"

"Oliver."

Something in her tone made him look up — this time with mild curiosity. She sat stiffly before him, exposing a great deal of bare leg, not much of skirt. Her short, dark hair curled about an intense, strong-featured face. Attractive? Perhaps. But not his type, thank God. Basically stupid, he decided. The sort that would soon be married to a rich man, have too many babies; her boyishness — charming now — would turn hearty and graceless. She would continue to be positive in a dreary way, her youthful passion gone. Ah, Time, the destroyer of all things, he thought, allowing himself a moment to admire the sturdy American-girl legs, the athletic thighs. It was almost a duty; such moments of sensual pleasure were far too fleeting, knowing what he knew.

"I should like to find out why you gave me an F on my last paper."

The T.A. read and graded the papers; Eldridge reviewed them hastily. Occasionally he added comments. But he could hardly be expected to recall individual ones unless they were brilliant — a phenomenon which, in English 188: Early American Novel, seldom occurred. He played for time. With a carelessly disguised false innocence he said, "Did I do that?"

Miss Oliver lunged toward him; the menace of her movement, her assassin's expression, caused him to recoil. She flung the paper down upon the desk, then resumed her stiff position on the chair. Violence evidently not an immediate threat, he collected himself. He toyed with his spectacles, put them on, picked up the paper, scrutinized it, recognized his handwriting, admired his pithy style:

"Really, Miss Oliver!"
"The study of English literature is one thing, your personal emotions quite another."
"Strong feeling is not a substitute for clear thinking."

He sighed, put down the paper. "It's extraordinarily simple," he said. "You didn't follow the assignment."
"It was a shitty assignment."
Oh, dear, this generation, Eldridge thought. A rich girl. He could tell from her voice as well as her costume. Permissive parents, undoubtedly. In her vernacular, a "Bad Scene." He said, "I asked you to relate the theological background of the Puritans to Hester Prynne's predicament."
There was a silence.
"You did not comply."
"What predicament?"
Genuine innocence, or false? He understood the latter. Yet he could not be sure. "Miss Oliver, I don't know what you mean. Have you read the book?"
"Yes, I read it." There was a kind of sincere amazement in her voice. "But I don't know what predicament she was in. So she got knocked up by that minister, what's his name —"
"Dimmesdale," he said mournfully.
"And they made her go around wearing that thing."
"You don't call that a predicament?" He was *almost* interested.
"I believe women should be as free as men. Hester Prynne was a fool."
"My dear Miss Oliver, I am not questioning your belief. But it is necessary to examine the situation in the light of the mores of the day. Could it be that you are without a sense of history?"
Silence.
"A sense of history, Miss Oliver, can help us understand our own mores more objectively. Moreover, we are none of us, even

yet, and despite your idealism, free of the heritage which is the background of *The Scarlet Letter*. It is part of us, Miss Oliver."

"I am attempting to make it not part of me."

Now he was truly bored. "Congratulations, Miss Oliver. I hope you succeed. I really do. But it has nothing to do with the fact that Hester Prynne was bound by her environment. It was that I wished you to comment upon. Could it be that you are lacking in imagination?"

"It doesn't matter what I'm lacking in, because I'm splitting —"

"Ah?"

"I'm quitting this — this factory."

"I trust not because of this little assignment." His tone was not compassionate.

"It's all bad vibes, Dr. Eldridge."

"I'm extremely relieved. Merry Christmas, Miss Oliver." He stood up, even gallantly extended a hand.

Which she took. "Merry Christmas, Dr. Eldridge. And Happy 1968."

2

In the "rich, permissive" home they waited. It was called Oonhall. The Olivers did not believe in the religious symbolism of Christmas, but they celebrated the feast enthusiastically, as their most important family rite. Hat, driving her pumpkin-colored Porsche, was on her way to join them. Battered luggage, bags of dirty laundry, tennis rackets and golf clubs almost hid her from view. Head skis curled over the back of the car; a bumper strip read MAKE LOVE, NOT WAR. Although momentous changes had taken place in her since she had seen her family last at Thanksgiving — she could easily, and with pleasure, foresee the Apocalypse — she could not imagine spending the holidays anywhere but at home.

Oonhall was in the foothills just outside of the growing suburban town of Los Robles. It was set upon five acres of what had once been country, what the Olivers still called "country," but what, in fact, was now part of the rapidly expanding San Francisco Peninsula. It was fifteen minutes by the new freeway to her house. She swung off the freeway on to the rural road and through the open gate of Oonhall. A sign upon the gate post said A MEMBER OF THE 4-H CLUB LIVES HERE.

She tore at high speed down the long, private drive. She passed the pinewoods and Becky's stable. In back of the stable was a jumble of empty, dung-encrusted cages, which had once contained rabbits, guinea pigs and hamsters; also, a broken dogcart, which her father, Teddy Oliver, had ordered from England, but which Hurwulf, the Oliver dog, had refused to pull. Farther up the hill was Loren's neatly tended herb garden. After this, the tennis court; after this, on the other side, a small, redwood shanty — Teddy's study, known as Fala, or "Hidden Place" in Oon. Beyond Fala, the Pasture, an unmowed acre of brown grass dotted with live oaks; in its midst, a rarely used swimming pool sick with black algae. Then a bend in the road revealed the large house, fitted into a hillside in layers as if it had grown there untended.

Teddy Oliver had designed the house himself, a task which Catherine, his wife, in her childbearing years, had left happily up to him. He had, at first, called in a fashionable architect and told him what he wanted. Nothing cold and modern and functional; nothing, in fact, which could be identified with any "period" at all. It was to have a decaying, haphazard look, as if it had somehow been happened upon among the oaks.

The architect had been delighted; a "decaying, haphazard look" would cost a great deal. He presented plans for what he considered to be a charming, informal country house. But his imagination failed; he had underestimated Teddy's daring. The drawings were "too architectural"; the architect, handsomely paid off, left with injured pride. Then Teddy, with a euphoria caused by the discovery of a latent talent, drew up his own plans, hiring an engineer only to see that the house would pass the building code and not fall down.

The basic, original structure was like a large, elegant barn; the closed-in porch, with its many panes of glass, added an airy look; a fanciful third-story turret with a widow's walk surrounded by an iron filigree fence — Loren's Tower — provided a Victorian Gothic touch.

The interior matched the exterior in its unpredictability. There were immense rooms with high-beamed ceilings and tiny, womblike chambers; there were narrow halls which turned corners, leading one unexpectedly into spacious, airy vestibules. There was a broad, straight staircase off the front hall and a hidden, curving, iron staircase off the back entrance, leading up to the Tower.

Light entered the dark redwood rooms mysteriously from clerestories and skylights; there were no vulgar "picture windows." But a miniature aperture in the living room precisely framed the shapeliest oak, if one stood in the proper place at the proper distance from it.

Teddy haunted junk stores and found discarded bathtubs with claw feet, marble basins, old iron barn hardware, an oak hatstand with a mirror for the hall. Antique porcelain knobs were attached to handmade doors of rough-sawn lumber. The warehouse, where his wife had stored the possessions she had inherited from the Laikens' Pacific Heights home, was explored. It yielded old chests, fiddleback chairs, wicker furniture from a country cottage, Oriental rugs to cover the pine floors and gold-leafed picture frames, from which Teddy removed sentimental oils of full-blown, Grecian-robed beauties decorating pastoral landscapes, replacing them, with the help of an art dealer in the city, with large, bright, nonobjective paintings by local artists.

There were also portraits of pioneer Laikens which Catherine had told him the San Francisco Historical Society had inquired after. She had ignored the letter; she would have been happy to have burned the portraits. Teddy had dissuaded her. Among them he had recently chosen Phineas Laiken, the founder of the family fortune, and hung him upon the living room wall.

Though Catherine had been an ordinary cook, her kitchen was not. The floor was pine; instead of modern cabinets, there were old-fashioned cupboards with glass doors. A heavy butcher's block, a marble pastry center, an extra bar sink from a hospital supply house and an antique poker table with the felt removed, surrounded by old, straight, farmhouse chairs, gave the kitchen a warm, used, family look.

If he had ever succeeded at anything, Teddy often thought, it had been Oonhall. It was so satisfactory that he even briefly considered becoming an architect. But this would have meant involving himself with other personalities, other tastes. Compromises!

Was it not enough to have designed such a home for his own family?

Until recently, Hat had thought so, too. But now, as she drove up before it, she saw it through other eyes. They were the eyes of the young man who had just liberated her mind and soul, and with whom she was in love. She had brought him home for a weekend and had found it necessary to apologize; it had been obvious that Oonhall's expensive rusticity was like Marie Antoinette playing shepherdess. It reeked of decadence, of money indulgently spent, epitomized, perhaps, by the portrait of Phineas, whose toughness had enabled him to survive the voyage around the Horn to the goldfields, and who had, she explained to the young man, exploited the poor Chinese for his own ends. Dignified, robust, utterly self-contained, this ruthless adventurer had gazed down at them from above the fireplace in the living room. Both young people had agreed that amends must be made.

Hat would make them. But now it was the Christmas season, and Oonhall's archaic splendor made it a most appropriate place to spend an archaic holiday. She would compensate for her bourgeois sentimentality later on.

She skidded to a stop on the graveled driveway. A wreath of field weeds hung upon the oversized front door. Clemente's work, she thought gaily. She climbed out of the Porsche and slammed its door. From an upstairs window, a round, dark face peered down: it was Mary Miller, the Olivers' "Mother's Helper."

A year ago, having exhausted all other minorities — Japanese, Chinese, Filipino, Mexican and Black — Teddy Oliver, at the suggestion of his neighbor, Mimi Alway, faced the last frontier and ordered Mary, a Hoopa Indian, from the Department of the Interior. Papers had to be signed, financial responsibility assumed, the home investigated. All this accomplished, Mary had arrived. She was shy, taciturn and unresponsive to the family's friendly overtures. She worked hard — scrubbed, cleaned and cooked — but her unresponsiveness had never changed.

This had disappointed the Olivers. Did not Teddy sponsor

good causes? Had he not brought up his daughters to be free of racial prejudices? Did they think any less of someone because she did housework for money?

Perhaps she was lonely? The Always had an Indian girl the same age; it was arranged for them to "get together" on afternoons off. Mrs. Alway had driven them to Carmel for an outing; they had sat together in the back seat without saying a word. It seemed that they were from different tribes or something — Mimi had reported with a wry little sigh. Nothing had come of it.

On Thursdays, Mary's full day off, Teddy drove her into Palo Alto in his Rover and gave her the money for the return cab fare. There was no public transportation in the Hills. The cab fare was ten dollars, but it was worth it, he explained to Mary, not to have a noisy, smelly bus driving past his home.

Teddy dropped her at the Greyhound station, from where she went to San Francisco. She would meet her brother Pete at the American Indian Center and attend evening services at the American Indian Baptist Church. This was all the Olivers knew of Mary's private life.

Mary reminded him, Teddy told his daughters, of one of those wooden peasant dolls you bought in Chinatown. The doll opened up and inside was a smaller, exact replica of it; this one opened and inside was an even smaller replica, and so on, until, at last, there was only a small, smooth, enigmatic wooden ball. One felt this way about Mary. No matter how much one tried, one got nowhere. How frustrating life was, despite well-intentioned efforts! But they must continue these efforts, they must not give up, it was part of the burden of being rich and secure to break down the barrier between the advantaged and the disadvantaged. What other hope was there in a world racked by wars and internal division?

Now Mary observed Hat from the window; then she closed it quietly and returned to her desk. She was practicing Intermediate Typing on Hat's old Remington. Unknown to the Olivers, she no longer traveled to the city on her day off; she left the Greyhound Station and walked two blocks to University Avenue to the Girl Friday Secretarial School. Tomorrow there would be a typing test; she could not afford to waste time greeting Hat or discussing the problems of emerging minorities with her.

Downstairs, in the large living room with its cathedral ceiling, sat Loren Oliver, who was fifteen, Clemente Lawrence, who was twenty, and Hurwulf, a fat, aging golden retriever. Clemente sat on a high-backed wing chair, sewing a patch on Becky's jeans. Her pale blond hair hung down her back like a silken sheet. She wore a blue cotton smocklike shift, the color of her eyes, and red Moroccan slippers on her tiny feet.

Loren lay upon the slipcovered sofa reading *The Mystic Mandrake,* one of a supply of books she had recently sent away for to the Elixir of Life store on Haight Street in the city.

Clemente said, "Do you think we should put the Monopoly game away?"

"What for? For Hat?"

"I was thinking of Aunt Harriet."

"For Aunt Harriet! Just because you're losing, Clemente! I have a monopoly of the railroads and Teddy's built two hotels. He always overextends himself. I think I have him cornered, but he doesn't know it. He'd be absolutely furious if you picked it up!" Loren rose from the sofa and wandered over to the refectory table, where the Monopoly game was spread out, and stared at it with a stern eye. She was small and compact, dark-eyed, with long, unkempt, rippling hair; she was dressed like a gypsy in an ankle-length red cotton skirt, a soiled white blouse which had belonged to her mother, and gold bangles in her pierced ears and on her thin brown arms. Her feet were bare and dirty.

She spun about in a frenzied little dance.

> *The Aunt, the Aunt, the ghastly Aunt*
> *She's coming to haunt*
> *And taunt*
> *And flaunt —*

"You've forgotten that I've met her," said Clemente placidly. "She was here for Catherine's Oonwald."

"Which she insisted on calling a funeral!"

"Did you explain there is no word for 'dead' in Oon?"

"I did more than that. I explained what Oonwald meant. 'Farewell to the Departed!' I even translated a Duna for her. I told her it was a kind of a hymn, which, of course, it really isn't. She said she preferred the Unitarian service for the dead."

"Clyde thought you shouldn't try to convert Aunt Harriet — at such a time," said Clemente gently.

"Oh, Clyde! He's just a caveman, basically. Let him stick to what he's good at — mending our fences and curing the swimming pool. Instead, he watches over us like a duenna. He acts as if Teddy isn't responsible for bringing us up. He actually had the nerve to tell Teddy I shouldn't be allowed to drop out of high school!"

"Forever why?" said Clemente, astonished.

"He doesn't think Teddy is capable of educating me."

"Well, he isn't," said Hat crisply as she entered the room.

"Welcome home, sister dear," said Loren, collapsing back into the depths of the sofa.

"Oh, Hat!" cried Clemente, her blue eyes sparkling with pleasure.

Hat and Clemente had been neighbors as children and "best friends" ever since. They were utterly different. Hat was tall and dark, with a direct, fearless air; Clemente, small and round and soft and golden like an angel.

"Teddy will begin and then forget to continue," Hat said, sitting down cross-legged on the floor. Hurwulf rose stiffly and thrust her moist muzzle into Hat's lap; she scratched Hurwulf's ears absentmindedly.

"It depends upon your definition of education," Loren said. "We have learned more from Teddy than from any stupid school. Besides, I know how to read and to observe. That's all that matters."

"I don't see how observing helps since you hardly ever leave the house except to visit the garbage dump or the Goodwill," said Hat. "I'm not for school myself. I shall make an announcement very soon about all that. But there are things going on in the

Outbar, as you insist on calling it, which you know nothing about."

"You're sounding more Big Sisterish every day. I know more about the Outbar than you may think. For one thing, you can learn a lot at garbage dumps. What people throw away can be more revealing than what they keep. You could do a thesis on it. I have other ways of finding things out, too."

"Sneaky, horrid ways!"

Loren smiled.

"Listening in on phone calls, reading people's mail!"

"We can discuss my character defects later. What's important now is Aunt Harriet's approaching visit. She freaked out at the Oonwald, but that didn't stop her from staying a month, thereby causing Teddy to take to drink."

"Oh dear," said Clemente.

Hat laughed. "Do you know why I'm named Harriet? She appeared at Catherine's bedside just after I was born and strongly intimated I should be named after her. Catherine found it easier to give in on what she called 'unimportant matters.' She did not consider that it might be important to me. Now I have to go through life with a name that reminds me of her."

"Does Clemente know why she's coming?" said Loren.

"For Christmas?" said Clemente.

"Of course, for Christmas. But she is also talking about Teddy remarrying. Teddy told me."

"Oh," said Clemente softly.

"It's my opinion," Loren said, "that she doesn't really want Teddy to marry at all, that, in fact, she never wanted him to marry in the first place."

Clemente looked shocked.

"It's my opinion that she has an unnatural, incestuous crush on Teddy."

"Everyone loves Teddy," said Clemente. "It's not *unnatural* to love him."

"And, at the moment, events are causing her to press her suit."

"To what?" said Clemente.

"Aunt Harriet has to find a new place to live. That spooky

Lexington Arms, which she calls home, is being torn down. One weak word from Teddy and she'll move in with us to care for the motherless brood. She refuses to recognize that the motherless brood is managing nicely, and that, as soon as Hat gets out of school for the summer, the motherless brood is going around the world together. Teddy and I were planning our trip last night."

"Which reminds me of my announcement," said Hat. "I am out of school. You are speaking to a Dropout."

"Oh, Hat, you're not serious?" cried Clemente.

"I'm deadly serious," said Hat. "That's what makes me different from Loren. I'm a Dropout with a purpose in life."

"There is nothing more boring than people with purposes," said Loren.

"But you were doing so nicely. We were so proud of you, Hat, when you were accepted at Stanford."

"You're right, Clemente. I was doing nicely for a time. It isn't hard. But that's just it. I'm not going to be 'nice' any more." Her voice grew fervent. "Being nice, for a girl, is just doing what the Establishment has programmed you to do. What does it mean? You go to college and take a few courses in art and English or music, then you marry a *nice* college boy and settle down and have a *nice* family. And that's it. Anything else is suspect. But I'm going to tell you more in detail, Clemente, as soon as we can have a private rap. I want you to understand. You lead such a sheltered life, you have no idea what's going on behind the scenes. We're in a Revolution, and I intend to stand up and be counted. Blacks, Chicanos, women — we all have to fight for our freedom. Take Mary Miller, for example, whom we have helped to enslave —"

"Mary has a new perm and is back-combing her hair," said Loren brightly.

"Did you tell her it looked better Indian style?" said Hat.

"She is very proud of it," Clemente said.

"She ought to be proud of her own ethnic background. I'm going to have a talk with her. She must develop more of a social conscience."

"Social consciences are a drag," said Loren. "I'm glad I don't have one. But now that you're a Dropout, Hat, we should get Teddy away at once. We can take Becky out of school; she'll be better off for it. We'll leave as soon as we celebrate this pagan rite."

"I shall miss you," Clemente said with a little sigh.

Both girls turned toward her. "Clemente is coming too, isn't she?" said Loren.

"Am I?"

"Of course she is," said Hat. "If we go."

"If?" said Loren.

Hat's face darkened. "It just might be that I have other plans," she hesitated. "It just might be if I go anywhere, I'll go by myself, though it may not have occurred to Teddy that I could manage alone."

"It could be very dangerous to abandon Teddy at this moment," Loren said savagely. "We can end up with a Wicked Stepmother if we're not careful."

"And Teddy isn't like other grown-ups," said Clemente. "It would be fun to go with him. We can finish the Oon legends along the way. I haven't done an illustration in months."

"Don't worry, I bet Teddy hasn't written a word, either," Hat said. "He's always getting ideas and working up others and then finking out. Remember, Loren, when he decided we ought to have a religious education?"

"Not *religious* — 'the myths of our culture.' "

"He started to read the Bible to us every day," said Hat. "We got as far as the 'begats' and he lost interest."

"That is exactly why he needs us," said Loren firmly. "He is impulsive; he has to be watched. He could do something disastrous for all concerned, and then regret it later, when it is too late!"

"Where's Becky?" said Hat to change the subject. Only moments before she had looked forward to Oonhall, to sharing the traditional rites with her family. Now Loren's concern about their father seemed like misdirected passion — childish, trivial — and Clemente's responses parochial. Perhaps coming home for Christmas had been a mistake. It was not a pleasant thought. If one no longer cared about what one had once cared about deeply, how could one trust the future? Would anything ever seem permanent or sacred again? She stared, very briefly, into an abyss.

Loren said, "Where is she always?"

Hat said, "Who?"

"You just asked where Becky was, for heaven's sake!"

"Did I? I wonder why? Well, then, where is she?"

"At Debbie Alway's house, of course," said Loren, giving Hat a searching look. "Always at the Always. That could be her theme song. It is her home away from home." As if to divert Hat from treasonable thoughts, she began to chant:

> *Always at the Always*
> *Always — away.*
> *Away at the Always*
> *Always away.*

"Shut up, Loren," shouted Hat.

"Then she comes back and bores us with the preparations for that ghastly Linda Alway's debut."

"She's not at the Always today," said Clemente in a calm, motherly, peacemaking voice. "Clyde took her to Hollister to the ranch. She had never been up in his plane before. They are going to bring back a Christmas Tree."

Hat lit a cigarette. The abyss had vanished, but a kind of sadness lingered on. Yet there was nothing to be done; one could not go backwards. Her sense of personal loss was part of her new and broader perspective. She said, "Clyde took Becky? I don't see how he can stand her. She's becoming more a part of the Establishment every day."

"Becky is only twelve," said Clemente.

"Twelve can be a very dangerous age," said Loren. "As for Clyde O'Mahoney, he's as bad as Aunt Harriet. He and Becky are a perfect pair. It's too bad there's such an age difference, they could get married."

Hat yawned. "Really, Loren, you're paranoid. What you don't seem to realize is that none of this matters. Clyde and Aunt Harriet and Becky will probably be liquidated eventually, as useless parasites feeding on society. At the very least, they'll be put out to pasture. And you will, too, if you don't develop more insight into the nature of the Power Structure."

"What about Clemente? Will Clemente be liquidated?"

"Oh, I'm sure I will be," said Clemente modestly.

"Clemente is not politically aware, but she's not on her own private Power Trip. There will always be room for people to help the new leaders. Clemente serves others, which is more than you do."

Clemente smiled gratefully at Hat.

"What about Hurwulf? Does Hurwulf have a place in your Revolution?" Loren rose languidly from the sofa and lay down beside the dog. "Are you going to have poor old Hurwulf liquidated, Hat?" Hurwulf rolled over and Loren patted her throbbing belly. "The last time Aunt Harriet was here she made us a cake and Hurwulf ate it all up. Didn't you, Hurwulf, darling?" Hurwulf's eyes grew glazed, her tongue panted; she thumped her heavy tail against the floor. "It's because we had her spayed after her last litter; she has no sex life. Now food has become her main passion. Aunt Harriet was furious; perhaps she sensed a correlate, having no sex life and being overweight herself. Listen, Hat!" — Loren sat up abruptly.

"I seem to have no choice," said Hat with a bored yawn.

"Fuck Clyde *and* Aunt Harriet, you may liquidate them both. But please spare Hurwulf! Let Hurwulf enjoy her useless old age! Will you, please, Hat? Promise?"

"Fuck you, Loren," said Hat.

Clemente put down her sewing. "We mustn't quarrel. It's Christmastime," she said.

3

"Have you ever considered remarrying?" said Harriet Oliver to her younger brother Teddy. It was after dinner on Harriet's first night at Oonhall; they were sitting on the glassed-in porch. Harriet was sipping a small glass of port with her dessert — a generous piece of the Blum's Chocolate Mocha Delight she had brought with her as a gift. Teddy, who did not eat desserts, was having a Scotch. In the distance the faint hum of the freeway could be heard through the still December air.

Harriet was in her middle fifties. She had white hair, was full-bosomed and plump. She was dressed in a plain, navy-blue silk "costume suit" and a single strand of imitation pearls. Her only coquetry was the powder-blue frames of her bifocals, whose rims were sprinkled with rhinestones; beneath these, her earnest blue eyes blinked with a vague wonderment. At the Olivers', this mannerism grew exaggerated, became almost a tic. They were the only family she had; she yearned to be among them, but they did not make her feel at ease. Her brother, for instance. She had always known he was smarter than she. Mama had said so; Mama had said he was "creative" and would do more than be just the owner of a small real estate office, like dear Papa. Mama had encouraged him to take the entrance exams for Stanford. How proud she had been when he was accepted! How proud Harriet had been, too; she was still proud of this dashing, if somewhat peculiar, brother. Why could he not let her simply bask in his superiority, as she so longed to do?

Teddy sat opposite her in a wicker chair — handsome, suntanned and lean. His unbarbered hair was still dark but for a shock of gray which fell in a lock over his forehead. He was wearing a wrinkled seersucker jacket, a black knit tie in his sister's honor, and a pair of worn khaki pants. He was fifty but looked much younger.

Were it not for this youthful quality and elegance of manner he would look like Papa, she thought. The same green-gray eyes, the same long nose and thin mouth. Yes — if you squinted slightly and imagined him in Masonic robes. There was something sensual and Oriental about him, something dark and enigmatic. Like Papa. But, after all, weren't all men part of a secret order, moved by forces she would never hope to understand? It was just that Teddy, the only man she was close to, seemed, somehow, even more so.

She was not clever like Teddy, but she had been a librarian (she had retired early, rather than try to master the new computers); she had taken a Great Books course and had read some Freud. Even this great man, she had learned, had despaired when it came to genius. How could she, an old maid whose experience in life had been so limited, hope to presume? And yet, was there not something she could do, should do, for a widower and three motherless children? Certainly, in an ordinary situation (the Olivers being to her, extraordinary), she might have filled a useful role — most logically, the management of their household. But she had not received such an invitation; she had resigned herself by now to never receiving it. Still, the one gift she thought she possessed — that of down-to-earth, old-fashioned common sense, ought not to be wasted. She felt certain there were women after him; despite her love and admiration for her brother, she was not as certain of his judgment in such a matter. She could not quite have said why.

"Ought I to?" he said now, with a comic little sigh. He seemed at ease, entirely genial, which encouraged her not to shirk her duty.

"It has been three years, dear, since that dreadful accident. You must begin to think of yourself. There are so many lonely women — I know from experience — who would give anything to care for you. But you must be careful not to fall into the hands of the wrong one."

"How does one tell?"

She never quite knew when Teddy was serious, but she did know it was a serious matter and deserved, therefore, a serious reply. "That's just it. It is not easy," she said solemnly.

"Perhaps you could give me some guidelines."

"That's what makes it so hard, dear. Every woman has her own methods — her little tricks and snares. If she is not worthy, she will try to appear so. One has to look below the surface. I can only give you an opinion on an individual."

"Do you have one in mind?"

She paused, flustered. Then, "I am acquainted with many single ladies," she said with dignity. Then, daringly, "Hazel Henderson, for example."

There was a silence.

"You have not met Hazel, Teddy?"

"No, I don't believe I have had that honor."

"Such a lovely person. She belongs to my Study Group. She was widowed four years ago; her children have married and moved away. I'm not so stupid as to think any of my Study Group would do, but Hazel used to be a psychology teacher at a junior college. She's very modern — sometimes almost too much for some of us. She calls us the Senile Singles, as a joke, of course. She's trying to reorganize our group, make us more up-to-date. She read *The Prophet* to us at our last meeting. A few of the girls were shocked, but Hazel says we have to think of . . . such things . . . as beautiful. She's a very advanced thinker, Teddy."

"It sounds as if she is."

"If you like, I could arrange a meeting. Something that would seem . . . spontaneous. It seems such a pity for an eligible bachelor to go to waste when there are also . . . eligible ladies."

"You make me sound as if I am a natural resource."

"It isn't only you," she said shyly. "There are your girls." Though fond of children, she had always been cautious not to give advice on the bringing-up of her nieces; she had never felt it would be welcome and needed to protect herself from being told: how could *you* know?

Moreover, how could she? Yet was there not something in Teddy's present geniality which seemed to invite her to intrude? Was this perhaps his way of saying I need help? She set aside the Mocha Delight, took a deep breath, and assumed her duty.

"Poor, dear Catherine was never strong. Your children used to run about like little wild animals."

"Little wild animals have often seemed nicer to me than some of the products of our so-called 'civilization,' " said Teddy with a note of pride.

This was ignored. "I can remember them frolicking naked upon the lawn in the summertime."

"We dressed them in winter."

"But they are now getting to an age when they are in need of a woman's guidance. Loren, for instance. She looks like a gypsy and reads such odd books!"

"She is not without goals. I believe she is studying to become a witch."

"And Hat tells me she is not going back to Stanford after Christmas. What plans she may have I could not get out of her!"

"When you do, I would appreciate your letting me know."

"And now you've sent little Becky off with that man!"

"You mean Clyde?" Teddy seemed genuinely amused.

"I have always thought it strange, Teddy, that a man of his looks — so masculine-appearing, you know — so rugged — should hang around another family instead of creating one for himself."

"Are you trying to say that Clyde is queer?" he asked mischievously.

"You mean —?" Her hands fluttered toward the cake, then, with an exertion of will, she brought them back and settled them upon her lap. "I just said he was extremely masculine, such an outdoors man. He's like . . . one of those Marlboro ads on television," she ended limply.

"Yes, he is, isn't he? But he could be queer just the same. It isn't necessary to look or act effeminate. But what if he were? Becky would be perfectly safe, then, wouldn't she?"

Harriet gave a little gasp.

Teddy laughed. "I am only trying to expand your imagination a bit. I don't really know anything about Clyde's sex life, thank God. All I know is he is an old friend and we couldn't manage without him."

Harriet rallied. "I only meant that it is a bit odd."

"I suppose it is, in a way. But we are an odd family, aren't we? Nevertheless, I had the impression, except for lacking a wife and mother, that we are a happy one."

Harriet said nothing. Familial happiness was in the same category as the upbringing of children. She had not experienced it herself. She could not pretend to be informed about it.

Moreover, as it was practiced here at the Olivers, she was not sure she even approved of it. Their "happiness" hung in the air like an exotic scent; there was an aura of secrecy, of private ritual, like Papa's Lodge, from which, like Mama, she had been excluded. It was a mystery which both baffled and challenged her.

"Perhaps being happy makes you more vulnerable," she ventured.

"More vulnerable — to what?"

"To things that happen. You can't count forever on their going along the same way, can you? Hat is nineteen. And Loren and little Becky will grow up. What will you do then?"

Teddy's mouth tightened slightly. He rose, went to the wicker sideboard, and poured himself another drink. "I suppose there will be marriages. Grandchildren —" His voice remained genial. He sat down again, stirring his drink by revolving the glass in his hand.

"That's exactly what I mean, dear, about a woman's guidance. Such things don't just . . . happen. The right young men need to be encouraged. Do I sound dreadfully old-fashioned? I suppose

I do?" Nervously, she reached for the Chocolate Mocha Delight. "I don't know what is old-fashioned and what is not. We just . . . are."

Harriet munched on the cake in timid, chipmunk fashion; her blue eyes blinked in rhythm with her munching. Then she patted her lips with a white handkerchief. In what she considered a casual tone, she said, "Who, by the way, is that young man who hangs around Hat?"

"Which young man? There have been several."

"The one who looks like an orthodox rabbi."

"Perhaps he is a rabbi."

"He arrives on a motorcycle. A very large one. He wears a — a knife in his belt."

"I believe his name is Arab."

"Arab? Does he have a last name?"

"If he does, he doesn't use it. He's one of Hat's Resistance friends from Stanford. A nonstudent at the moment, I think. They are planning to overthrow the Establishment together."

"He and . . . Hat?"

"Oh, there are others. Dog and General Disarmament and Jack-from-out-of-Town. The General's in jail at the moment. He attacked a newspaper photographer when they picketed the R.O.T.C. He refused counsel and defended himself and lost gloriously. Hat was crushed; she wanted to go to jail, too, but she slept too late and missed the demonstration."

"I wish you wouldn't tease, Teddy. You have three daughters who will, since you were fortunate enough to marry a wealthy wife, come into a fortune. You lock yourself up all day in your study and come out at night to play games. You are perhaps shirking a responsibility." She reached for the cake again. "I say three girls, yet there always seem to be four. Does Clemente Lawrence . . . live with you?"

"Clemente? No, I don't think so. She has her own mother. You remember her parents, I think. They lived here in the hills when Clemente and Hat were little. Then they were divorced and moved away. But Clemente and Hat have kept up their friendship all these years. Her mother, as a matter of fact, will join us at

Christmas. She spends most of her time in foreign parts, doing research for her books. She has collected at least two husbands in the meantime, but she is single at the moment. She has reassumed her first married name for professional reasons." He considered. "Yes, now that I think of it, perhaps Clemente does live with us. She comes for extended visits; this one has lasted a year. I think she finds us jollier — and more stable."

"Do you support her, Teddy?"

"Clemente's father has remarried and vanished. But her mother is the soul of generosity. When she receives her royalties, once or twice a year, she showers Clemente with presents — art books, jewelry — once an Irish wolfhound puppy from Dublin who died in customs."

"What about her daily room and board?"

"Clemente pays for that — by being Clemente."

Harriet sighed. "I have always thought there is something not entirely open about that girl. She is hard to know."

"That is because you are not used to angels." Teddy rose and added more whiskey to his glass.

"Are you drinking a great deal, dear?"

"Not . . . ordinarily."

Should she comment on this? Papa had drunk more than had been good for him; perhaps it ran in the family. But Teddy did not like to be compared to Papa. She did so want to be sensitive to his peculiar moods. At the same time she did not want to shirk her duty. "Perhaps you are a bit nervous; perhaps there is another reason for Mrs. Lawrence's visit?"

"Besides visiting Clemente? If there is, I am not aware of it."

"Oh, Teddy. Men are so innocent. From what you have told me about her marital history, I should advise you to be on guard."

Teddy grimaced.

"Like her daughter, she may be looking for more stability."

"Leah thrives on instability, I'm happy to say."

"When women are lonely, they do desperate things —"

"I believe you are more on the side of lonely women than single men."

"I have an understanding in that direction."

"Moreover, I don't think you trust my judgment."

"Certainly, it was excellent the first time," she lied politely.

"I have sometimes wondered if you really think so."

Again, Harriet reached for the cake; this time she polished it off. "I'm sorry," she mumbled with her mouth full. "You know that isn't true. I'm sorry if you ever had the slightest suspicion that it could be."

"As I recall, you were disturbed because Catherine was a Roman Catholic," he said lazily.

"It was not our Tradition, Teddy. But she wasn't Catholic, anyhow, as it turned out. She never went to church."

"She visited the convent next door. She went on Retreats there. And her nuns said a mass for her soul."

"I can't help what her nuns did. Besides, you gave them all that money in her memory. It wouldn't surprise me if you still give them handouts. As for the Retreats — they were a sort of rest cure, weren't they? That's what Catherine used to say. They waited on her and fattened her up; she came back refreshed. I imagine she paid for it through the nose, but she could afford it. I'm not used to nuns; I have always found them, well — spooky — but if they helped dear Catherine . . ." Her voice was accusing.

"The nuns of the Convent of the Precious Blood are groovy cats," said Teddy with a little smile.

"They are what, dear?"

"They're extremely hep. They don't just hold Retreats for rich, suburban women; they have conferences on poverty and racial problems — that sort of thing. They are taking off their habits and wearing modern dress."

"I prefer the habits. At least one knows who they are."

"You seem to lack an ecumenical spirit."

"I am not as broad-minded as you," she said humbly. "I try to be, but there is so much going on nowadays — it is difficult to keep up. I know you all think of me as a kind of a fossil, but you are the only family I have."

"Sister, dear, allow me to apologize. I promise not to tease you again. Let's have a jolly Christmas. Cook for us. We are tired of buffalo meat."

"Buffalo meat?"

"That's what Loren calls Mary's cooking. Make us goodies. Buy Loren shoes. Help Hat plan her future. It is true we are a motherless family and can use direction. I'm not sure I'll be able to satisfy your matchmaking propensities, though. I really believe I am quite contented as things are."

"Perhaps," she said stubbornly, "you are not as content as you think."

"You know more than I, then. You act as if you sense a dark secret."

"I always sense dark secrets here. But maybe it's because I'm obtuse and an old maid and don't understand happiness, as you have suggested."

"I'm sorry if I suggested such a thing. I don't really pretend to understand it myself, though, like everyone, I have spent my life in its pursuit. But is it something to be analyzed and dealt with quite so objectively? You remind me of an efficiency expert. Happiness, I think, remains a mystery."

"I am a practical woman," said Harriet, "and — and a Unitarian. Mysteries have always seemed immoral."

"In that case you may find us utterly depraved," said Teddy pleasantly.

4

HAT was visiting Mary Miller in Mary's room. It was the tidiest room in the house. Mary had painted the walls herself, powder blue. She had washed and brushed the white rugs on the floor until they were soft and fluffy. She had washed and ironed the white curtains, and tied them back every morning with a new blue satin ribbon from the dime store, so that they hung in a flounce. On her bed was a freshly ironed blue and white sprigged muslin spread with a ruffled hem. On the table beside the bed was a white pottery lamp with a frilly white lampshade, also from the dime store, with its shiny plastic wrapper still on it.

After Catherine's death, Loren had changed the decor of her Tower room, and Mary had rescued Loren's cast-off antique whatnot, along with the miniature articles which Loren had once collected. There were a pair of tiny gold glass slippers, numerous china dogs and cats, pieces of doll's furniture, a set of See-No-Evil, Hear-No-Evil, Speak-No-Evil monkeys, a Walt Disney skunk, and an assortment of tiny liquor bottles from airplanes, which Clyde used to bring to Loren before he had bought his own plane. To this collection Mary had added a green satin pincushion with a scene of Fisherman's Wharf stamped upon it and a tiny, pottery cable car, made in Japan, from Chinatown — souvenirs of field trips organized by Miss Shelton, the director of the Indian Center.

Over Mary's bed was a framed colored picture of Jesus as a shepherd, leading his lambs through a green pasture. On top of the chest of drawers were two photographs in cheap gilt frames from the Fashion Photo Studio in Eureka, the nearest large town to the Hoopa Reservation. One was a pastel-tinted picture of her parents, their wedding portrait. Her father wore a dark suit jacket and clip-on tie, loaned to him by the studio for the occasion. On his head he wore a broad-brimmed fedora, his own. Her mother was wearing a flowered cotton dress with puffed sleeves. They sat, stiffly posed and unsmiling, against a black velvet hanging. Their dark eyes stared straight ahead with a modest but firm expression; they had the immortality of statues.

But Mary's father had died from TB when she was six. Her mother's hair was now white, her face filled with many tiny wrinkles. She suffered from arthritis. She lived on the reservation but took a bus into Fort Klamath every day to work in a laundry, where the steam heat made her pain more bearable. They were not immortal, they were not statues; Mary tried not to think of their realness because it made a funny, hollow sickness inside of her.

The other photograph, in black and white, was of her brother Pete. It was his high school graduation picture. Unlike Mary, who had gone to school on the reservation, Pete had attended high school in Eureka; he had been a star fullback, a popular boy whom the kids had nicknamed Chief. In the photograph he wore his white letterman's sweater. His white shirt was open casually at the neck; he had a relaxed, easy posture and an open, cheerful smile. His dark eyes were friendly and filled with confidence.

But Pete had changed, too. When Mary first came to work for the Olivers, she used to meet him at the center, where he came for the dances. But the last time she had seen him there, over four months ago, he had looked bad. His hair was long and dirty; his eyes had a queer, glazed look; his voice had turned into a mutter, and the happy, easy manner was gone. He had borrowed twenty dollars from her and had not appeared again. Mary had gone back for two months, hoping to find him. Then she had started Girl Friday and no longer was able to go into the city on her day off.

Mary sat, now, upon a straight chair, her chunky body dressed in one of Catherine's old skirts and sweaters, a scarf covering her hair, which she had set that morning in fat, pink plastic curlers. Hat was stretched out on top of her clean bedspread, talking to her in an intense, rapid voice.

"You may not realize it, Mary, but you and I are in the same boat," Hat was saying.

Mary stared at the picture of Jesus over Hat's head and did not answer. She felt bad, because Jesus had taught her you were supposed to love everyone, but she did not love Hat. Hat was forever prying into her life on the reservation, or talking about something she called her "ethnic origins." For that matter, she did not love Loren, either, who was snotty and would not let her in to clean her bedroom. She did not love Mr. Oliver, who had asked her once to call him Teddy. (When she had refused, he had stopped calling her Mary and addressed her as Miss Miller.) She heartily disliked Clemente, who was always trying to take over the kitchen or offering to help with the housework. The only member of the family whom she felt at all warmly toward was Becky, who treated her as she had expected to be treated, as a maid in a white man's household, a concept Mary had acquired from movies she watched on the TV set Mr. Oliver had put in her room.

There was no family TV. Mr. Oliver called it the "Boob Tube." Loren had one of her own in the Tower, on which, very late at night, she watched monster films or what she called "old flicks." Sometimes Mary thought the Olivers would be easier to work for if they would only watch the programs she did, and learn the proper way to act.

"I mean it, really, the same boat," Hat was saying. She fumbled in her jeans pocket for her cigarette package. "Cigarette, Mary?"

"No, thank you, Miss Oliver."

"We'll get to the 'Miss Oliver' bit in a moment, Mary. But let me explain first. You see, it's this way. Like, we're both slaves."

Mary continued to look at the wall.

"I am a slave, being a middle-class white woman; you are a slave, being a member of a racial minority. Our people, my forefathers, put a fast deal over on your people, who were noble and natural and uncontaminated — unspoiled, that is, by rotten civilization. Being Puritans, and therefore, sexually repressed, they — my forefathers, that is — put women down, too." She dropped ashes on Mary's bedspread. "Are we communicating, Mary?"

Mary nodded yes, hoping she would get rid of Hat sooner by agreeing. Hat reminded her of Mr. Oliver, with whom it was necessary to employ the same tactic.

Yesterday, he had come into what Mary thought of as "her kitchen," carrying a paper sack, which he put down on the counter and opened.

"I've just been to the Cheese House, Miss Miller, and selected three cheeses," he had said. "It's nice to know cheeses. This one is feta, a Greek cheese made from goats' milk. It's eaten with olives, or sprinkled on salads or spinach. This one is Fontina from Denmark. And this one is a dessert cheese, Brie, from France, to be eaten with fruit. Let me give you a sample of each."

He made her taste the nasty, smelly stuff; as soon as he was gone, she rushed upstairs to brush her teeth. Mary felt the same way now about the things Hat was saying as she had about tasting the cheese.

"You know that picture over the fireplace, Mary? The painting of the old cat in the fancy gold frame?"

Mary nodded. Didn't she dust it regularly?

"I could tell you a few things about him that would blow your mind. He was my great-great-great-grandfather. Well, I forget how many 'greats'! And he was a pig! That's how we got our money, Mary. Because my ancestor had people like you work in his mine for peanuts, and what's more, he treated them like dirt."

Mary thought this was a most irreverent way to talk about one's ancestors; she wished that Hat would stop.

"It bothered my mother; he was on her side of the family, and she wouldn't let my father put the picture up. But after her accident, he got it out. He said it has historical interest, it really ought to be in a museum. That's the kind of world we live in, Mary. Museums filled with portraits of pigs like that. That's our history. Did you know that even George Washington kept slaves?"

Mary didn't.

"That's what I mean. We've all been brought up on lies. Take your religion, for example. If I were you, I'd go back to my own tribal practices. I'm sure they were very beautiful."

"I was brought up Baptist," said Mary firmly.

"Part of the Establishment's scheme for putting you down, Mary."

"My brother talks that way, Miss Oliver, and I think he may be in trouble with the law."

"The law is the Establishment, Mary, and I respect your brother for his stand. I'd like to talk to your brother, Mary. He lives in San Francisco, doesn't he? Why haven't we ever met him, by the way?"

Mary's face darkened. "I worry about him a lot, Miss Oliver. But I told him not to come around here. He's always after money. I don't want him pestering folks. I give him what I can."

"I should be happy to donate to his cause, Mary."

"Please don't, Miss Oliver."

"My name is Hat, Mary. You must stop thinking of yourself as Lower Class. When the People take over, as they will, the Class System will go. You either have to be with the Revolution or against it. Tell your brother I'd like to meet him someday." Hat stood up. "I have to split now and do some Christmas shopping." She walked over to the dressing table and crushed out her cigarette in the empty glass bowl where Mary kept her hair rollers. She looked at Pete's picture. "This is your brother, isn't it?"

"Yes."

"He looks far out. I can see him on horseback, with a bow and arrow, hunting for game. I really can. Is there anything around for lunch?"

"I'll fix you a sandwich, Miss — Hat."

"If it isn't too much trouble. I'd make it myself, but I do have to dash."

"Do you want roast beef or tuna?"

"Roast beef would be groovy, thanks." She walked to the doorway, then paused and turned around. "Power to the People, Mary," she said cheerfully. "Right?"

She waited patiently until Mary nodded in agreement, then she went out.

5

THE large room just off the furnace stall in the Olivers' basement was called the Playroom; it had never functioned as such. When the girls were little, they had preferred the upper rooms and the company of their parents.

There was a dirty Navajo rug upon the stone floor (Hat had offered this to Mary, but she had refused it), a discarded blue-velvet sofa, an abandoned Ping-Pong table, and shelves of extra canned goods and now-mildewed toilet paper which Teddy once, on an impulse at household organization, had bought in wholesale lots.

Here, also, were stored discarded purchases from Teddy's shopping spree on his and Catherine's trip to Europe — a piece of a Sicilian donkey cart, a Florentine putto, which resembled a damaged department store doll with wings and genitals, and the remains of an Italian marionette theater, its proscenium arch adorned with faded pastel cupids; it had seen one production of Cinderella and one Oon Drama.

On the sheetrock wall of this subterranean chamber, Clemente was painting a Family Mural of the Olivers. Using poster paints, she worked in a broad comic-strip style, after Giotto.

Clemente had been working on the Mural on visits to the Olivers during her vacations for the last two years. But now that she had completed her formal education, which had consisted of high school in various parts of the country where her mother had temporarily settled to do "research," and a few months of art school in Mexico City while her mother wrote a book about Montezuma entitled *The Feathered Chieftain*, she was determined to finish her work.

It was already planned; she had done a cartoon on brown wrapping paper and presented it to the family for their approval.

"We must not be like John D. Rockefeller," said Hat.

"Or Michelangelo's pope," Teddy said.

The general consensus was that it was not right to interfere with artistic inspiration; the artist must be left alone to practice her sacred work.

The first panel showed the family playing croquet upon the lawn. Becky was a baby, sitting in her carriage. Next to the carriage lay Hurwulf, who still had her youthful figure, surrounded by her first litter of pups. Loren, Hat and Teddy held mallets; Teddy was about to drive a ball through a wicket, a fierce expression upon his face. In the background, Catherine was crossing the lawn, bearing lemonade upon a tray. In the mock-up, her figure had been more solid, like an older Hat; upon the wall it had turned shadowy and distant.

The second panel showed Teddy, Becky, Loren and Hat on a walking trip in the Sierras, which had taken place shortly after Catherine's Oonwald. Becky, Loren and Hat were each carrying backpacks — the Ultimate Light Pack — which Teddy had bought for them after studying catalogues and visiting numerous sporting goods stores. Teddy, dressed in lederhosen and knee socks and boots, was being borne upon a litter over a mountain pass by four rangers. (He had fallen and broken his ankle.) In his hands he held a small book. Clemente had painted in the title: *Conifers of the Sierra Nevada*. During rest stops, as he lay on his bed of pain, they had brought him pine needles, and he had identified them for everyone's instruction.

Hat marched at the front of the group; Becky and Loren brought up the rear. Catherine was to be shown in the form of a small angel hovering over the procession. Clemente had worked on the angel and then rubbed it out; she said she could not keep it from resembling a sea gull.

"And where are you, Clemente?" Hat had asked her. Clemente had also been on the trip; she had bandaged Teddy's ankle and held a wet kerchief to his sweating brow.

"This is the Oliver Family Mural."

Hat, who had taken Art Appreciation, reminded her that even Giotto had painted himself in as a member of the crowd during one of the miracles of St. Francis. "Besides," she added, "you are a member of our family."

But Clemente would not change her mind.

She was now at work upon the third panel, which was entitled "Hat's Solo Flight." The family was shown at the Palo Alto Airport, gazing up into the sky, watching Hat at the controls of Clyde O'Mahoney's Cessna Skylark, which he used to fly to and from his ranch near Hollister, and in which he had taught Hat to fly. Hat wore an old-fashioned pilot's helmet and was waving down at them from the cockpit. The Cessna did not have an open cockpit; this was artistic license in order to have a good view of the panel's heroine. In the foreground, somewhat foreshortened, stood Clyde. It was a good likeness. Clemente had captured his tall, slightly stooped, wiry body, his weathered, sunburned face. He wore his old white Stetson, a present from Catherine — beneath it, his sandy hair curled down in sideburns. His small, pale-blue eyes had crinkly laugh wrinkles around them, his nose was small and round like a button, his mouth was large and twisted sideways in a wry grin. He wore faded blue jeans and one boot; his hand was cupped over his mouth as he — again, artistic license — shouted directions up to Hat, his pupil.

Clemente was painting in Clyde's other boot when Loren, wearing a long maroon satin skirt from the Goodwill and a black velveteen bodice fastened with drawstrings, which she had stolen from the costume room at her high school after a performance of the *Gypsy Baron,* slipped into the room. She was carrying a piece of fudge cake on a paper napkin.

"Aunt Harriet is trying to fatten us up," she announced, and handed the cake to Clemente. Clemente put down her brush and began to eat. Loren surveyed the new panel with a critical eye.

"Clyde is not a member of our family," she said. "You don't put yourself in, but you put in Clyde."

"I am the artist," said Clemente smiling.

"Clyde refuses to speak Oon."

"Catherine didn't speak Oon," said Clemente.

"Ah, but she understood it," said Loren fiercely. "She understood things. Teddy said when he took her to France she surprised him with beautiful French, even though in boarding school she had been too shy to speak a word of it out loud."

Clemente said, "I have often thought that you must miss her the most. Hat is older, and Becky is too young."

"Why should I miss her any more than I would miss her if she had gone on an extended trip?" said Loren, angry now. "You'll become an Outbar, yourself, Clemente, if you're not careful."

"I'm sorry."

Loren changed her tone. She gazed thoughtfully at the Mural. "I am encouraged, though," she said. "I don't believe you will have to add a Wicked Stepmother."

"Oh, dear, I hope not. At least, not wicked."

"Any stepmother would be wicked in this case. Oh, can't you see her, Clemente. Trying to be clever, sucking up to us, reading books on psychology, having long discussions about our 'problems' with Teddy — but never, no matter how much she tried, even sincerely, fitting into the Oliver household. How could she? It's an impossible situation. In the long run she would decide we should be sent off to an understanding boarding school for our 'own good.'"

"Perhaps," said Clemente, "you don't think I fit in. It is true that you are an unusual household."

"You aren't a stepmother, Clemente. A stepmother plays a different role; her loyalties would be utterly different." Loren sat down with hunched knees upon the rug. "However, as I said, I have cause for optimism. I have analyzed why people marry."

Clemente finished her cake slowly. Then she stuffed the napkin into the pocket of her smock and sat down on the sofa to listen.

"The first," said Loren, "is money."

"That's a shocking reason, Loren!"

"You have to put yourself into the position of someone who is not rich. Or not as rich as we are. Very few people are."

"I'm not rich, but I could never imagine —"

"That's because you've always been cared for. Your mother may be careless about financial matters, but you know that Teddy would never let you starve. That's because you're like St. Francis — you offer spiritual sustenance in return for a crumb of bread. Rich men have always fed saints. But let me tell you, it's extremely common for people to marry for money. Money matters to most people. It matters to me, even though I have enough at the moment."

"Olivers aren't interested in money," said Clemente.

"In that way, I'm not an ordinary Oliver. Hat may not think I'm interested in her Revolution, and I'm not, in the way she is. But you never can tell what might happen, and I am planning for my security. Not money. Jewels. I've looked into it a bit, and jewels are what you carry if you have to escape over a border. Jewels can be sold for money anywhere. Take the Oon jewels, for instance."

"The Oon jewels?"

"Catherine's jewelry, which she inherited but never wore. She didn't care for personal adornment; it embarrassed her to be thought wealthy. But Teddy keeps them in his safe; he showed them to us. He says they're worth tons more than they were even when she inherited them, and they were antiques then. The bracelet is for Hat and the earrings for Becky and the necklace for me. I hope to add to it with the money I'm saving. Jewels are a good guard against inflation and convenient if you have to split the country."

"I do think jewelry is nicer than money."

"But we were talking about why people marry. Teddy doesn't need to marry for money, because he already did."

"Loren, you know that's not true."

"I didn't say he didn't love Catherine. He loved her passionately from the moment he saw her in her dingy, cheap little room, playing the Pea Princess. She wanted to identify with the common people, but Teddy recognized her disguise at once and knew she needed someone to take care of her. Her having money just made him freer to do so. It was their Ronwar — each helping the other in his own way. It was very beautiful and can never happen again. And Teddy has money now, so we can eliminate that reason."

"Well, I'm glad we can."

"Now, secondly — children. That is the reason some people marry, I believe."

"And Teddy has children as well as money," said Clemente with a little sigh.

"We're enough, wouldn't you say?"

"Most people would think so."

"Third — companionship. Here again, that's taken care of. He has us."

"But that won't be forever, will it? You'll go away sometime. You'll probably go to college, Loren, eventually."

"College? Not me. You never went to college, Clemente. Why do you think I should?"

"I'm not as intelligent as you are," said Clemente simply.

"Schools destroy your brains by programming you," said Loren. "I will not be programmed. I refuse to sit there while they stuff things down you, like they do in France with geese. To make goose liver. I'm surprised it took Hat so long to find that out. No, I shall be completely happy to be Teddy's companion in his old age. We understand one another completely."

"You don't think you might — fall in love?"

"I have considered that possibility and rejected it. I don't think my Ronwar will decree it. I'm not like the other girls at school, who moon around after boys. They all seem stupid to me. I can't imagine 'giving myself' to anyone, as they say in books. Or they say, he 'took' her. I don't wish to be 'taken.' In that way, I agree with Hat. But Hat thinks she is going to find some kind of equal, beautiful relationship, in which nobody has any outdated sex hang-ups, where 'nobody's on top.' I believe those are her words. But I don't even think that. I'm too cantankerous. That's something that only happens rarely, with very rare people, like Catherine and Teddy. I believe I'll make a groovy old maid, though Hat doesn't approve of that term. But I want to finish why people marry."

"Please continue. I'm really very interested."

"Another reason is sex. That is a very compelling force, though probably a person like you would not recognize it."

"You don't think I'm sexy?"

"Angels aren't. That's why the lower parts of their bodies are always neutral."

Clemente glanced down at the lower part of her body a bit apologetically.

"Oh, you're all there, Clemente. I don't mean that. It's your spirituality. Spirituality overcomes lust."

"But what about . . . Teddy?"

"Well, in the first place, Teddy is getting along; sexual drives diminish. Besides, if he felt physical satisfaction were necessary, he could take a mistress."

"Would you approve of that?"

"A mistress would be better than a Wicked Stepmother, because she would lack certain rights. Moreover, she could be abandoned whenever she grew tiresome."

"That doesn't sound like something Teddy would do."

"Teddy is a man, Clemente. We must be realistic."

"I'm sorry, it's just all so . . . abstract." Clemente rose and went over to the Mural and examined it. "Have I caught Clyde, do you think?"

"You're changing the subject."

"I don't mean to."

"When people change the subject, they usually have some reason. Do you think I'm horrid?"

"No, not horrid. But you read so many books, it gives you a different way of looking at things. I lack your analytical mind. I never read. I was always a disappointment to my mother for that reason."

"Saints don't need to read, they just exist. You couldn't analyze and plot for your own self-interest if you tried. But somebody has to think of these things around here."

Clemente smiled gently and picked up her paintbrush and began to work again on Clyde O'Mahoney's boot.

6

"WAS it fun?" Clemente asked Becky, who had just returned from Hollister with Clyde.

They were sitting in the kitchen drinking mugs of tomato soup which Clemente had made. It was Mary's day off, and Teddy had taken Aunt Harriet to see the Christmas displays in the stores.

Becky wore faded blue jeans and an old striped T-shirt. Unlike the rest of the Olivers, she had gray eyes, freckled with green; her sandy hair was cut in bangs over her forehead and clipped neatly just beneath her ears by Clemente. She was known as a "wholesome child."

"No problems here," Carter Alway had said to Teddy as he patted Becky's head.

As a result, her sisters found her dull. Loren had referred to her as the "changeling" and had hinted darkly that she must have been adopted.

Teddy, blessed with "what every parent and teacher longs for" — the words of Becky's junior high school principal — sometimes worried that her lack of problems was a problem in itself. He made clumsy, sporadic efforts to make up for neglecting her. The efforts were not rebuffed, they simply went unnoticed. Was this not ominous? To be rebuffed might mean, at least, that she had built up defenses against a thwarted need. He comforted himself by deciding he had done such a good job with this third child that he no longer had a role to play.

"We did stunts," said Becky, "in the plane."

"You're so brave."

"As soon as I'm thirteen, Clyde's going to teach me to fly, like Hat."

"What about Loren?"

"Loren prefers her books. Clyde said I would be the best pilot of all."

"I'm not sure I'd care to go up with you. You're too careless. You've spilled your soup all over your shirt."

"Clyde says you need courage and that's what I've got. I might become a stunt pilot for an air circus."

"Where is Clyde?"

"He's putting the Tree in the barn. Then he's going to play tennis with Hat."

"I promised Teddy to make decorations."

"Why couldn't we buy some this year? The shiny kind."

"Teddy believes people should do things with their hands. It's more honest."

"Well, I wish we could buy some. I don't mean I don't like your decorations, Clemente, but why can't we be more like other people once in a while? You should see the Always' house. They have all their oak trees lighted. And the Schmidts have a plastic Santa on their roof."

"Teddy," said Clemente severely, "would call that vulgar."

"Did Aunt Harriet find a wife for Teddy?"

"If she has, it has not been announced. No candidates have been around."

"You sounded just like Loren when you said that," Becky said, her mouth filled with soup.

Clemente blushed. Her own way of talking was simple and lacking in artifice, but she had lived so long among the Olivers that she sometimes unconsciously took on their mannerisms.

"Anyway, Mrs. Alway has a candidate."

Clemente said, "Who?"

"She's going to invite all of us to Linda's debut party, where there will be a Mrs. Collier to meet him. Mrs. Collier has had a very tragic life. Her first husband ran off to Las Vegas with a lady veterinarian. He took half the electric blanket — it zipped — and the TV set. So she got a color TV to replace it. Her second husband threw her hair dryer at her, she had to have the scar removed by a plastic surgeon. As long as she was having that done, she had her whole face lifted, too. Her philosophy is to try to get something good out of something bad. She can't really afford to come to the party; she lives in Chicago now. The Always would like to send her a ticket, but they are afraid her pride would be hurt. She would prefer to 'borrow, beg, or steal' than to take charity. But she wouldn't miss Linda's debut for the world. Loren says Aunt Harriet is more ghastly than ever."

"She didn't seem that bad to me, but then I am not as perceptive as Loren. Do you want more soup?"

"Yes, and make me a cheese sandwich, Clemente. Yellow cheese, toasted on both sides, with a pickle in it. Please hurry, because the Always are picking me up to go to the Grand National. We have the box seat right next to John Wayne's."

7

IT had been a dry autumn. Day after day the sun burned feebly through a thick, smoggy haze; foliage had lost its glitter; it was neither hot nor cold. Even now — December — no crispness in the air hinted at winter; it was limbo-like weather, no season at all.

Clyde and Hat, carrying rackets and cans of balls, walked side by side across the brown lawn toward the tennis court. Hat had put on white shorts. Her legs were still brown from summer; her short, dark hair and long stride gave her a boyish look. Clyde wore his Stetson and the khaki shorts he kept at Oonhall; the pocket of his thin, checked shirt bulged with a package of Camels. His angularity, his slight stoop, his easy saunter had a kind of elegance next to Hat's awkward briskness.

He stepped ahead of her to open the court door. It stuck. He gazed at it contemplatively, then pushed it gently, lifting it at the same time. It opened with a squeak. He opened and shut it several times, listening to the squeak with a rapt expression, the way Teddy sometimes listened to a section of a Mozart quintet. He analyzed, diagnosed, as Hat waited. The next time, she thought, he would bring tools and repair it, eliciting Teddy's respect and gratitude. She tapped a foot impatiently, then walked away, across the court.

Her sneakers clung to the soft, sticky asphalt, making little sucking sounds. Weeds had sprung up in the cracks; she sidestepped robin dung. The robins had stripped the pyracantha bushes, leaving naked, thorny branches; they had gorged on the berries and got drunk and sick. Teddy had meant to replace the vines with canvas, but had not yet done so; he had also meant to replace the net, which had large holes in it and drooped in the center. She took a position on the far side of the net in front of the weathered, buckling backboard.

Hurwulf followed her, settling down in a pool of pale sunshine; feathered rump up, head down, thrust forward toward the court, she beat her tail happily against the blacktop. She had watched many games here, long ago, when the court was the center of a small social life.

Teddy had had the court built shortly after building the house. He had played tennis at Stanford and meant to take it up again. He did not care for football or baseball, but tennis was, he used to say, a civilized sport. He had hired an instructor, taken a series of private lessons, and played a stiff, uninspired game. Despite his shortcomings, he had enthusiastically organized a foursome — Clyde, Catherine, Mimi Alway and himself. Then a "tennis elbow" had set in. While forced temporarily into inactivity, the idea of raising peacocks occurred to him. The peacocks roosted on the fence; their irresponsible habits had almost destroyed the court. Teddy had finally given them away to a zoo, but by that time his interest in tennis had waned.

Clyde and Catherine, however, continued to play. Clyde played aggressively; his strength made up for his lack of skill. The surprise had been Catherine. Hat could still see her in her white tennis dress — part of her old debutante wardrobe — which she had produced from her closet, absently brushing her shoulder-length chestnut hair back from her dark eyes, serving a long, hard shot to Clyde. She had had lessons as a girl and had excellent form. Usually languid, she seemed to revive on the court, revealing a hidden energy; she played a lively, unselfconscious game.

Clyde had taught Hat when she was a child, and Catherine would sometimes rally with her, helping her to improve her backhand. But when Teddy suggested the girls take lessons, she had demurred; she had had too much of that, she said, when she was growing up.

In the old days, before Catherine's death, there had been two other players who used the court on Sundays: Mad Fred and Dr. Zimmerman.

Mad Fred, so-called because of his eyes — tiny, blue, darting sparks set in a larger-than-usual sphere of white — would arrive in his old pickup. He was in his late fifties — grizzled, heavyset, a fleshy, mottled red face with a grumpy expression; perhaps "half there." His costume never seemed to vary: a sleazy, flowered Hawaiian shirt of many colors, a battered straw hat, faded blue denims and sandals, which exposed white, heavy-veined, dirty feet.

Beneath the shirt was a surprise. This was Lulu the Hulu. Tattooed upon his white, flabby thorax, this dainty creature, half naked in a grass skirt, would, if Mad Fred were in the right mood, dance to his disciplined breathing. If he were not in the right mood, no amount of pleading would persuade him; Lulu, he would say, was not in dancing spirits today.

Mad Fred was devoted to Teddy because during Teddy's term of office on the board of the Los Robles Hills Neighborhood Association, Teddy had saved Fred's Place, a dilapidated saloon which had once been an old roadhouse of doubtful reputation. The Neighborhood Association had wished to petition the State Board of Equalization not to renew Fred's liquor license, claiming that it was a nonconforming use in what had become a residential neighborhood and was apt to attract "undesirables." In an inspired speech to the board, Teddy had persuaded them that the tavern, having been there longer than the homes which had sprung up around it, should be declared a historical monument. Now a small plaque adorned the wall next to the entrance.

> This structure built by Felix Garcia in the 1850's served as a gambling retreat and meeting place for Mexican-Californians. Acquired by Fred Robinson in 1945, it continued to serve as a well-known and popular public house.
> Plaque placed by Los Robles Hills
> Neighborhood Association. May 24, 1965.

While he tended bar, Fred announced to his clientele that Teddy Oliver had immortalized him.

Dr. Zimmerman was a psychiatrist who had escaped from Austria before World War II. He drove down from the city, where he had his office, in his Jaguar XKE with Bobsie, his serious, social worker wife, a Bennington graduate.

"Bobsie does not approve of my car, but it gives me happiness, and she approves of my happiness," the doctor would explain.

Bobsie had flat breasts but ample hips; she looked as if she had been built for bearing children, but not for nourishing them. She was, in fact, childless. She devoted herself to helping her husband, whom she considered brilliant but impractical.

Teddy had been one of Zimmerman's patients. He had had no unusual anxieties, he had explained; he had merely wanted to explore his subconscious. He spoke of this as one would speak of exploring a mysterious and exotic land. The result was unconventional; he and the doctor, who was soon known as Zimmy, became fast friends.

They would retire together to Fala to discuss Zimmy's original ideas of therapy, which he hoped one day to be able to put into practice, and which he illustrated by drawing numerous graphs and charts embellished with little arrows, demonstrating the way A interacted with B, the way B reinteracted with A, the way A then re-interacted with B (C, D, E, and so on, naturally complicating the situation). "This, of course, is the role of the group therapist," said Zimmy.

Teddy had nothing but praise for these conceptions. He insisted that Zimmy must write a book.

"But first I must have an operational clinic," said Zimmy. "What I do now is our bread and butter, but I chafe under the limitation."

While they talked, Bobsie, who did not care for competitive sports, nor, as it turned out, the Olivers, whom she felt to be frivolous, sat upon the lawn reading psychiatric journals.

The doctor had a large, bald head, a black, stiff mustache and wore thick-lensed spectacles. For these jaunts into the country he wore a white knit shirt with a tiny green crocodile on its pocket, Bermuda-length white shorts, white "tennies" and the same black silk hose he wore with his business suit. He would emerge from Fala and go to the swimming pool, where Mad Fred waited, drinking Heineken beer.

"And now we play, yes?" he would say eagerly.

Mad Fred, who talked very little, nodded in a gloomy way. Removing his sandals, he would put on a pair of Teddy's sneakers; then he and the doctor would play a set.

The little girls, who saw few adults apart from Clyde, the Always, teachers, hired help and Aunt Harriet (whom they half included in the hired-help category), would hide behind the pepper tree, giggling and spying on the odd couple through the pyracantha. They could not decide which of the two players was the funnier — Zimmy, who looked like a goblin, or Mad Fred, who resembled a huge troll.

When the set was finished, Zimmy, who always lost, would rush to the net to shake Mad Fred's hand; this was the hidden spectators' favorite part. Mad Fred always seemed astonished by this ritual; the doctor would have to grope for his hand across the net.

"Good, very good, no?" Zimmy would say, while the little girls covered their mouths to suppress their laughter.

At the age of four Becky lost interest in the grotesque. She began to wander further afield, made welcome and feeling at home in neighbors' houses; the Outbar held no fear for her. At last, Hat, also, declared she was too old for such childish activities. Clemente did whatever Hat did. This left Loren, who still, sometimes, sneaked out by herself to observe the activities on the court.

Only Loren, therefore, watched the nuns from the Convent of the Precious Blood, who came to play tennis at Teddy's invitation after Catherine's death.

The convent was on fifteen acres, next to Oonhall; ten of the acres were leased out as a walnut orchard. The main building was no longer used for Retreats; it had become a training center, a kind of Halfway House for the "new nuns" whose ecumenical spirit Teddy so admired.

Under the supervision of the mother superior, Mother Humilitia, who had been instrumental in the change, seminars were held there; members of the "advanced" clergy of all denominations and from many countries, as well as noted sociologists, psychologists, theologians and social workers, gathered for this purpose. In the back of the convent, in a low adobe building, were rooms for lay people who came for Retreats twice a year, as well as for nuns and priests recovering from an illness or an operation or in need of a rest. It was here where Catherine had gone for her "rest cures."

But except for the nuns, the court was seldom used any more. Clemente's father was gone, the Always had joined a local tennis club, and Mad Fred claimed a gimpy knee, which left the doctor, when he came to visit, without an opponent.

Now Clyde, somewhat to Hat's surprise, had suggested this game. That she had not played for a year, that she had more important things to do, did not dissuade him. Genial goading — didn't she want to stay in shape for her Revolution? Was she afraid she couldn't keep up with an old man like him? — made her give in sulkily.

Clyde was no longer the old family friend, part of the comfortable, familiar landscape of home. He stood for everything she was against. Could one, ought one, to play games with the Enemy? Moreover, she sensed that lately, in his unobtrusive way, he watched and assessed her, in much the same cool manner he had studied the squeaky gate. She found this both infuriating and oddly exciting.

"You remind me of your Pa," he said once in his offhanded tone, after listening to her political opinions.

"How?" She knew that her philosophy differed now from Teddy's — what did he mean?

"All your ideas. Your head must buzz with 'em. Doesn't it make you dizzy having so many ideas?"

She was angry with herself for having asked. Evidently, to

Clyde, "ideas" were all the same. "It's better than having none," she said scornfully.

"Like me?" he grinned.

"Yes, like you!"

"It all comes out the same in the end. The big fish eat the little ones." He had glanced at her mockingly. "Darwin. How's that?"

"Tremendous. Only Darwin was a scientist and science has led us into our beautiful technocracy. Like we have the bomb. Groovy."

"But just the same, the big fish do eat the little ones."

"Nobody says you can't try to stop them."

"Well, I reckon you can organize the little fish and then they can knock off the big fish and become the big fish themselves. But I don't see how that is going to change things much."

"If all the big fish are as cynical as you, they deserve to be eaten."

Clyde had chuckled merrily.

Now she felt she had accepted his invitation to play tennis not because it might be fun to play tennis, but because of this new, charged atmosphere which had arisen between them. Did she hope to convert him or did she merely enjoy the squabbles? She suspected it was the latter and felt demeaned.

The two opponents faced each other across the net. Hat noticed with peculiar satisfaction that Clyde had grown a little tummy, which bulged now over his shorts, that his sandy sideburns were sprinkled with gray.

"Rally?" he said. He dropped a ball and hit it across to her. She swung and drove the ball into the net.

"What's the matter?" he crowed, hitting another one across. "You in love or something?"

Furiously she ran for the ball and returned it; he hit it back down the center line; she scurried backwards and made it. Ping went the ball against her racket; the gut hummed. She had forgotten what a nice sound that was. Ping, hum. Ping, hum. The vibration in her hand, her sweaty grip on the leather handle, the sun on her muscles suddenly relaxed her.

"Let's start a game," he said.

She served. Her ball bounced deep in the service court. She was congratulating herself when it came spinning back towards her, landing on the baseline. Too late. Clyde grinned. "Love, five," she said. She served again, this time concentrating harder. No thoughts of anything except that furry orb. There. Another good one. This time she was ready and returned his ball with her backhand. He ran to the net clumsily and smashed it over. But she was there, scooping it up; she lobbed it over his head.

"Five all," she said. And went on to win the game and then the set.

"Congratulations," said Clyde with admiration.

They sat down together in the sun next to Hurwulf. Hat pulled a weed from the court and tickled Hurwulf's head with it.

"Well, how are things since I left?" said Clyde.

"Managing, thanks. Teddy's not drinking in the daytime. Our dinners are rather uptight with Aunt Harriet, though. And Loren's mad because they've never finished the Monopoly game."

"Becky tells me Loren's worrying about Teddy falling into the hands of a scheming woman."

"Loren's more involved in — bourgeois family life. She's wasting her time, since it's doomed."

"I'm not a family man myself, but I'd hate to see that happen."

"Maybe if you were a family man, you'd change your mind."

"Not if my family were anything like the Oliver family."

Hat sighed restlessly.

"Is it doomed, too?"

"Loren, at least, will make a fighting stand. The fact is, I think she's afraid of the Outbar. I mean, the outside world. She gets all her notions from books."

"I've never especially favored intellectual women," Clyde said lazily.

"Is it all right to be an intellectual man?"

"Worse for a woman, makes 'em argumentative, no good in bed."

"I suppose you think Blacks should just sit on their front porches and strum banjos?"

"Come again?"

"You are forcing people into stereotyped roles."

"Sorry. I think that women should sit on front porches and strum banjos. But to change the subject slightly, does Loren still think she's too good for school?"

"She wants to get Teddy off to Europe as soon as possible. She is afraid he is weak and might succumb and betray Catherine."

Clyde was silent for a moment. His blue eyes turned lighter, almost transparent. "She has appointed herself the guardian of Teddy's morals?" he said at last.

"She's bossy and enjoys spying."

Clyde reached for his Camels, offered one to Hat, who refused. "What about you?" he said.

"Me?"

"How are you getting along?"

"I . . . am formulating plans."

"Good. To do what?"

"I'll tell you when they're formulated. I'll tell you one right now. I'm with Loren about school. It doesn't do anything for me."

"What did you expect it to do?"

Hat's face became dreamy; it were as if she had slipped swiftly into another, brighter world; then, just as swiftly, she returned, her mouth twisted into an ironic curl. She said, "It's all part of the Establishment. When I get out, what will have changed? I'll know a little ancient history and a little ancient literature, but nothing . . . relevant. I'll be basically the same person I was when I started."

"I hope so," he said dryly.

"You may hope so, but I hope to change — for the better."

"I like you the way you are." He grinned, then added slyly, "You're awful pretty — for a girl."

"Clyde!"

"Yes, ma'm?"

"You wouldn't say that to a man, would you?"

"Tell him he's pretty? I'd be damned if I'd do that."

"That's just it. You put me down without even realizing what you're doing. It's your tone, as well as what you say. You see, women are a minority, just as much as Blacks and Indians."

Hurwulf rose and thrust her muzzle into Hat's lap; Hat pushed her away; her face grew darker. "I'll get out of school, and then what? I'll be expected to marry and produce babies and — that's that. Anything else would be suspect. I'd be an outsider, a freak."

"You're terrific when you get all worked up like that," he said. "You remind me of Catherine."

"For God's sake, you once said I reminded you of Teddy."

"Well, you're kind of a mixture of both. You're full of ideas like Teddy, and you're gutsy like Catherine."

"In what way was Catherine gutsy?" she asked scornfully.

"She used to beat me at tennis like you do."

"Christ, we're not on the same trip at all."

She leaped up, then clumsily reached for her racket; Clyde intercepted her and presented it with a comic courtly bow. She snatched it from his hand, then stood there facing him, her body trembling with defiance. "You have a thing about Teddy and Catherine, don't you?"

"Your parents are — were — mighty fine folks, Miss Oliver."

"I'm not interested in a Sunday School lecture." Her voice broke slightly. Then, "Thanks for the game."

"Thank you, my dear."

She marched proudly and dramatically off the court.

Clyde picked up his racket and a can of balls and went over to the backboard and hit a few balls against it thoughtfully. He did not leave the court until Hat's tall, angry figure had disappeared from sight.

8

INSIDE the house Hat found Becky finishing her soup. Clemente had gone into the basement to work on the Mural. She said, "Stop making that nasty noise when you drink."

"Shut up yourself," said Becky.

"You just feel smarty because Clyde took you off in his plane."

"Well, what do you feel smarty about?"

"I'm sorry if I acted cross. I'm tired from playing tennis. I mean, I'm bored. Bored with everything. I can beat Clyde now. He's getting old."

"You're getting old," said Becky. "Old and ugly."

"Do you think so? Actually, the other night I found a gray hair."

"Soon there'll be lots."

"Of course Clyde never knew how to play tennis to begin with. He was a poor boy. Although that didn't seem to make him simpatico with the oppressed."

"He is a self-made man," said Becky, slurping up her soup.

Hat sat down and lit a cigarette. She inhaled it greedily. Then she stamped it out in an ashtray and lit another. "What did you do with Clyde, by the way?"

"Flew around. He says I'll be the best pilot — better than you."

"Who cares? Did he say anything else?"

"He told me his adventures. About being a blackjack dealer and a bronc buster in a traveling rodeo and a merchant seaman and —"

"Big deal. He loves boasting. Teddy just eats his stories up. Catherine did, too. I can't imagine why. I suppose it's because they led such a sheltered life."

"He told me how he met them. He said they drove up to his ranch because they were looking for land. Teddy wanted to be a farmer, and he told them all the bad parts, like the weather and bailing the cowboys out of jail, and talked them out of it. He said there isn't such a thing as a gentleman farmer."

"He ought to know."

"And we talked about horses and planes and about which was best."

"Better."

"We decided they were both good in different ways."

"It sound fascinating, I must say."

"It was," said Becky smugly.

9

TEDDY had spent the morning going over things in Fala.

Fala had been constructed when he had begun his novel. At that time the children were small, and the study was built far from the house at the bottom of the Pasture. It was announced that it was a Sacred Sanctuary. Catherine, pleased with his aspirations, protected its sacredness for him. Even now, when the novel — only an outline, really — lay at the bottom of a drawer, Fala still kept its aura, like an ancient shrine where once a religious rite had been practiced. Teddy was always allowed to work there in peace. Even Mary left it alone. Only Clemente, on her own impulse, appeared unobtrusively once a week, tiptoeing about to dust and sweep.

The small, shingled, brown cottage had three rooms — the workroom, a bath and a tiny bedroom like a monk's cell, in which Teddy used to rest and think between sessions at his desk.

On the walls of the study and bedroom were framed black and white photographs he had taken during his and Catherine's brief European tour. (She had refused to take the children; she had been dragged across Europe as a child and had found it a miserable experience. Neither felt they should leave them longer than a month.)

The photographs were not of ordinary tourist attractions, but unusual scenes, which he thought might go into a book tentatively titled *Oliver's Europe.* A soapbox orator in Hyde Park; a gypsy family in the Luxembourg gardens with their trained goat, which climbed a ladder; a fire-eater in the Piazza Navona, an immense man with overdeveloped muscles and long hair; an acrobat named Sonny Boy, who rode a motorcycle on a tightrope at Lake Como. Later, he had considered changing the title to *Mountebanks of Europe,* by T. Oliver. But a month was not long enough for a book, and Catherine would not return.

Fond of music, he had also installed a stereo sound system — a McIntosh tuner, a Dyna amp and preamp, a Sony turntable, an Ampex professional tape deck, and Altec Lansing Voice of the Theatre speakers — a project which had consumed most of a month. Life, alas, was not long enough if one wanted to do the right thing. Even choosing recordings, he sometimes thought sadly, was almost a career.

Now he was seated at his Olivetti, typing by hunt-and-peck method to the *Goldberg Variations,* the music punctuating his activity without intruding upon it.

>Scientific, Ltd.
>Chicago, Ill.
>
>Dear Sirs:
>
>Could you kindly send me your catalogue on astronomical equipment? I am interested in setting up a small observatory.
>
>>Sincerely yours,
>>Theodore Oliver

>Editor
>San Francisco Chronicle
>San Francisco, California
>
>Dear Sirs:
>
>The Committee on Ecology for the Save Our Bay League, of which I am privileged to be a member, has been making an ex-

tensive study of the ecology of San Francisco Bay. We have come across a surprise, though a splendid one. There are sea lions in the slough which Hardeman Homes, Inc. is proposing to fill in order to build their new subdivision. These animals — *Zalophus californianus* — have evidently wandered in from the sea some time ago and made the slough their home. There is one bull lion, four females, and a number of cubs. Speaking for the committee, I feel certain that Mr. Hardeman would not wish to wantonly murder these representatives of our vanishing wildlife. But when the slough is filled, what then? Only the pressure of public opinion can save this family.

Sincerely yours,
Theodore Oliver

He put the letters in envelopes which were embossed with his letterhead and addressed and stamped them. Then he began to tidy his desk. He filed away stock reports and a folder of bills marked "Paid." He returned the new Bean's catalogue, which he had been reading, to the bookshelf of catalogues and *Consumer Reports* above the stereo. Then he opened another folder, marked "Tax Deductible Items," which contained a fat inner folder marked "Conservation," the cause to which he was lately most devoted. He opened the inner folder. In this were brochures from many organizations he contributed to — groups concerned with population growth, the blocking of new freeways, zoning laws, the preservation of wildlife, the promotion of bicycle paths, the fight to keep industry out of the Hills, a local battle to prevent homes being built in his neighborhood on anything less than three acres. Some of the brochures had his name on their letterhead under Sponsors. The advance of what was called "civilization" by engineering minds and business interests must be stopped. The pine trees which hid the freeway from his view were, at best, only a half measure. He wrote out checks to two of these organizations, then he rose and stretched, put on his old corduroy jacket, which hung over his chair, and leaving the music on and the door open, walked out into the Vineyard. He had rather planned to look at his novel again this morning; it would be an antidote to his sister's visit. But the day was too lovely; he would take a short stroll first, perhaps think about it in the open air.

The novel was to have been the tale of a young man who left civilization and came to live on a small, primitive island off the west coast of Mexico — a spot which Teddy had once briefly visited on a fishing trip. The young man lived as the natives did; he built his own adobe hut and took the native girl, Felicita, as his mistress. Soon the people began to come to him for advice and help. With meager medical knowledge, which he had learned from some mysterious source, he cured their diseases and eased their sufferings. He taught the people to build better homes and better fishing boats. Although kind and friendly, there was something distant and aloof about him; his only rule was that the people were to discourage tourists who came from the industrial world. There had been a legend on the island that one day a savior would come; soon it was assumed that the young man was he. At last, fearful of destroying their fresh new faith by having it turned into dogmatic ritual, he vanished. But they found relics belonging to him and set up an outdoor altar in his memory. The padre, his enemy, told the people that the young man was bad, that he had lived in sin with a woman and was not a member of the established Holy Church. He made them tear down the altar brick by brick. That night there was a terrible earthquake in which Felicita was killed; the padre told them that the real God had punished her. The people went back to their joyless way of living, in fear of the padre and his God. Eventually only a few old men and women remembered the "good days" when the young man had lived among them.

It was to have been as simple as that — though of course filled with symbolic meaning. The old and decadent morality, the dead religion versus the new Avatar. Teddy had taken a course in Spanish in order to learn enough of the language for the book; he had studied a little Mexican history, especially the history of the Mexican Indians (though his was to be an unnamed tribe); he had even developed a stylistic method which would differentiate between the Spanish language of the padre and the Indian patois. But, somehow, the characters had never developed properly; the pace of the book sagged.

Once, swallowing his pride, he had forced himself to show it to Leah Lawrence for her advice. He was quite certain from reading her historical novels that she would never grasp what he was up to, and he had been right.

Leah had put aside her own work and read Teddy's unfinished manuscript conscientiously. Then she had made certain suggestions.

"Your young man, the hero, where is he from, for instance? He simply appears one day upon the island? The reader would want to know about his past."

"We know very little about the past of most avatars," said Teddy. "They appear at some point in history, transform people and events, then vanish."

"We know about Jesus's childhood, don't we?" said Leah.

"All of that was written later and is uncertain."

"Just the same, couldn't you make your hero have a bit more flesh and blood? In the love scenes, for example — he isn't very sexy."

Teddy, cursing himself for ever having asked her — what did she know of either saints or sex? — thanked her and put the manuscript away. It had lain in the drawer ever since. Perhaps, someday, he thought . . .

But it was really not so much being a novelist that mattered — it was just that he would have liked to have been something on his own terms. He had the time, the financial resources, certainly, he felt, the sensitivity. What else was missing? What, for example, did Leah Lawrence, seemingly so foolish, so lacking in delicacy, possess that he did not? Was this the reason the woman always rubbed him the wrong way?

The music accompanied him, now, into the Vineyard which surrounded Fala. Music, he thought, to think of unfinished projects by. The Vineyard was another. Black, crooked stumps in tidy, well-spaced rows which, despite his extensive research on wine-making, despite nourishing and coddling, had produced —

no grapes. His dream of a wine cellar with his own private label — Oon Winery (Clemente had even done a mock-up) — was not to be fulfilled. Not a writer, not a photographer, not a vintner. He sighed.

"Why does one need a title?" Zimmy had asked. "Why is it necessary even to work if you don't need to? It is your damn Puritan ethics. Martin Luther did the same thing to us. You are you, aren't you? A good husband? A good father?"

It was true that these activities he had mentioned had taken up much of his free time. The schools, for instance. Catherine had been adamant about sending the girls to public schools; she, herself, she felt, had been stifled in private ones. But there had been much to be desired of the California public school system; for years he had contributed his time and energies toward improving it. He had been on numerous committees, president of the local grade-school P.T.A., a member of the Los Robles School District Board of Trustees, a campaigner for bond elections and sex education in the schools. He had helped with homework (which had required learning the New Math), had consulted with his daughters' teachers and school psychologists; he still had files of STAT and STEP tests, reports, grades. Catherine had scarcely bothered to read them; he had scrutinized each one carefully, weighing, assessing, the result against his knowledge of that particular daughter. He, not Catherine, had gone to the "Conferences," those fear-inspiring meetings with teachers designed to show that the schools were not impersonal.

Both Hat and Becky had passed the classroom criteria. They were good students, "active in extracurricular activities," "group-oriented," "creative," "possessed leadership qualities," were "well-adjusted," and "college material."

It was Loren who had caused Teddy to lose interest in the schools. Loren was at first, politely, an "underachiever," and "did not live up to her potential." Later, this "potential" itself was questioned. She seemed to be "lacking in interests"; nothing "captured her imagination"; her work, when she handed it in, was not "creative." She was "withdrawn," "uncooperative," and "destructive to classroom morale." She had refused to salute the flag, not for any "interesting ideological reasons," but just because, she had said, "it was too boring"; she would not take P.E. for the same reason; she was not well-adjusted socially; she was "immature." Mr. Oliver must not feel bad; he had two other successful daughters; perhaps Loren felt inadequate trying to live up to the high family standards. But she must, at least, be encouraged to do what she was capable of doing. Was not that all that was asked of anyone in this world?

The "denouement" had come last year, while Loren was a ninth grader in junior high. Western Civilization was studying The Myths of Our Culture. They were to do a paper and a "project."

For her paper, Loren chose the Birth of Avatars and researched it with unaccustomed enthusiasm. She included the birth of Zeus, of Christ, of Buddha, of Venus, and ended with the appearance of the child Superman from the Planet Krypton, discovered upon the doorstep of the Kent family. This last phenomenon was not appreciated by the teacher and she was given a D for facetiousness.

The "project" assigned to her was to make the Parthenon out of sugar cubes, which she did with the help of Clemente. She then left it upon the living room floor, where it was eaten by Hurwulf. She refused to make another. A note came from the teacher saying that if the project was not handed in, Loren would fail the course.

Teddy replied, humorously delineating the disaster, adding that he intended to take Loren on a "field trip" soon to see the "real thing." Would that not do?

No, it would not.

Could she not then make the Roman Forum, as she had already done the Parthenon?

The Forum had already been assigned to someone else; the projects were to be put upon display for Public School Week; a Parthenon, not two Forums, was needed. There was virtue, moreover, in completing a task despite difficulties. Had Mr. Oliver ever heard of a Freudian accident? It might be worthwhile seeking some outside psychiatric advice.

The schools, Teddy had concluded, would always be products of lower-middle-class aspirations and mores, of small minds and little imagination, of people who talked about "creativity," but who, upon facing the real thing, felt threatened. It was an ugly atmosphere of chalk dust, rules, educational lingo and puritanism. He had resigned his positions, refused to join committees, and, for Public Service, turned to the Peace Movement, where, he decided, the real action now was.

To be surrounded by the young instead of their brainwashed parents and teachers was a new pleasure. Passive Resistance appealed to him; he had marched, attended meetings, Be-Ins, Teach-Ins, donated money. Like Hat, he had considered going to jail; perhaps he could write his memoirs as a prisoner, as so many famous men had done before him. He had toyed with titles: *Inside, Looking Out, A Time for All Good Men, Stone Walls Do Not,* by T. Oliver.

But, just as he was contemplating this bold step, the Peace Movement had turned violent. He was willing to go limp; he could not approve of Molotov cocktails. He made a few impassioned speeches; the young radicals had looked bored. They still accepted his financial contributions, but he began to sense that they were leaving him out of their planning. Even Hat stopped discussing Resistance tactics with him and no longer encouraged him to participate. He had felt the rude chill of ingratitude.

He turned then to Conservation. Saving a redwood grove or a herd of sea lions had a simpler, more uncomplicated virtue to it; it was, perhaps, not as dramatic, but one knew where one was. Redwood groves were not nonachievers who made "Freudian slips"; neither did they manufacture bombs in basements. Conservation had given Teddy a new sense of civic satisfaction.

In his personal life, he concentrated more fully than ever upon his family. Here he could be in control, could instill ideas of beauty, grace and love, so lacking in the schools, into their everyday existence. Without Catherine, this seemed even more important. Games, trips, pets, holidays, their secret language, their private little jokes — he had created all of this; in the end, this would be his monument. Zimmy had said so. Clemente was even now celebrating this creation in her mural.

But this morning it did not, somehow, seem enough. His sister, who knew exactly how to get under his skin, had managed to undermine his faith even in this. The record had stopped; he walked slowly back toward Fala. Fighting his peculiar despair, he thought again of his novel — of the young savior, the innocent, native girl. He would dig it out and begin again.

Coming out of the sunlight into the dark room, he was startled to see a woman bending over his desk dusting. Her quiet, deft movements reminded him of someone — Felicita. It was just in this humble, modest way she would have cared for the young man's house.

"Oh, Teddy, I'm sorry. I thought you were through with your work," Clemente said. She looked up at him with an earnest, apologetic smile.

"My dear, I am."

"I wouldn't have bothered you for the world."

"Clemente, you never bother anyone. As a matter of fact, I was feeling just a bit depressed. Your presence cheers me."

"Depressed?" Her look of concern would have been amusing had it not been so comforting. "Is something wrong?"

"No, nothing. That's the problem with depressions. There is usually nothing to hang them on. I hear this sort of thing happens to aging men. Probably my dear sister worked me up a bit, talking of all of you leaving."

"Who is leaving?"

"After all, she is quite right; children do grow up and begin their own lives. Well, I must put up with it, as one does with rheumatism."

"Teddy, you're not old." Clemente dropped the dustcloth on the desk and approached him. "You could never be old; your spirit is so . . . young. Why, I'd rather be with you than people my own age any day." She laughed childishly. "I can't imagine abandoning you."

"Clemente" — his hand came to rest lightly on her shoulder —

"you ought to be a nun or a missionary or something. Heal the sick, the halt, the lame —"

"I think probably I'm better at dusting," Clemente said with a shy smile.

10

MARY did not go to Girl Friday on her day off. She had put off writing her mother a Christmas letter because she had no news of Pete. Reluctantly she skipped class to go to the Indian Center.

From the Greyhound station in San Francisco she took a city bus. Used now to Los Robles Hills, the dingy section of the city they drove through suddenly frightened her. It seemed to be all parts and pieces — half-finished freeways; overpasses which ended, like a nightmare, in midair; the rubble of torn-down buildings; the blank stares of buildings waiting to be torn down. Because of the construction, the bus had to take detours; it jolted over abandoned streetcar tracks, over ruts and holes. After half an hour, she got off and walked the two blocks down dark, lonely, littered streets to the old two-story structure which housed the Indian Center. The center was upstairs; downstairs there was a vacant store, still filled with empty showcases.

Mary climbed the filthy steps; rock music filled the landing. She stood in the doorway, gazing shyly into the room. It was crowded with people her age, standing in small groups or sitting on chairs which lined the wall. The ceiling was decorated with red and green crepe paper and there was a small Christmas tree upon a table.

Miss Shelton came to greet her. She was a middle-aged, stringy, white woman, who wore a limp, red-wool dress and a sprig of holly fastened to her bosom. Her eyes, behind rimless glasses, looked at Mary calmly. "We haven't seen you for a long time, Mary," she said, in a matter-of-fact, careful tone, as if she were talking to a timid, high-strung animal she did not want to frighten away. "Are you still studying secretarial work?"

Mary nodded.

"We're very proud of you; you must be very proud of yourself. And how are things at home with your family?"

"They're all right." Then she blurted out, "Have you seen my brother, Miss Shelton?"

Miss Shelton answered her in the same careful way. "No, we haven't, Mary. But the police stopped by here the other day to ask us about him. I'm afraid your brother may be in bad company. But you mustn't let that spoil your Christmas. We have a lovely group of young people here tonight. The Baptist Choir is going to lead us in Christmas carols. Won't you come in and have some punch and cookies?"

Mary shook her head and started slowly back down the stairs.

"One of our young people is going to recite a poem he wrote about the Great Spirit." The director's voice was higher and faster, a kind of pleading, seductive note had replaced the businesslike tone.

This sudden show of emotion frightened Mary more; Miss Shelton's words, the loud music, even the gay decorations filled her with an awful desolation. She ran down the stairs and out into the dark and silent street.

11

"When I was in college, the girls were all called names like Trinki, Blitz and Cubby," Teddy said. It was a Sunday afternoon, a week before Christmas. Mad Fred and Teddy sat on old lounge chairs beside the murky waters of the swimming pool, drinking Heineken beer. By profession, Fred was a mournful listener. He put a cigarette into his mouth, let it dangle unlit, and listened.

"They had long legs and husky voices, like boys."

Fred nodded solemnly. He knew. He was from a wealthy eastern family; he had gone to Yale for a year, or perhaps two; at times, it seemed, he had even graduated. Then he had come West. Owing to an obscure ailment variously described as a horseback injury, a degenerating disk, and an unnamed hereditary disease, he had missed the war; with some family money he had bought Fred's Place, living in one of the back rooms. He had been there ever since. He had married, or had he? He had no children, or, perhaps, he did? His unconventional life gave him a faint air of vice which appealed to Teddy's imagination.

"I was just a small-town poor boy," said Teddy. This was not true; his father had owned a flourishing real estate office — Oliver's Realty ("A Little Down to Feather Your Nest"), in Siskiyou City, in northern California. But Fred's presence worked upon his fancies like a drug; even the truth sometimes took on a storybook quality.

"I was a rich black sheep," said Fred.

"I didn't date them; I was afraid of them."

"Damn right, too. Bitches, all of them," said Fred. "I've watched them grow up. They pick a fight with their husbands and then get into their Cadillacs and come down and bore me. You know what I mean, you know that kind of broad. Catherine never did that, Teddy. She had class."

"Drinking upset her stomach," Teddy said. This was true, but he said it for another reason. He knew that Fred would never accept such a commonplace explanation.

"No, she was a classy dame," said Fred. "She didn't like me, Teddy, but she was classy just the same."

"Why didn't she like you, Fred?"

"Ha!" Fred chewed on the cigarette, then remembered to light it. This activity, done with a slow deliberation, enhanced the suspense. "Well, she only liked classy people," he said at last. "I was repulsive to her; she shrank from my presence. To her, I was the scum of the earth." He dragged on the cigarette, removed it, and took a swallow from the bottle. "Scum, filthy, rotten to the core," he said, and belched happily.

"I doubt if she felt that," said Teddy, gently urging him on.

"She did," said Fred, "because she was classy. Hat is, too. Hat was the first to recoil from Lulu. I saw her look of distaste. No, I saw it; it was there. Mad Fred, she was saying to herself, is a dirty old man. She will save herself for someone stalwart and clean-limbed." He belched again. "I saw her playing tennis with Clyde the other day. It gave me a start. I thought it was Catherine."

"I wouldn't exactly describe her friends as clean-limbed at the moment."

"A passing fancy. Her Prince will come and care for her, as you did for Catherine."

"Hat's quit Stanford, Fred. She says college is a Bad Scene."

"That's unimportant. Girls don't need education. That's purely a modern notion which will change in time. Hat will become a wife and mother, the mistress of a lovely home —"

Teddy smiled and sipped his drink. "My sister thinks *I* should remarry," he said.

Fred nodded gravely.

"She doesn't think I'm providing the proper environment for my daughters. What's your opinion of that, Mad Fred?"

"Why don't you ask Zimmy?"

"I'm asking you."

"Then I say fuck your sister, Teddy. That's what I said to mine. Go your own way, seek your own destiny. You're a woman's man. You surround yourself with them. Maybe another classy dame will come along. But it's none of your sister's beeswax."

"No one," said Teddy, watching Fred's face, "could replace Catherine."

Fred nodded again; his mad eyes glittered like a satyr's.

"You don't think anyone could, do you?"

"What I say is, wait and see. Who can predict?" His tone seemed to indicate that he could, if he chose.

"I have a lot of plans, Fred, but they don't include marriage. I'm going to take the girls on a trip to Europe. When we return, I want to finish my book. I'm also thinking of building an observatory to study the stars. The entire universe is up there, like a big map, waiting to be read. Then, there's Zimmy's life dream — his clinic. I still want to help him with that if I can."

Fred grunted. "I hope he's better with nuts than he is at tennis," he said.

"He's an extremely brilliant man, Fred. He deserves a backer."

"I thought you'd been through all that. Isn't that what you used to talk about down there in your study?"

"Yes, but Catherine's lawyers panicked. We would have had to use capital. She wasn't well at the time and I didn't want to push it. I'm not really sure she liked Zimmy, anyhow."

"Capital," said Fred dreamily. "I used my capital years ago. I can remember the ruckus. Using capital, Teddy, is some kind of mortal sin. I'm not sorry, though. I have what I want. And I have a plaque to go with it, thanks to you."

"You're an easy man to please, Fred."

"I am. I never really wanted very much. Like, right now, a new roof. I can't pay for it, but something will happen. It always does. I need a new roof before winter."

"You're a lucky man, too, if that's all you require."

"You're telling me!" said Fred.

12

To explore the world of the sephiroth you must disentangle yourself from the world of everyday life. A man cannot wander through the landscape of the sephiroths until he is free from all physical sensations, thoughts and worries which keep him tied to his usual surroundings. The physical and mental exercises of the cabalists are designed to achieve this.

Loren, lying on the sofa, put down *The Black Arts* and gazed with mild curiosity at her sister.

Becky, dressed in jeans, cowboy shirt and cowboy boots, was entering the living room with the mail. She threw it down upon a table, then scrambled through it, extracting a white envelope which was addressed in a prim, childish hand to The Oliver Family. This she opened greedily.

"It's come," said Becky. "This is it! I addressed it myself two days ago. I helped them with the invitations."

Free from thoughts, thought Loren. Unable, at this moment, to achieve this goal, she said, "What invitations?"

"To Linda's Coming-Out party. We're all invited. January twenty-eighth. I'm going to get a new dress and grow a ponytail."

"A debut," said Loren, "is just an outdated sexual rite. It means that Linda Alway is pubescent and may be courted by the males of her tribe." She picked up her book again. Then, "Is Linda Alway the one who appears in horse shows?"

"She won five blue ribbons at the Cow Palace, and First Place in Jumping. You should see her dress, Loren. They were going to order one from France, then Mr. Alway got mad at de Gaulle so they ordered it from Spain instead."

"Is this the party where Teddy is to meet Mrs. Collier?"

"She's coming all the way from Chicago."

"To meet Teddy?"

"Don't be silly, for Linda's debut."

"Perhaps Teddy will prefer the ravishing, virginal Linda to the aged, menopausal Mrs. Collier?"

Becky giggled. "Stupid, Linda is eighteen."

"She is undoubtedly precocious for her age. The motion of the saddle makes girls lustful. If she doesn't run off with a stable groom, she will probably marry an older, rich man who is expert at sex."

"Well, I hope you don't come to the party, Loren. If you said things like that, I'd just die of embarrassment. What's that?"

"What's what?"

"That noise."

There was a loud humming sound, and the house shook. Becky ran to the window. "It's Santa Claus," she cried.

"He certainly makes a disturbance. I thought he came quietly, at night, when everyone was asleep."

"It's Santa Claus in a helicopter! I can see him! Come on!" She ran out the door, through the porch, on to the driveway.

Loren followed at a dignified distance.

The tiny, quivery craft hovered above them; they could see the pilot, wearing a red elf's cap, and Santa Claus himself, waving. Hurwulf, awakened from a nap on the lawn, barked crazily.

"Hello Santa! Wave at Santa!" shouted Becky.

"It's just some old alcoholic they hired because he has a red nose," said Loren.

"Shut up, Hurwulf. Hello, Santa! Hello! They're going to the shopping center to land. Where's Hat? Let's make Hat take us."

Becky ran back into the house; Loren followed. "Hat?" screamed Becky. "I wish Clemente could drive. Where's Hat?"

"Can you imagine Clemente on a freeway?"

"Here's Hat. Hat, please drive me down to the El Rancho. I want to see Santa Claus land. He's passing out free presents! Then you can take me to Saks to look for a dress. Teddy says you have to."

"Shut up, Becky," said Hat. "If you shut up, I'll take you down, but you'll have to hitchhike back. I have other things to do besides going to Saks. I hate the way those stores smell, like brothels."

"How do you know how a brothel smells?" said Loren.

"You shut up, too," said Hat.

"I'm going to get a pink velvet dress with a high waistline," said Becky. "Linda's dress is wine-colored, to go with the theme. Mrs. Alway thought pink would blend nicely. It's like getting married; you're supposed to harmonize with Linda but not overshadow her. Linda's the moon, and we're all little stars."

"That's why I'm not going," said Loren. "I would hate to detract from Linda's great moment." She turned toward Hat. "Since you're so obliging, I'll hitch a ride, too. I have a little shopping to do myself and — Did I say 'A-N-D'?"

"Did you say what?" said Hat.

"I don't want to speak the word. Can't you spell?"

"I really wasn't paying any attention to anything you said."

"I think I said it."

"Well, tough shit. What if you did?"

"I'm practicing a discipline. I don't want to say 'A-N-D' for a month. Now I shall have to punish myself by cutting my arm with a razor. I hope I have the courage."

"Clyde's right," said Hat. "You're getting balmy."

"Balmy to an Outbar, which hardly concerns me."

The reader board of the El Rancho Shopping Center said:

    5 days til Xmas
    Good Will Tord Men
    Best Food Mayonaise 59¢

The buildings of the center — California-ranch-style with shake roofs and carved wood signs — were decorated with blue and silver foil, which sparkled in the sunshine.

The helicopter had landed; in the parking lot a crowd was gathered, hiding Santa Claus from view. Hearty chuckles and jolly Ho, Ho, Ho's were coming from a loudspeaker.

Loren left Becky on the edge of the crowd. Trailing her long, limp, maroon crushed-velvet gown, over which she wore a piece of bedraggled rabbit fur, Loren walked through the Boy Scout Christmas Tree lot. Its stock was almost depleted; a few shoppers roamed the aisles between the remaining trees like giants in a ravaged woods. She walked on past the supermarket, called The Country Store, to Ye Bottle Shoppe.

In front of Ye Bottle Shoppe was a Living Creche — populated with a sheep and a goat and a camel. The camel had nasty bald spots and a sour expression; he was kept isolated from the sheep and goat and the plastic Holy Family by a fence. A high school boy, in white sheet and burnoose, holding a shepherd's crook, tended the animals.

Loren stood in front of the fence.

"You again?" said the boy.

"You got it?"

"I have half a lid. I'm saving one joint for the camel. Twenty bucks. You got the bread?"

"I'll give you fifteen."

"I can see you have the Christmas spirit, all right. Eighteen-fifty."

"Sixteen is final. I want acid, too."

He grinned. "White Lightning?"

"You've got some?"

"Rare, quality stuff. Six bucks a pill."

"Show me."

He glanced about, making certain no one was watching; then, lifting his burnoose, he dug into his jeans pocket and produced a small cough-drop box. He opened it, displaying four white pills.

Loren examined them critically. "Five bucks," she said.

"Come on. When you try it, you'll know it's worth more."

"I'll give you sixteen for the pot and five-fifty for the acid," she said firmly.

He shrugged his shoulders and handed her one pill; then, digging into the camel's feed bag, he brought out a paper sack of pot. She thrust some crumpled bills into his hand and added a fifty-cent piece.

He counted them carefully. Then, "The sack's on the house. Merry Christmas."

"It will be interesting, if not merry. My aunt is here; she knows a Widow Henderson with advanced ideas, whom she wants my father to marry. There will also be a debutante party, where he will meet a Mrs. Collier. However, I'm not too worried, as none of the mentioned candidates are nubile."

"Nubile?"

"It means you can still have babies. I don't mean that he wants babies; he just prefers the company of young people and he has that already."

"Having a baby is far out," the boy said. "My sister has this groovy little kid. She's only two, but she looks like a miniature grown-up. She wears this intense little dress and classy little boots."

"Your goat is nibbling at the Christ Child."

"You stoned, by the way?"

"I smoked my last joint several hours ago. My crop did very badly this year, which is why I'm here. Well, so long. I hope the camel has a good trip."

"He needs something." The boy held up his crook as if it were a bishop's staff. "Peace!" he proclaimed.

"Peace!" Loren turned away, back into the crowd.

Santa Claus was climbing back into the helicopter, followed by a flock of children. The loudspeaker began a Christmas carol.

Joy to the world, the Lord is come.

Loren hummed the tune under her breath, being careful about the "ands."

13

"THEY had long legs and husky voices, like boys," Teddy said. Mother Humilitia smiled agreeably. She was paying her Christmas visit to the Olivers, bearing walnuts from the convent's trees in a burlap sack tied up with a red ribbon. From the porch window, Teddy could see the four young nuns she had brought with her playing doubles on the court. They looked like old-fashioned schoolgirls in midi-length, navy-blue cotton skirts, white blouses, dark stockings and tennis shoes. Sister Gabrielle from France, Sister Mary Aloysius from Montreal, Sister Mary Modesta from Belgium and Sister Juanita from Mexico. All, according to Mother Humilitia were linguists; two were social workers, one was a pediatrician, Sister Gabrielle was a scholar in early medieval history. Such an array of talent on his tennis court! Teddy felt deeply honored. But his greatest social triumph was Mother Humilitia herself, who sat opposite him sipping a sherry as he drank a Scotch.

"I was shy with them, but then I'm still shy with the ladies," he said with a boyish grin. He took pride in speaking to her freely on any subject, as he would to any intelligent woman. It was, in fact, a kind of game.

In both her manner and appearance, Mother Humilitia looked like an old-fashioned mother superior. She was in her late fifties, of Mexican-German origin. She was tall and bony with dark, hollow eyes beneath metal-rimmed spectacles; her skin was like pale saffron; she had a corpselike aspect. Unlike her charges, she dressed in the traditional habit of her order — a long, black gown, starched white collar and black bonnet. High, black, witchlike shoes peeped from beneath her skirt. Though he knew from her reputation, and from what was going on at the convent, that she possessed a lively mind and broad vision, she had steadfastly refused to reveal this part of her nature to him. How he longed to talk to her of the mysteries of her religion, of esoteric matters — Manicheans, Gnostics, Arians — exotic cults whose names intrigued him, but which he knew little about. He had even tried dropping references to demonstrate the eclecticism of his tastes; on former visits, he had brought up St. Thomas Aquinas, St. Augustine, St. John of the Cross. Today, upon the wicker table in front of her, was a book by Teilhard de Chardin, displayed in a way in which she could not miss seeing it. But none of this had worked; her favorite topics with him seemed to be the weather, news of his daughters and the deteriorating physical condition of the Convent of the Precious Blood.

Sometimes he wondered why she bothered to come? She must know people of her own faith who had tennis courts and who donated even more to the convent than he. In respect of Catherine's memory? But Catherine had only attended the Retreats; she had never officially rejoined the church. Did Mother Humilitia want to convert him? If so, she would not so firmly confine her conversation to trivialities. He would have liked to think she simply enjoyed his company, but why then did she remain so formal and elusive? He felt both frustrated and challenged by her presence.

"For someone so shy with ladies, you almost have a convent here yourself," she said merrily.

"Yes, a household of virgins." He kept his conversation as bold as possible within the limits she set. "It's a responsibility, Mother. My sister thinks I should remarry. What is your opinion of that?"

"How could I have an opinion?"

"You knew Catherine. Do you think it would be possible to ever replace her?"

"I'm not sure one replaces people as one does furniture. Every soul has its uniqueness."

"Then perhaps I should marry for the sake of my daughters?"

"Why should anyone marry except for his own sake?" Her tone indicated she was not to be seduced.

"Ah, but you see," he went on stubbornly, "my sister feels they are not growing up in the proper environment."

"I am not an environmentalist, I am afraid. That is, only when it is, unfortunately, a practical necessity. Our chapel floor, for example, is infested with termites. I have just received two estimates to repair it, but it is beyond our means. However, I shall not worry. God will provide. He always does. Nothing is perfect here on earth, only in the City of God."

He felt a mild triumph; he had forced her to discuss her theology. "I'm afraid that's where I stumble," he said, taking advantage of the opening. "I guess that's where I become a heretic."

"You can't just become a heretic," she said in an amused tone. "You have to be a heretic from something."

So he was not to be allowed even this! "But I do believe in something," he cried. "I believe in — in the power of love."

"Love?"

"That which is within all of us."

"You believe then in the perfectability of Man?"

"If I didn't," he declared passionately, "I'd throw myself off a bridge somewhere."

"Oh, mercy. Dear me, please don't. We should miss you. And, as you said, your family needs you."

She was not, he saw, taking him seriously. In her eyes he was not even a sinner, not even, no doubt, worthy of hell. She had consigned him to some sort of pallid limbo reserved for nonentities.

"I'm not sure my family really does need me," he said, disheartened.

"Come now, Mr. Oliver —" She chided him like a child.

"No, they are growing up. Hat is leaving us. She's going to

work in the city after the holidays. She feels like your young nuns; she wants to join the Revolution."

"She's old enough to make up her own mind. And your other girls? Loren and Becky?"

"Becky is busy with her friends and horses. Loren is the one I can still count on. Our family life means a great deal to her. She has imagination; we are very close. We speak the same language — I mean that literally. We call it Oon."

"Perhaps she will be a linguist, then," said Mother Humilitia with her brisk, professional cheerfulness. "And the other girl — the one who lives with you — how is she?"

"You should know her better, Mother. She is not Catholic, but she is a saint."

"I should like to. One meets few saints. But I must leave." She stood up. "It has been most pleasant."

"May I offer you another sherry?" he said, rising with her.

"Thank you, but I have an appointment with the third pest man. However, we shall be singing carols in the chapel on Christmas Eve; that is, if our floor holds up. We should be happy to have you and your family join us."

"I'll give them the invitation, but Christmas Eve we always open our presents, Mother."

She nodded and extended a long, bony, transparent hand. "Merry Christmas," she said warmly, "to you and yours. Tell them we shall remember Mrs. Oliver in our prayers."

"Remember all of us, Mother. And thank you for the walnuts. We shall enjoy them." He accompanied her to the porch door, held it open for her. He did not want to say what he said next, but the words slipped out, as smoothly as a Christmas greeting. "Don't worry about the chapel floor, Mother. Send the bill to me. That will be the Olivers' Christmas present to the convent."

"God bless you," she said tranquilly; her expression did not change.

Damn the woman, he thought, as he watched her walk toward the court, where she had left the convent's station wagon. How did she manage to make him feel like such a fool?

He went back to the wicker bar and took out a beer. Then he

noticed the sack of walnuts. He untied the ribbon, took a walnut out, cracked it between his palms, and popped a piece of the meat into his mouth. It was bitter, and he spat it back out into his hand.

14

ON the same evening when Mary visited the Indian Center, her brother Pete hitchhiked in stages down the Bayshore to the Los Robles off-ramp. Here, since no one would pick him up, he walked to the nearest service station in town and asked directions to the address which Mary had given him. The service station man looked at him suspiciously, but when Pete explained he was going to visit his sister who worked for some rich people, he showed him on the map how to get there.

He walked the ten miles, first through the town, then down dark country lanes where the houses, set high up on hills, far from the road, sparkled with Christmas lights. As he passed each house, dogs barked savagely; some of them even ran into the lane and snarled at his heels.

Pete was wearing blue jeans, a man's white dress shirt with the sleeves, which had become ragged, cut off at the elbows, a heavy, jeweled, black belt and a pair of combat boots from a surplus store. His black, lanky hair was long; around his neck he wore a nickel medallion which said "Jackie." He had pawned his black plastic jacket, and he shivered in the cool night.

Pete was not dressed this way because, like Hat's friends, he wished to model himself after an outcast from society; Pete was the real thing. He was nineteen years old and in trouble.

When the motherfucker of an army doctor had turned him down, he had hitched a ride to San Francisco, and, with as sure an instinct as the rich find their neighborhoods, he had found the Tenderloin. There he shared rooms with other derelicts and took odd jobs when he could find them. He had washed dishes, cleaned up vomit off the floors of transient hotels, and acted as a bouncer in a topless bar frequented by sailors.

He tried, during this time in his life, to figure out the city; no longer a star athlete at Eureka High, he thought if he knew where he was, he might know who he now was. He read discarded newspapers out of ashcans. Since being turned down by the army, the big news, like the war or about the President, which his teachers had called Current Events, no longer interested him. What caught his fancy were the little items about people on the back pages. A liquor-store man was held up and robbed; a spic shot up his family; a gray-haired old lady was raped in her apartment by a young white man wearing a Halloween mask.

The lovelorn column also fascinated him. In it people wrote out their troubles for everyone to read; they were funny, unfamiliar problems, like having a mother who wouldn't let you wear mini skirts, or a husband who spent his night out with "the boys"; but the peoples' names were strangely reminiscent of names of Indians he had known — Disgruntled Wife, Sick-at-Heart, Stay-at-Home, Still Growing.

Also, the obituary column intrigued him. You could sound pretty important and still not make the front page, like he could, if he died right now, in the Eureka newspaper: "Local athlete passes in San Francisco."

In the city papers, most deaths were part of Vital Statistics. "Pioneer Woman" had only three paragraphs; "Business Mogul," two; "Well-known Dentist," "Bay Area Artist," "Philanthropist," one each. The less important people were in a column entitled "Deaths." He imagined himself there. Then somebody told him you had to pay to get even this small notice in.

Death in the city was like the other Vital Statistics — like the Sun, Moon and Tides, Rainfall, Snow Report, Temperatures and Road Conditions. He found this interesting.

The odd jobs grew scarcer, and he turned to what the reservation minister had called a "life of crime." Pete never really thought of it this way. This "life of crime" just consisted of keeping reds, speed and pot in his room for an old junkie he had met at the café. Various people, sent by the junkie, would visit his room; Pete would sell them the stuff, and the old man would give him a cut.

This activity usually took place in the daytime; at night, he wandered the Tenderloin, crowded with pimps and prostitutes of both sexes — alcoholics, drug freaks, bands of baby-faced sailors and an occasional party of well-dressed white folks visiting the Minerva Café for the Greek music and dancing. On reds himself, then speed, he wandered in a dream. He made no lasting friendships; sex, which he had experimented with in various forms, no longer interested him. He could not even remember who the Jackie of the medallion was, nor even which sex Jackie had been.

The Indian Center, which he had gone to for its parties before he had been turned down by the army, seemed as much another world as the reservation. For a time, he remembered his mother, and the memory had caused pain; now, blissfully, he forgot her, too. A few times, wandering through Golden Gate Park, he had gone off the path and walked over pine needles; their dry odor and crunching sound reminded him of northern California. But sensations now were numbed, and he preferred this.

In one still-alert part of his mind, like a kind of safety catch, was the thought of his sister Mary. But the last time he had seen her she was scarcely recognizable; her manner had been more like the manner of the thin, sparse, white lady who ran the Indian Center than anyone from his present life. Mary had given him money, then lectured him like a schoolteacher. Still, he had enough to keep him going for the present, and the future did not exist any more.

Then something happened. The junkie for whom he was fronting stopped coming with the stuff; he heard from somebody else at the café that he had been busted. That was two nights ago; he had not returned to his room since. He had two dollars in his pocket; he left the Tenderloin and made his way down the peninsula. In the still unfogged region of his mind he knew of only one person who could help him.

He walked, now, beneath a new underpass, then down another dark lane, through an open gate which had a sign on it which read A MEMBER OF THE 4-H CLUB LIVES HERE, and up a long, graveled, private road. At the end of this road was a very large lighted house with a small, orange sports car parked in front of it. It was nine-thirty at night; he was cold, hungry, dazed. He rang the Olivers' doorbell.

A girl with long, silky, blond hair and a soft, round face answered. She looked at him oddly with startled blue eyes, then she quickly closed the door, except for a crack.

"I'm looking for Mary Miller," Pete muttered.

"I'm sorry, it's Mary's day off."

"I can wait," Pete said.

"I'm afraid I can't say when she will be home. It's usually quite late. Perhaps you had better come back another time. Whom shall I say called?"

He stared at her dully; all he understood was that he had to see Mary — Mary was his last chance. This understanding sent a slow impulse to his motor reactions, and he put one boot into the crack.

The girl uttered a low cry.

"What is it, Clemente?" another girl's voice asked impatiently.

"Someone . . . for Mary."

The speaker came to the door. She was a tall girl with dark, curly, short hair. Across her forehead, restraining her hair, was a blue and white beaded Indian headband. Her dress was short, made of natural-colored suede, with fringe on the bottom. She was barefoot. Pete could remember Halloween costume parties at his school, where kids dressed like Indians. Was it Halloween? He had thought it was nearer Christmas, but perhaps he had made a mistake.

The girl looked at Pete with large, brown, thoughtful eyes. "Why you must be Mary's brother," she said in a husky voice. "I bet you're Pete!"

Pete nodded.

"For God's sake, Clemente, ask him in."

The blond girl let go of the door, and Pete walked into a large, warm hall.

"Come on into the living room," the girl commanded. She went on talking as she strode ahead, leading him into a larger room. There were soft rugs, big paintings on the walls — bright blobs of color; a fire burned in a stone fireplace, and a fat, furry dog lay in front of it asleep. The dog opened its eyes, blinked at Pete, and then curled its tongue in a yawn and closed its eyes again.

"Mary's not home. It's her day off, but to tell you the truth, I'm not sorry," the girl was saying. She spoke in a low, rapid, husky tone. "I've been wondering if you'd ever show." She squatted down, Indian-fashion, beside the fire, and motioned for Pete to join her. He chose a small straight chair instead. The girl smiled up at him, running her fingers through her hair. "I've been dying to talk to you, and frankly speaking . . . alone." She laughed, as if at some secret pleasure. "You want a beer or something?" she said.

He was faint from thirst and hunger, but he shook his head no.

"Okay, this is the thing, Pete. I'm concerned about Mary."

"Mary?" he muttered.

"Mary, your sister," she said, and laughed again, this time at his stupidity. "She isn't half dumb, you know. If she were given a fair IQ test that wasn't based on Wasp standards, she'd probably come out very well. But she's got to get over her slave mentality; she's absolutely loaded with hang-ups." She was gazing at him with a kind of joyful anticipation. "We're communicating, aren't we?"

Puzzled, he nodded.

"I thought we would. I could tell by looking at your picture on Mary's dresser. Mary told me you've stopped going to that Indian Center that's run by some honky. I mean, she doesn't think it's rotten, and that's the problem. She's just got a ghastly permanent on top of it. I've tried talking to her, but I get nowhere. It's a real hassle. But, I gather, from what she says about you, that you're one of us." She smiled encouragingly.

Pete stared at her dumbly. Her voice and manner suddenly brought back another, faraway world. He was sitting in a classroom; Miss Somebody-or-Other, a white teacher, was talking to him; her voice was enthusiastic; she was smiling in the same way, urging him on — to what? He could no longer remember.

"I mean, you're with the Revolution, aren't you? You're not just going to accept your position in life because that's what you've been told to do by the Establishment. I can tell you're different from Mary, and I admire you tremendously for it. I really do!"

The strange room, the warmth from the fire, her lean, brisk boyishness made him feel fainter. He held his eyes wide open, trying to keep from passing out.

"I want to help Mary and you, too," she was saying. "The thing is, at the moment, I'm terribly tied up with another aspect of the Power Struggle; we're fighting the campus Establishment. As soon as Stanford starts, we're going to picket the R.O.T.C."

I mustn't pass out, Pete thought.

"I'm also awfully involved with the Women's Liberation Front. But it's all the same bag. Power to the People, right? I wanted to give Mary some money for the Indian cause, but she wouldn't take it. You will, won't you?" She leaned eagerly toward him; there was a kind of harsh wistfulness in her manner. "I mean, if I write you a check, you'll see it gets to the right people? As soon as this R.O.T.C. thing is over, if I don't land in jail, which is a definite possibility" — she gave a little sigh at this thought — "we'll get together. By the way, have you ever been in jail?"

He had not been following her conversation. Jail? Why was she asking this? Could she know, or had she guessed about his problem? He shook his head no, firmly.

"Too bad. I was hoping you could give me some tips. Oh, well, it doesn't matter. I'll learn soon enough, I suppose. I understand the food is ghastly, and I'm definitely considering a hunger strike." She uncrossed her knees and twisted around, sensuously stretching her long, brown, bare legs out upon the rug and propping her head up on one arm; her face, turned toward him, was flushed with excitement. "You know what we're going to do, Pete? We're opening a headquarters in the city. S.D.S. But, actually, it's going to be part of the whole scene. Blacks, Reds, Chicanos, women — we're going to liberate the Third World. Maybe some of your group would like to contribute to our underground newspaper. We're awfully short of Indians at the moment." She sat up abruptly and glanced at a tiny gold watch upon her wrist. "Hell, I have to split," she said. "I wish we could rap more, but I promised to pick up my little sister at a neighbor's. My father's out; he's showing my aunt the Christmas decorations, isn't that wild? You can stay here and wait for Mary, if you like. But I'll give you the donation first, in case I don't make it back in time. Clemente, will you be terribly sweet and get my checkbook for me?"

The blond girl, who had been standing in the doorway all this time, disappeared.

"Will twenty help? I'm kind of low right now with Christmas and all. You know how it is." She sighed. "If I were playing it absolutely straight, I guess I'd sell my Porsche and give the money to the Resistance, but you have to have some kind of transportation if you're going to get anything accomplished, right?"

Pete nodded.

The blond girl came back, and the tall girl wrote out the check. "There," she said, and handed it to him. She stood up. "I'm really sorry I have to leave, but maybe you'll still be here when we get back. If you're not, phone up and get our office address in the city. Promise?"

She was walking into the hall toward the door. He followed her. "Well, Merry Christmas and all that, if I don't see you," she said, and opened the door. She said, "Oh, Clyde!"

A thin man in a Stetson hat stood on the doorstep. He took off the Stetson and smiled at the girl, then he looked over her at Pete. His eyes narrowed suspiciously. Pete understood the look. After the confusion of this crazy house he found it almost comforting.

"I was on my way up here to pay you a visit," the man said in a slow, measured tone. "I stopped at the filling station in town, and they told me you were going to have a visitor." His eyes stayed on Pete as he talked.

"A visitor?" the girl said impatiently.

The thin man nodded his head at Pete.

"Well, you don't mean Pete, for heaven's sake?"

"I sort of did."

The girl laughed. "Clyde, this is Mary Miller's brother. You know, Mary, our maid. He's waiting to see her, and we've just had this beautiful talk."

The man stretched out a hand; after a moment, Pete realized what he wanted and stretched out his, awkwardly. The man shook it without changing his expression. "Nice to meet you, Pete," he said. Then he turned to the tall girl. "Is Teddy around?" he asked.

"Teddy? No, he's taken Aunt Harriet out, thank God. Clemente and I are going to pick up Becky."

"What about Pete?"

"Well, what about him? He's going to wait for Mary, aren't you, Pete?"

Pete did not answer. The man was silent, too.

He seemed to be thinking. Then he said, "I'll tell you what. Why don't I drive Pete up to the road and drop him off? He can come back another time and see Mary."

"Well, I don't know. Why don't you ask him what he wants to do? I'd take him myself if I didn't have to run stupid errands. Come on, Clemente." The tall girl and her friend brushed past the man and went out into the driveway.

"Okay, Pete," said the man; this time his voice was sharper.

Pete followed him out. The two girls had already climbed into the Porsche, the tall girl in the driver's seat. She started the car, and, spinning the wheels on the gravel, sped out of the driveway.

The man gestured for Pete to get into his Cadillac. They drove down the long drive, then out on to the road; the man did not say a word. When they had gone about two miles, the man stopped the car. "You live in San Francisco?" he said.

"Yes, sir."

"Okay, the highway's just up ahead. I'm heading south, myself. Just one thing, though. I don't think it's a good idea for you to come back here unless Mr. Oliver is home. You can telephone first and make arrangements for a visit. Do you understand?"

"Yes, sir."

Pete got out of the car, and the Cadillac swung around and drove off into the night.

He felt better out in the cold air again. He walked a short distance toward town, then he turned back. The road here was bordered by tall eucalyptus trees, and he stayed behind these until he reached the Olivers' gate. Avoiding the drive, he made his way through some pine trees, then he crossed the lawn, keeping in back of the oaks. The house stood before him; there were no cars, now, in front of it, but the lights were still on inside. He walked slowly around the house, hugging its side. It grew darker. He stumbled once over a bicycle which lay on the ground and hurt his knee. But the pain made him feel more alive and kept him going. He came to a back gate, which he pushed open. His face bumped against a clothesline. He found the side of the house again, and a back door. He tried the door; it opened, and he slipped inside. He was in a narrow hall. At the end of this hall was a strange, curving, metal flight of stairs, which he assumed must lead to the second floor. If I'm caught up here, he thought foggily, I can say I'm looking for Mary's room.

He climbed the staircase. It ended at an arched doorway. He opened the door; instead of a second floor, he found himself in a single, separate apartment — one large, round room, like a cave, with another open door, which he saw led into a bathroom. The room was lit eerily with a green light, which came from a lamp with a green glass shade hanging from the domed ceiling. All around the room were windows with cushioned window seats beneath them. On the seats were piles of comic books and science fiction. There were straw mats and cushions upon the floor; a brass bed, which was unmade; the walls were covered with strange posters. One was of the heavens, with stars, moons and planets wheeling dangerously; one of letters of the alphabet in a peculiar pyramid order; one was the head of a hairless man, marked off in sections with a number in each. The most terrible was that of a goat with wings and breasts and a star upon its forehead between its immense curving horns; its black, bearded face watched Pete thoughtfully. A sweet, heavy odor filled the air; it seemed to come from a small, glowing cone upon a plate in the center of one of the straw mats.

Pete found the room frightening, and he wasted no time. He moved quickly to a small bureau and began to open its drawers. He rummaged clumsily among jewelry, sweaters, girl's underwear, nightgowns. Except for a small flashlight, which he slipped into the pocket of his jeans, there seemed to be nothing worth his search.

Then he noticed a fourth, narrower drawer, with no knobs, at the bottom of the bureau. Beneath scarves and more sweaters he felt something hard and square and metallic. He pulled it out. It was a small, black, tin box with a lock upon it. It would not open; he shook it, heard coins, and thought, paper money. He slipped this into the other jeans pocket, then pushed the drawer closed with his foot. He was tiptoeing toward a closet when he heard a voice behind him say, "Hello." He whirled around and found himself facing another girl.

The girl stood, staring at him. She was in her early teens; she wore a long, green, wool-fringed skirt and a fringed shawl and beads around her neck. Her dark hair fell straight down her back. Her eyes were large and dark, and strange. He felt a thrill of terror.

"Who are you?" said the girl. Her voice was calm.

"I'm Mary Miller's brother," he muttered. "I'm looking for Mary."

"Mary's not home. This isn't her room, anyway. It's my room." The girl came closer. "Nobody's supposed to enter my room. As a matter of fact, it's usually locked. But I just went down to the kitchen for a moment." Her eyes examined him, up and down, with a kind of cold curiosity. Then, suddenly, she reached out and grabbed his medallion. She examined it for a moment, while he stood there frozen.

"Jackie," she said. "Who was Jackie?"

He did not answer.

She dropped the medallion.

"Was Jackie someone you loved?"

He stared at her helplessly; he could feel the weight of the box in his jeans. "You don't see Jackie any more?" she said.

"No."

"Did Jackie betray you or did you betray Jackie?"

He was faint again, as he had been downstairs. He felt himself trembling. He did not know what to say to this strange girl.

"You certainly are nervous," she said. "You need a fix or something?"

He shook his head and moved towards the door.

"Aren't you going to wait for Mary?"

"No. I . . . haven't time."

The girl shrugged her shoulders and turned away; she seemed to have lost all interest in him.

He brushed past her, out of the door.

Outside again, he ran as far as he could, away from that terrible house. At last, exhausted, he slid into a ditch beside the road. It was damp and cold. He slept for a while.

When he awoke, it was late at night. The black sky was sprinkled with many tiny stars. He was stiff and light-headed and so chilled that he shook uncontrollably. Then he remembered the box. With difficulty, because of the shaking, he pulled it out of his pocket and put it on a flat rock. Finding another rock, he attacked it clumsily and savagely, smashing the flimsy lid. He pulled the lid off with trembling fingers and dropped it into the ditch. Then he stood up, took the flashlight out of his pocket, and examined the contents of the box.

Inside were a few coins, some Zig Zag papers, a roach holder, a plastic sack of grass, a photograph of a woman, four pills — probably acid — and six beautiful twenty-dollar bills.

Pete dropped the box and the photograph in the ditch and thrust the rest of the contents of the box into his pocket. The check the tall girl had given him was no good; he could never cash it. But the money would get him some food and another bed until he got something moving again.

15

"INGREE flin Mary's brother strunlos," said Loren to Teddy late the next morning, as she followed him out the door on his way to Fala. "Ingree flin li money box."

Teddy stopped. "What did you say?"

"I don't have to translate for you, too, do I? Well, I suppose I have enriched the language on my own, some. I said, Mary's brother was here last night; he stole my money box."

"How do you know that?"

"I met him in my room. He told me he was Mary's brother. He was an Indian. The box is gone."

Teddy sighed. "How much was in it?"

"One hundred and twenty dollars and sixty-four cents."

"Oh, damn," said Teddy.

"I have been saving for four months."

"Oh, hell. I suppose he shouldn't come again. As a matter of fact, Clyde called last night to warn me he didn't like the fellow's looks. I'm afraid I pooh-poohed the whole thing. Now Clyde will think I'm dreadfully naïve, won't he? He'll be able to say, 'I told you so.' Damn."

"I'm more concerned about my money than what Clyde will say. I am thinking of calling the police." She was not thinking of calling them even though, if the acid was discovered, she could claim that Pete had put it there. She was happy, at least, she had put part of the pot into a coffee tin.

"Oh, for God's sake, we can't call the police," Teddy said. "I'll make the money up to you."

"There is a principle involved," said Loren, who did not believe there was a principle involved.

"I'll give you a hundred and twenty dollars to forget your principles."

"My principles are worth more than that. They're worth at least a hundred and fifty. The extra is for the emotional trauma."

"One hundred and fifty, providing you don't say anything to Mary or anyone else, including Clyde. It would only upset Mary, and it would strengthen Clyde's tendency to be oversuspicious. It's very sweet, the way he looks after us, but we don't want him to think we're too helpless." He reached over and rumpled Loren's hair. "Fair enough?"

"Fair enough."

"I admire a woman of principle."

She grinned. "There was a photograph of Catherine in the box," she said.

Teddy stiffened. Money was impersonal; the photograph was not. He was experiencing the sensation of ravaged intimacy which goes with being robbed. "Well, there are other pictures around," he said firmly, trying not to show his shock.

16

THOUGH it was known that Clemente's mother was coming for Christmas, she had been vague about the date of her arrival. She had arrived in New York from London, where she had been doing research at the British Museum, stayed there for a time, evidently in somebody's empty apartment, and was now winding her way across the United States in what she called "my caravan."

A series of postcards preceded her. Teddy suggested that they follow her trip upon a map. The first card, from Savannah, Georgia ("one of North America's early planned cities"), seemed to suggest she was taking a southern route to avoid bad weather. But the next card was from Concord, Massachusetts ("I walked over the bridge that arched the flood."); the next from Springfield, Illinois ("I have finally visited Lincoln's tomb."); the next from Fort Laramie ("so interesting when you think of the Oregon Trail"); and the last from Salt Lake ("from here I shall follow the route of that unhappy Donner Party"). After that — silence.

"Let us hope she did not follow it too literally," said Teddy, reading the *San Francisco Chronicle* at the breakfast table two days before Christmas. A storm had risen in the Sierras, imprisoning skiers in resorts; highways were closed, chains required at even low altitudes; no one was crossing the Summit.

But in the early evening of that same day an old Ford station wagon drove up in the driveway, a horn tooted, and they all poured out of the house to greet her. How had she made it?

Leah, stepping out of the car, smiled happily and began a round of kisses. But they were not to be put off so easily. Had she carried chains? Had she put them on herself? How had she got past the highway patrol? How had she driven at all in such a storm?

Storm? She would not have called it a storm, not really. Yes, it had snowed; she had followed a snow machine for a while, which had cleared the way for her. It had been most exhilarating because, except for the machine, there were no other cars at all upon the road; it had been like traveling through a vast white wilderness. She had found it easy to imagine herself as one of those ill-fated pioneers. Her imagination had soared even further. With no familiar landmarks, everything transfigured into shapeless white humps, she thought she understood the experiences of mystics. In this visionary state she had reviewed her life and come to certain new conclusions — conclusions, in fact, which would affect them all.

No, she had not carried chains; they were a nuisance to put on and not at all necessary.

Teddy, looking with dismay at the wagon, which was filled with household possessions — he noted, among other items, a swivel chair, a rug, a portable heater, a card table, a number of cardboard boxes, a mattress, an empty birdcage — guessed that its weight had kept her from skidding. Did she, he also wondered, mean to stay forever? He asked her politely what she would like brought in.

After some moments of indecision, she settled upon four suitcases, a typewriter, a typewriter stand, a desk lamp, the chair, and a tiny portable safe which contained, she said, *Strongbow,* "such a magnificent creature" that she could not afford to lose him; she must keep him beside her even while she slept. As for the rest — she gestured toward the still-crowded car — it could stay there for the moment; she would not settle in tonight.

Clemente and Aunt Harriet hurried into the kitchen to help Mary add to the meal; the others quickly vanished. Leah, without bothering to tidy up, joined Teddy in the living room for a cocktail. She sat on the sofa, her good legs crossed, a run in one stocking, wearing a travel-worn red jersey dress, which clung tightly to her full breasts and hips, and some of her heavy Berber jewelry on neck and arms; her reading glasses hung on a chain around her neck.

The family resemblance between Leah and Clemente had always disturbed Teddy. Leah's gold hair (a brassy, artificial gold), her blue eyes and vague, sweet smile, her overrouged cheeks and carelessly applied lipstick gave the effect of a blowsy, tarnished angel. Everything was a bit too bright, like those cheap reproductions of virgins one saw in Italy or Mexico. And, yet, despite her haphazard toilette, she was still a handsome woman. She had attracted many men, three of whom had married her. She was also an amiable woman. All of her marriages had ended most amiably.

"An artistic career and marriage simply do not mix," she would announce cheerfully each time. She was apologetic about this career; a bad fairy, it seemed, had pronounced a curse over her cradle and there was nothing to be done — she must spend her days, and many of her nights, tappity-tapping, as she called it, on her old Remington, utterly oblivious to the ordinary domestic rhythms other people followed.

When, years ago, Leah had lived with Clemente's father, down the road, the Olivers and Lawrences had known each other in an informal, neighborly way. Even Catherine, who usually spurned women friends, took Hat there to play, or to fetch Clemente, and would stop and have a cup of coffee with Leah. But, mostly, this had been Teddy's job.

Teddy and Leah would sit down together at the dining room table, where Leah worked, always cluttered with thesauruses, dictionaries, encyclopedias, mail from her agent in New York, reams of yellow paper, manila envelopes, unsharpened pencils, scissors and paste, filled ashtrays, and sprinkled over all, a fine film of dust and cigarette ash. The family ate in the kitchen; Clemente had learned, by necessity, as a little girl, to cook and clean house and care for her own clothes. Teddy, tidy himself, had been repelled by Leah's lackadaisical housekeeping, yet he had enjoyed those moments. Leah's warm vagueness was different from Catherine's removed, aristocratic air; he admired the latter more, but Leah was a comfortable contrast.

Moreover, he respected her talent. Though her books were not what he called his "cup of tea," he had read them with a kind of bored awe. Obviously, beneath her scatterbrained surface — the seeming lack of focus — was a disciplined mind. How, otherwise, could she have sorted out patterns from the chaos of history, and, putting one sentence after another, building paragraph after paragraph, chapter after chapter, come up with the story of Montezuma, Queen Eleanor of Aquitaine and her Troubadors, the Young Milton, the Young Cromwell, the Romance of Jane and Thomas Carlyle, the Children's Crusade, the Life of Muhammad, and God knew how many others. The paradox in her nature fascinated him.

She had begun to chatter as soon as she had arrived, and she was still talking; in the confusion he had not yet unraveled her train of thought. He made them both Scotches and began to concentrate.

"When I see all this it makes me feel so fortunate," she was saying. "Perhaps I should feel guilty, but I feel fortunate. Do you think that's wrong?"

"Wrong?"

She fumbled in the large leather bag at her side and brought out a crumpled cigarette package. He rose to light her cigarette. She took a deep drag, then leaned back and smiled at him sunnily. "I am speaking of domestic felicity," she said. "I did not provide this for Clemente, but she has you."

"We feel fortunate to have Clemente," he said. "At the moment, she is painting the Oliver Family Mural on the Playroom walls."

"Clemente is plastic; I am verbal. I would prefer to be plastic; it is more therapeutic, working with your hands. In insane asylums they have patients paint, you know; they don't have them write. I am all nerves and mind and passion. And yet . . . I worry about Clemente. There is a certain passivity . . ."

"I don't think there is anything to worry about." He realized that he did not much want to talk about Clemente with the mother who had abandoned her, that he felt an irritation at her sudden, (but probably only polite) concern.

"But it isn't Clemente that I want to talk about. Not at the moment."

He was surprised at his relief.

"I mentioned a recent vision."

"Yes?"

"Visionaries are often gauche. I am going to be. I am going to violate the etiquette of a guest in a home. I am putting *Strongbow* away."

"Pardon?"

"I am going to leave him sitting in his safe, fascinating man though he is."

"Oh, yes, the safe." It seemed simpler to just listen, rather than to stop her and start again from some commonly known point. He remembered that she talked this way, and that, eventually and surprisingly, threads connected; sense was made.

"For some time now I have had the uncomfortable feeling that my interest in the past is an escape from . . . the present. The Twentieth Century has whirled about me, and I have succeeded in ignoring it. *Strongbow* is a great temptation, but I intend to be firm. I am entering the present. I am determined to write something modern, to set my scene in the Now. Last night, as I was driving, it came to me. I have found my subject. It's to be called *The Happy Family*. It will be fiction — a novel. My inspiration is to be . . . the Olivers."

He winced.

"The everyday, ordinary, sweet rhythms of domestic life, the emphasis on personal relationships, as opposed to large events. The crises will be only those which everyone must face — the pangs of young love, the struggle to know who one is, what one should do, the inevitability of old age, of death . . . "

"Won't that all seem rather tame — after *Strongbow?*"

"The noise of battle? The clash of swords? That's just it. There won't be any. Nothing spectacular. A celebration of life's little joys and sorrows. The real stuff of existence."

"Like the *Reader's Digest?*" he said. "My Most Unforgettable Family?"

"I shall guard against sentimentality. I shall look at you with a cold eye. I shall shut myself up in my room and emerge only at mealtimes and to do research. If I don't appear, forget my existence. I can survive on scraps at odd times."

"You are going to write it *here* — at *Christmastime!*"

Leah sighed blissfully. "You have said just the right thing. It is exactly what Crane Simmons would have said."

"Who is Crane Simmons?"

"The dashing, youthful father."

"And why would he have said that?"

"Because he could not imagine someone not celebrating the moment — in this case, Christmas. He is a festive man. I have failed to live that way; instead of fully experiencing the Now, I am thinking of how I could put it down in a book. You will celebrate the holiday; I shall record your celebrating it. That is my curse. I want to do a rough draft while everything is fresh, while I'm fortunate enough to be close to my subject."

"Aren't you afraid we will begin to act unnatural, knowing we are being scrutinized?"

"It would be impossible for the Olivers to act unnatural under any circumstances." She began to dig in her bag again. "Moreover, you are all sophisticated enough to understand artistic license. The Olivers will merely be my taking-off point. After I stuff myself with domestic details, I shall leave and write a book about an entirely different family, a fictional family. You will recognize a few things, but it will not be you. Art is not life. Oh, here they are!" She produced the cigarettes again, stuffed one in her mouth.

He rose to light it.

"There is no getting around it, writers are monsters, we have no scruples, there is a serpent in our bosom, thank you, Teddy dear." She rewarded him with a beatific smile.

He sat down hurriedly.

"I said that art is not life, but your life is a work of art. There is no need for you to cram existence into a book or a painting, to make form out of chaos. You have achieved this out of the very stuff of being. The everyday, boring details of life are turned into graceful rituals, conversation into dialogue, tiny disasters into comic relief, tragedy into triumph. I want to thank you for providing me with my inspiration."

"It looks as if we can't stop you," he said dryly.

She wiggled about on the sofa, crossed and recrossed her legs; her dress crawled up to her thighs, bracelets jangled. "I want you to tell me everything about the Olivers!"

He looked at her with a distaste combined with a peculiar fascination. The woman was vulgar, and he detested vulgarity; she was thick-skinned, insensitive. She wanted to reduce him and his family to characters, probably even caricatures, in a sleazy novel. He felt violated, outraged. Why, then, did he not put a stop to it at once?

"Let's begin with Hat," she was saying. "Naturally, she will not be called Hat. She will not even *be* Hat. But reality gives me a springboard from which to soar."

"Hat has quit Stanford; she is going to live in the city. She is interested in radical politics."

"You must be very proud. You have brought her up to be independent, filled with an inner fire. I shall have to find a young man for her who is worthy. She cannot love an ordinary male. He would have to be someone who wants to change the world along with her, don't you think? Someone who refuses to go to that awful war, who tears up his draft card or — I am thinking — a Black?"

"I don't think I could predict —"

"No, no, of course you can't. That's my job. I'm only musing aloud. Now, Loren. What is that unusual child up to?"

Teddy's repugnance grew stronger. He felt as if he were in the hands of a shameless gossip columnist. "Loren — Loren and I have always been very close, as you know. She is helping me plan our trip abroad. Aside from that, she dislikes school, and school dislikes her. She grows herbs and reads about magic. And she is working on our Oon language."

"Natural, part of the elements, utterly without guile. Of course she dislikes school, and of course school dislikes her. She is not Apollonian, she is Dionysian. Her intelligence is not deducible. She thinks with her being. She is like the gentle rain or sunshine. Perhaps she should take up Modern Dance."

"If so, we should start her training."

"No, it must come from within, not be superimposed from without. Dancing would be part of her existence, as much as eating and sleeping. At the end, she dances naked before kings but refuses the jewels they offer. She is not interested in money, material possessions or fame. She gives herself but demands nothing in return. How does that sound?"

"Imaginative, though I am not certain I recognize Loren."

"Art has a higher truth than reality," said Leah severely. Then, "Becky! What is happening to little Becky?"

"She is busy with her horse and her friends."

"She feels a kinship with animals, doesn't she? Could it be she goes to live among them, like St. Francis, dressed in rags?"

"I have not detected that tendency, yet, but then I only pay the bills."

"Timid among people, not at ease with the opposite sex, retiring in nature — but fearless among our wild friends . . ." She sighed happily. "A beautiful, unusual, gifted family — and they owe all of it to you!"

"Would you care for another drink before dinner?" he asked nervously.

She inclined her head yes, then took out another cigarette; he stood up and bent over her to light it. As he did so, she flashed up at him a blatantly seductive gaze, then she giggled. In horror, he almost dropped the lighted match upon her lap.

Leah's eyes were those of Clemente's, but the expression — so different. Amiable amorality, he thought, as opposed to innocence. A fallen angel versus a real one. He knew why he had to keep Leah here now, why he would let her write her book. It was to prove to her that they were everything she was saying they were.

PART TWO

17

WHEN you have no family, Christmas can take on a larger dimension; it was this way with Aunt Harriet. For her, it was as if the whole calendar revolved around this feast.

In June, she began her preparations, picking up odd presents and storing them away like a squirrel, sending for catalogues, potting plants and putting up preserves which would be used later for gifts. In July, she began to knit ski socks, sweaters, scarves and hats for the Oliver family, most of which, not being to the recipients' tastes, were destined to be given to the Indian Mission Relief Society of Mary Miller's church. In August, she ordered her cards; in September, she made out lists and checked addresses; in November, she entered the kitchenette of her apartment in Oakland to produce indigestible plum puddings, fruitcakes and sweets for a family who had no sweet tooth, apricot cordial for Teddy, who did not care for liqueurs.

That the Olivers were now motherless increased her energies; they must be provided with a proper Christmas, and who but she would see to this? That Teddy, not Catherine, had always directed these seasonal festivities did not occur to her. But, despite her willingness, her efforts were sabotaged all along the way.

A proper Christmas, for example, meant opening presents together as a family, at one time — preferably on Christmas morning. When packages arrived in the mail, from the Zimmermans, from the Always, from a cousin of Catherine's — she tried to intercept them and hide them away. But they were discovered and opened at once. This lack of ceremony seemed to her indicative of a deeper lack: of the weakening of family ties which she had predicted.

Nor did Teddy help. He doled out large checks early, and permitted the girls to buy their own gifts. Becky already had her "debut" dress; Hat had purchased new tires for her Porsche; Loren had put her money away in some secret place, "like a French peasant," said Teddy.

Only Clemente, who was not an Oliver, seemed to observe the proprieties; but even Clemente blossomed out two nights before Christmas in a long, pale-blue kaftan, a gift from Teddy, which matched her blue eyes. (Teddy had wanted to see it on her, in case it did not fit.)

What would be left when the sacred day (or, rather, night, for the Olivers, being Night People, observed Christmas on Christmas Eve) arrived? Harriet felt it necessary to double her efforts to make up for the haphazard early start; she retired to her room and embroidered three new cases for the sunglasses which her nieces wore and constantly misplaced. The cases would help, she thought (that they also would be misplaced was too much for her limited imagination).

But what perhaps puzzled her most was that beneath this careless, untraditional approach, she sensed a kind of family solidity and solidarity, which came out in most peculiar, even shocking ways.

Clemente made cookie dough; Loren took half of it, rolled it out, and cut it with a gingerbread man cookie cutter; then, to Harriet's dismay, she added bits of dough here and there to form gigantic breasts and oversized male "parts."

"Oh, Loren has made her lovely Porno cookies again," cried Hat.

They hung the disgusting creatures on string, balancing them to form a "mobile" for the hall. That odd Leah Lawrence, who kept so much to herself, typing all day in her room, went into ecstasies over them. But both Mary Miller and Harriet had to avert their eyes, and poor little Becky announced that she could not bring her friend Debbie Alway into the house as long as it hung there.

"I warned you that you would find us depraved," said Teddy to his sister, with a wicked twinkle in his eye.

And, yet, somehow, Christmas Eve arrived and was observed — if not as she would have wished it, at least in the Oliver fashion.

18

"HEY, thanks, neat, Hat," said Becky.
"Show the rest of us," cried Clemente.
"It's a set of curry combs and brushes," said Becky, handing it around.
"It's really for Spot, but that's the same thing, nowadays," Hat said.
"Which is why I'm presenting her with this," said Loren, offering Becky a clumsily wrapped package.
"How groovy, Loren. What is it?"
"Stupid, it's a collector's item for horse fanciers. It's part of an old stirrup I found where I shop."
"Where does she shop for that sort of thing?" Aunt Harriet wanted to know.
"Probably at the Goodwill or Salvation Army," said Hat.
"Hardly," said Loren huffily. "They don't carry antiques. I found it at the Los Robles city dump. It wasn't free, either. I had to pay the garbage collector a quarter."
"Did you wash it, dear?" said Harriet.
"The Los Robles city dump is very high class," said Teddy.
"And here's something for Hat and for Teddy," Loren continued. "It's an old African witch charm, a love amulet to ward off bad vibes. You put them under your pillow while you sleep."

"Where did you get it?" asked Hat. "That is, if it isn't rude to inquire?"

"Not at all. You get them free at the Voodoo Shop with every five-dollar purchase."

"How thoughtful of you to protect us, Loren," said Teddy.

"There's an extra something in your package, Teddy. Be careful, it's fragile. It's for a special occasion."

Teddy unwrapped a crooked, thin, brown cigarette. "A joint? Just for me? How touching!"

"I rolled it myself. It's real hashish. It's too expensive to give everyone. I'll provide you with instructions later."

"You don't smoke, do you, Teddy?" said Harriet, peering at the package with her nearsighted eyes.

Teddy whisked it away. "Only on *very* special occasions," he said.

"And here is a jar of dried rose petals from my herb garden," said Loren to Harriet. "You put them in your underwear drawer."

"We did this when I was a girl," said Harriet, diverted from Teddy's gift. "How delightful, Loren."

"Doesn't Clemente get a love amulet?" said Hat.

"I have something else for Clemente. Angels don't need protecting."

"A cookbook. *The Black Art of Cookerie*. Thank you, Loren."

"What sort of cookbook, dear?" said Harriet.

"It's just so Clemente can feed Loren her special macrobiotic diet," said Hat.

"It's so I won't poison my system with Mary's buffalo meat," said Loren.

"Where is Mary?" said Harriet.

"Teddy drove her to the bus station this morning so she could go to her church," said Clemente.

"First we gave her presents," said Loren. "Teddy gave her a check, Becky and I gave her handkerchiefs, and Hat gave her an Indian basket in order to teach her about her artistic heritage. She said, 'Thank you, Miss Hat.'"

"Shut up, Loren."

"No words of evil passion on this Mithraic feast day," said Teddy.

"Am I late?" cried Leah Lawrence. She rushed breathlessly into the room, wearing bright orange stretch pants, a tight black sweater, antique Mexican stone beads, and carrying a large paper sack under her arm. "I'm no good at wrapping things. I tried and gave up, but here we are, autographed all around." She opened the sack and passed out shiny copies of her new book, *Passionate Interlude: The Story of Liszt and Lola Montez.*

"How terribly thoughtful of you," said Harriet. "I shall present it to my Study Group."

"There are a few purple passages, I must warn you!"

"My Study Group is very advanced. We did *Love in the South Seas* by Margaret Mead, and Hazel Henderson did *The Prophet*. So long as things aren't dirty just for the sake of dirt — that's my philosophy. There's so much rot crammed down your throats these days, don't you think? But I don't see how one can object to Liszt. He was a genius, and geniuses are apt to be a bit odd. What he did in his spare time was his own affair. That's my opinion."

"It was his spare time that she wrote about," said Loren.

"I think it depends upon Aunt Harriet's definition of rot," said Hat. "I believe that anything is all right as long as it gives pleasure and doesn't hurt anyone else. There are laws on the books that even forbid certain sexual acts between married couples just because somebody in the Bible said it was wrong. It's all the fault of our stupid Judeo-Christian taboos. Take fellatio, for example —"

"Take what, dear?" said Harriet.

"Hat is trying to say that certain mores have become archaic," said Teddy, interrupting. "For instance, orthodox Jews don't eat pork because the Bible forbade eating animals with cloven hoofs. I can't remember why at the moment. I must remember to look it up —"

"Or sodomy. What's wrong with sodomy?"

"Is that from Sodom and Gomorrah?" said Aunt Harriet.

"I'm sure I don't know what it's from, I just know it is, and if two consenting adults can't —"

Teddy held up a hand for silence. "Listen to this part of the record, everyone," he said. "I have always liked these lines."

They listened.

> *In what manner should I bear a child,*
> *who ever a maid*
> *Have lived chastely all my life past and*
> *never man assayed?*

"Perhaps she didn't know where babies come from," said Loren.

"A baby," said Teddy, "is still a miracle."

"They are beginning to produce them in test tubes," said Hat. "Then women will be liberated at last, and the whole family structure will change. Perhaps there will be no families at all."

"I am glad I shall not live to see that day," said Harriet firmly.

"Perhaps Jesus *was* a test tube baby," said Hat. "Perhaps they possessed a knowledge we have since lost."

"Hat, you are upsetting your aunt," said Teddy lightly.

Hat sulked. What she could not say was that Christmas was upsetting her. The elation she had always experienced on this feast day was somehow missing. Where had it gone? Shocking her aunt was merely the defiance that springs from disillusionment. It was a limited but agreeable way of expressing how she felt.

"Christmas," Teddy was saying, "is a mystery, not, of course, for the reasons we have been told, but because life itself is mysterious. Science cannot explain all. I won't have it. Love is our only hope and Jesus, that remarkable man, was filled with that. Let us share his spirit. Would anyone care for a drop of Christmas brandy?"

No one did.

"Then perhaps I shall have just a bit."

Clemente ran to fetch the bottle. In the meantime, Becky

passed out her gifts. Nylon panty hose for all the girls, a black dress tie for Teddy.

"She doesn't want us to disgrace her at Linda's debut," said Loren. "But you needn't worry, Becky, because I won't be there, thank you just the same."

"I'm not sure I will either. I may be out of town, but thanks, Becky," said Hat.

Clemente, who had returned with the brandy, opened hers. "They're beautiful, Becky, and ever so useful on other occasions, but I'm afraid I won't be at the debut either," she said. "I mean, I wouldn't feel comfortable with all those people. I'm not used to large, grand affairs, I guess. I'm just a homebody."

"Who has never had a home," said Leah dramatically.

"Our home is her home," said Teddy, accepting a glass from Clemente and raising it to her.

Clemente blushed.

"If you're all not going to the debut, you must RSVP. The caterer has to have a count," Becky said.

Then Hat handed out colored enamel peace-symbol lapel pins, the money from which, she explained, would go toward the new Resistance printing press.

Thanks, again, all around.

"Clemente has not passed out her presents," said Becky.

"They aren't much, really. I made them myself." She presented every one with a small package, each wrapped in a different Japanese rice paper.

"Funky," Loren said, opening hers. It was a symmetrical plastic paperweight, embedded with tiny carefully selected pebbles and weeds.

"A work of art, we are deeply honored," said Teddy.

"How extremely kind of you, Clemente," said Aunt Harriet, gazing at the strange object with her nearsighted eyes.

"Clemente is plastic; I am verbal," murmured Leah.

"Where is Clyde?" said Hat suddenly.

"He left presents and said he'd be back for dinner," Becky told them importantly. "His plane was vandalized at the airport; he has caught the criminal and made a citizen's arrest."

"He's always talking about making citizen's arrests, now he has had his wish," said Loren.

"So some poor young man will be in jail on the holidays," said Hat. "He should have blown up the whole plane while he was at it."

"But the young man committed a crime," said Becky.

"He was probably protesting the fact that some people can afford private airplanes, while others, like himself, don't have enough to eat," Hat said.

"If I know Clyde, he will just give him a good talking-to and let him off. Just frighten him a bit, you know," Teddy said.

"A bully man," said Loren contemptuously.

"What if it were your — your precious savings, Loren, or your Porsche, Hat? What would you think about that?" said Becky.

There was a silence. Then Loren said, "Well, at least she thinks."

"She has posed a very interesting question," Teddy said.

"If someone took my savings," Loren said thoughtfully, "and I could catch him, and I had a gun, I would shoot at his feet. But I would not bully him. I would not make any speeches about morality and observing the law, like Clyde will no doubt do. I would just get my money back."

"If someone stole my Porsche, and I saw him do it," said Hat, "I would talk to him — not about bourgeois morality, because I don't believe in it myself. But I would explain to him why I need the Porsche, that I am using it to work toward an equal distribution of wealth."

"I'm sure he would be very interested in that," said Loren.

"I would try to make him see the big picture," said Hat.

"And what if you don't succeed?" said Loren.

"Then — I guess he'll have to take it," said Hat. "It isn't easy living up to your ideals, if they're as high as mine, but I'm afraid that's my trip." She sighed.

"Can't we open Clyde's presents?" said Becky, who was no longer interested in the problem she had presented.

They opened them. For the ladies there was perfume — French and expensive; for Teddy, a bottle of Haig and Haig.

"I believe Clyde is trying to tell us something," said Hat.

"Perhaps he is trying to tell us we smell bad," said Loren.

"I think it's yummy; I'll wear it for the debut," Becky said.

"Would you like to buy mine?" Loren said. "We can check the price in the stores, and I'll sell it at a third off."

"Really, dear, I can't help saying that is not the proper spirit," said Harriet.

"Half off?" whispered Loren to Becky.

"I think it's my turn, now," Harriet said. She handed out the sweaters, glasses cases, jam, cakes, and cordial, amid extravagant, if hollow cries of surprise and gratitude. "And now, I have something very special for Teddy!" She smiled proudly and handed him a package.

Teddy unwrapped it. There was a silence. Then, "Really, Harriet, you shouldn't have . . ." Then, "I honestly don't feel right in accepting it." Then, "It's extremely thoughtful, but no — I would not feel right."

"I did hate to give it up, dear, but I have no children, and it should remain in the family. And I was so struck by the resemblance to you."

"What is it?" said Loren, peering over Teddy's shoulder. "Or, rather, who?"

"It's a photograph of your grandfather, dear," said Harriet. "You never knew him."

"Our grandfather. Far out! Where did he find that groovy sultan's costume?"

"That's his Lodge robe. He did look handsome in it, didn't he, Teddy?"

"Yes, very. What a nice frame, too. Thank you again, Harriet. It was most considerate."

"Where is that costume now?" said Loren.

"I'm not sure. I think he was buried in it. Is that allowed, Teddy?"

"I'm afraid I don't know; the arrangements were made before I arrived."

"Oh, damn, I'd love to have it. I wish I'd made the arrangements," Loren said.

"His Lodge did it for us," said Harriet.

The photograph was passed around.

"It's camp," said Hat.

"It's what, dear?"

"Oh, damn, why did they have to bury him in it?" said Loren.

Teddy retrieved the photograph and hid it tactfully among his other gifts.

The telephone rang. Loren ran to answer. "It's for Hat," she screamed. "It's Arab, Hat!"

Hat rose to take the call.

"What did Arab give you for Christmas, Hat?" said Becky.

"Arab doesn't believe in presents, not while people are dying in Vietnam. Hang up in here, Loren. I'll take it upstairs. And be so kind as not to listen in."

"Such a lovely Christmas," said Harriet, picking up pieces of tissue paper and ribbon off the floor, and folding the paper into tidy squares.

"A lovely Christmas of a Happy Family," said Leah. She appeared to be taking notes in a small, spiral-bound notebook.

19

"YOUR life is a work of art," Leah had said. "You make form out of chaos." Her remarks had the effect on Teddy of stirring up that very chaos which she believed he had mastered. An obscene, shapeless monster, it lay just below the surface of his consciousness; that was where he had trained it to lie. But, now, as if in some sort of retaliation for Leah's claim, it seemed to toss and heave ominously.

But this was ridiculous, he told himself. No doubt he was just suffering from a transient depression. But — on Christmas Eve? Then he suddenly recalled something Zimmy had once told him. Christmas, he had said, was the worst time of year for the widowed, the divorced, the old, the outcasts — in short, people who had no families they could count on. Teddy, in Fala, where he had gone after the presents were opened to attend to some correspondence — this had been, at least, his excuse — was not helped by this sudden memory.

He did fall into Zimmy's category, being widowed; moreover, he missed Catherine deeply — more, in fact, than was perhaps quite normal after three years. But he could scarcely qualify as a man without a family. The feast just celebrated was proof of this alone; he recalled Leah's eyes misting over with sentiment as she had observed them.

He put on a Mozart sonata, then sat down at his desk, cluttered with gifts he had brought with him and with unopened cards and letters. The music soared and ebbed. A sublime theme. A pattern. Had Mozart fought against this brooding shapelessness? Was the sonata only a master's attempt to pretend it wasn't here? Was it only a superb illusionary effect? Was this, after all, what art was? If so, he had misundersood it; he did not like the sonata; it was even possible he did not like music at all. He turned it off and opened a card from the Zimmermans.

It was a hand-blocked card — a black peace symbol on white, rough paper — like a child might do in kindergarten using a potato. Bobsie's work. Bobsie believed in handicrafts with a fervor which made up for her lack of artistic talent. She wore her own jewelry and her own sandals, her own woven, peasant-style skirts. Away from his office, Zimmerman sometimes appeared in her efforts. A Mexican-style embroidered shirt, clumsily wrought cowhide sandals, and, in place of a tie, a piece of hideous silver jewelry — a twisted, turdlike clot upon a chain; it had an erotic symbolism, something to do with the unity of male and family elements, of lingam and yoni, of fire and water — Bobsie had explained it once in her humorless way. He turned the card over; on the back was a note in Zimmy's handwriting.

Dear Teddy,
    The New Year. Beginnings. Rebirth. "Begin, and then the work will be completed," said Goethe. Bobsie and I have had a long talk. I am forty-six. I should wait no longer to begin to practice what I preach in my yet, alas, unfinished book. Not an office, but a domestic environment in which to receive, not my patients, but my "guests." Preferably in rural surroundings, close to Nature, animals, trees, the soil. Also, within easy access to Stanford and the city — where I hope to do some lecturing and promotion of the book. We would live on a day-to-day basis with one another, a true Group Encounter. Bobsie is willing to sacrifice our precious domestic privacy to this. She will lead the Sing-Ins, the Body Awareness sessions, feed the chickens, assign the chores, allowing me to work with the guests (few in number) and write the book. My working title — *Ecstasy for Every Day*. What is your opinion of that?

Yes, we are going to do it. There is no turning back. Our financial resources, as you know, are limited, but how else does one accomplish anything if one doesn't make the break? We have even gone so far as to drive about looking for sites, not exactly a rewarding task in the Bay Area. The price nowadays for a tree? It is shameful! For this particular problem, we should especially appreciate your advice.

A Happy Holiday to you and yours,

Zimmy

His advice? His opinions? The Zimmermans were often ludicrous, childishly pathetic, lacking in style. And yet was this not true of many sensitive people who had clung to their idealism and refused to compromise? If he lacked genius, could he not at least recognize it, support it, perhaps even help guide it, and be in on the excitement thus engendered? T. Oliver, patron of the arts and sciences. Briefly, his imagination soared.

A miniature farm, inhabited by toylike figures. The brilliant doctor, the self-sacrificing Bobsie, the adoring guests, "few in number." He looked down upon them as a child looks down upon a dollhouse with its roof removed; he felt exhilarated, godlike. But there would be much to be done — careful thought would have to go into it. He put the card aside for the time being.

Then he took out his checkbook and wrote a check for six hundred dollars to Fred Robinson, Esq. The Esq. would make it seem like a little joke, the spirit in which it was intended. He typed a short note to accompany it.

Dear Fred,
If there's anything I can't stand, it's sitting in a bar drinking good Scotch and being rained on. Happy New Year.

Teddy

He addressed this letter, then opened other cards. Your Friendly Cleaners, the director of the Nature Conservatory, Green Oak Mortuary, Suburban House Cleaning Service, Bryce Investment Counseling, El Rancho Bottle Shoppe, Citizens for

Peace, Estate Gardening. Et cetera. Et cetera. More gloom descended.

He picked up Harriet's present. His restored father. The thin mouth, the veiled gray-green eyes beneath rimless spectacles, the ridiculous turban, the Oriental robes. "Camp," Hat had called it. His father, in his favorite role, was now a collector's item. He might as well have been Napoleon or Clara Bow, except that an original picture of the last two would have fetched a higher price. Was this what mortal aspirations came to? He stashed the photograph away in a drawer.

Then his eye fell upon the book Hat had given him. *Fell's Guide to Sunken Treasure Ships of the World*. He poured himself a glass of Haig and Haig, took the book and the glass into his monk's bedroom, and lay down upon the bed in the darkness and shut his eyes.

The Scotch was warm; the outside of the glass repulsively damp. He had no ice down here. For a moment he allowed himself to plan a kitchenette. A bar sink, small stove, refrigerator, Swedish faucets? A marble cutting board?

He opened his eyes and set the glass down upon the bedside table. The redwood ceiling was illuminated by wavering lights, reflections from the house, where they were playing charades. The charades had been his idea, but they had grown tiresome.

He lay staring at the lights. They flickered and ebbed, formed and reformed in a tantalizing manner. A pattern would be established, then, mercurially, change.

Change. Metamorphosis. Life. Death.

"I was struck by your resemblance to dear Papa."

Here, of course, was the reason for his anxiety. What the hell was his sister up to, giving him that photograph? What, in fact, was Harriet always up to? Pulling him back, down, with a kind of stubborn female persistence; ignoring his polite reluctance, ignoring the way he tried to lightheartedly change the subject; almost, but never *quite*, pushing him to the point where he would need to tell her outright that he did not care to be reminded, to be forever pulled and tugged down and back to where she was trying to take him; stopping cleverly just on the brink of having to hear this disclosure; then waiting for another opportunity to jab, push, pull. She had a kind of instinctive shrewdness he did not possess. The portrait had been her wiliest ploy. Like a slow-moving, seemingly dull-witted beast, she had waited patiently and then pounced. Christmas, surrounded by family — he had been trapped. Zimmy had never been so brutal.

"He did look handsome — didn't he, Teddy?"

He and Harriet and his mother, surrounded by friends and relatives, sat in camp chairs upon the roof of Oliver's Realty, like royalty reviewing the troops. Below, Main Street, transformed by flags and bunting; a surging mass of people — the whole town was out! Fathers held children on their shoulders; small boys climbed lampposts; heads leaned out of the windows of the M and M Department Store, Shultz Pharmacy, the Union Building. Then Chief of Police Bailey blew his whistle; people moved back on to the sidewalk — ten deep; the high school band struck up "The Star-Spangled Banner"; the people on the rooftops and the people below stood at solemn attention, the men with their hats over their hearts, as, down the street, following the Boy Scout Honor Guard, marched a red-fezzed army of men; at their head, Ed Oliver, like a turbaned pasha from the *Arabian Nights* — ballooning trousers, a scarlet sash, a shining scimitar hanging from his waist, and curved red leather slippers, like gondolas, upon his feet. All the floats and drum-corps majorettes and clowns which came after him could not dim this majestic image in his small son's eyes.

His father would return long after Teddy had gone to bed; he would sleep late the next day, emerging, at dinner time, the same balding, tight-lipped Ed Oliver of Oliver's Realty. The exotic costume had vanished, replaced by blue serge suit pants, shirt-sleeves and suspenders; the imperial manner by a defeated stoop and bleary eyes. In vain would Teddy search for some remnant of the splendor which had been his father's only yesterday. He looked for it in his voice as he mumbled grace; in the cold, vacant eyes as he bent over mashed potatoes and gravy; in his remote stiffness as he laconically responded to his wife's conversation. He tried to find out the secret by following him around, but his office and his numerous Lodge activities kept him away from home much of the time. Moreover, his mother had a way of discouraging their intimacy; she was even against his helping in the office. It was as if some supernatural agency had permitted his father to walk among them as a god one day a year, then brutally returned him to his mortal form.

"I never knew my father," he had told Zimmerman.

"Who knows their fathers?"

"My daughters — I don't want that kind of relationship with them."

"For that matter," said Zimmerman, lighting up a cigar, "who knows anyone? We are all strangers to one another in this world. Sometimes I look at Bobsie and think, I have never seen her before. Who is this stranger who shares my bed? Do you really believe you know your wife? I am not speaking in the biblical sense, but do you think you know her? As for daughters — it is even more difficult. It seems to me you go beyond the call of duty, that you do an excellent job."

The shadows on the ceiling formed and reformed like a kaleidoscope. He snapped on the light to make them vanish; he took a sip of the warm Scotch. Then his hand fell upon the book he had brought in with him; he picked it up and read the frontispiece.

> *The $3,000,000 treasure ship in New York Harbor.*
> *Wagons at the bottom of a Texas lake, filled with Spanish gold.*
> *The $15,000,000 General Grant, wedged in an underwater cavern.*
> *12,000 carats of uncut diamonds sunk in the Bay of Biscay.*

Who knew? he thought. It was never too late. It wasn't, of course, the money. It would be the quest.

AMATEUR DIVER FINDS FORTUNE IN GOLD BULLION — HISTORICAL FIND! SPORTSMAN RETRIEVES MONTEZUMA'S GOLD OLIVER DISCOVERS SILVER INGOTS IN 40 FATHOMS.

Full fathom five thy father lies;
Of his bones are coral made;
Those were pearls that were his eyes —

SPORTSMAN FINDS FATHER AT BOTTOM OF SEA

Nothing of him that doth fade,
But doth suffer a sea-change
Into something rich and strange.

He heard the noise of a motorcycle in the driveway. One of Hat's friends.

He let the book slip from his fingers, shut his eyes, and slept.

20

IT was three days after Christmas. Hat, dressed in a black leather mini skirt and shiny, knee-high black boots, entered the living room; she carried a battered, expensive suitcase which she set down upon the floor with a dramatic thump.

Loren, who was lying in her favorite place upon the sofa, put aside her book and gazed with mild curiosity at her sister.

Hat said, "Good-bye."

"So you are off to seek your fortune in the Big City. Good luck, sister dear."

"Yes, I shall undoubtedly need it."

"I don't want to spoil your fun, but you are already possessed of a fortune."

"There are other kinds."

"Like living with Arab?"

"Whoever said —?"

"I am precocious, and you leave letters around."

"You're not precocious, you're just a snoop. I suppose you've told everyone about Arab."

"Who would be interested?"

"Did you tell Clyde?"

"I never talk to Clyde. He's not exactly a brilliant conversationalist. Though I don't see why you're keeping it such a dark secret. Arab isn't exactly my type —"

"I can't imagine who would be."

"But there's nothing wrong with living with him, if that's your trip. Do you feel guilt?"

"Guilt? Of course not. But Clemente would worry, for one thing. I want her to understand, but she seems so far away when you talk to her, somehow. I decided I could explain things better to her when I write."

"You had better print it in big letters, then. She never reads." Loren picked up her book. Then, lightly, "What about Teddy?"

"What about him?"

"He would understand, wouldn't he? He claims to be broad-minded about such things."

"I don't feel much like telling Teddy, that's all. I'm just not in the mood to hear him say I'm in Lodown, or whatever the word for joy is in your Oon language. And I don't much want you making up an Oon hymn for the occasion. And I don't want it in the Family Mural. This is my thing, and I want to keep it that way." Her voice had turned high, uncertain.

"Well, don't get uptight. Nobody cares."

"The only thing I feel badly about, as I told you, is Clemente. It might be nice if you would help her occasionally. Your macrobiotic diet takes more time to fix."

"What is Time?" Loren gazed sadly at her sister. "Merely a meaningless pattern imposed upon the Now by stupid Outbars. Besides, nobody ever makes Clemente do things. We have Mary. Nobody tells Clemente she has to knock herself out —"

"Well, I hope you help her just the same. That's the only thing I felt guilty about — leaving Clemente."

21

DINNER was finished. Since Christmas, Teddy had insisted on candlelight. He had just bought a Spanish-style, circular wrought-iron chandelier, which he said ought to have been in a movie star of the twenties' villa. He had had it unelectrified and put in candles. Now twelve flames multiplied themselves in the glass of the French doors. Soft candlelight and reflected candlelight cast flickering shadows on the faces of the girls, and soft candlelight and soft reflections, he hoped, obscured the bags beneath his eyes — he had not slept well lately.

Clemente padded, barefoot, from dining room to kitchen and back again, clearing. Teddy and Loren and Becky still sat at their places; Leah had not appeared. Teddy sipped a brandy; Loren nibbled at pine nuts; Becky was eating a second piece of the chocolate pie which Clemente had made because it was Teddy's favorite.

Since Hat had gone, Clemente had become even more motherly, as if she were trying to fill the void. She would allow no one to help her; Mary Miller, who had never learned to serve properly, and who, moreover, made Teddy nervous because he did not really approve of being waited on by servants, had been reduced to menial chores; she ate her own dinner happily before the TV.

"The Poor Relation and the Errant Daughter have gone," said

Loren to Teddy. "The Peripatetic Mother has settled in to observe us like guinea pigs. We shall never finish that particular Monopoly game. I feel it in my bones. Clemente may as well put it away."

"Perhaps it's too late to finish that one, but we could start another," Teddy said.

"No, we must concentrate on planning our trip."

"I have in mind a Greek island," said Teddy. "An isolated one, where we can all run naked and sip wine and contemplate the wine-dark sea. We must examine the atlas. Clemente, how does that sound to you?" He looked up at her as she removed his plate.

"I don't think I ought to be consulted. I mean, if I go along —"

"If?" said Teddy sternly. "What is this 'if'?"

Clemente blushed. "I should like to, of course. But will you leave without Hat?"

"Hat will return," said Teddy complacently. "Her Ronwar will urge her back to us."

"Her Ronwar has taken her away," said Loren.

"It isn't her Ronwar," said Becky, scraping her plate with her fork. "It's Arab."

"Arab is her Ronwar for the moment," Loren said.

Teddy sighed. "I have always made it a point not to interfere with my daughters' destinies. Love is too enigmatic and elusive a thing for other people to pronounce upon. Still . . . Arab? I hardly know the young man; he is not sociable. He has even gone so far as to tell my daughter that her father is the worst sort!"

"Worst sort?" said Clemente.

"He thinks of me as a gentleman liberal, a weak Do-Gooder, who does not understand the basic horrors of the Power Structure, a member, in fact, of that very Power Structure myself. No doubt I am on his list to be liquidated. But I shall not interfere. The future is in his hands. He will not compromise; he will sacrifice himself, no doubt, as easily as he sacrifices others. Perhaps he will build a Golden Age on the ruins of the old. Let us hope so; there could certainly be improvements. I don't find his manners and his hairiness aesthetically appealing, but I suppose niceties must be sacrificed in a Revolution. Obviously, Hat finds him attractive. Love is mysterious —"

"It is not love so much as an experiment," said Loren.

"All love is an experiment," said Teddy. "Life is an experiment, both glorious and perilous . . ." He poured himself more brandy.

Clemente sat down next to him. "Sometimes I wonder what my Ronwar is," she said shyly.

"I should be happy to cast your horoscope for you," said Loren.

"I think, perhaps, I would rather wonder."

"I believe," said Teddy thoughtfully, "that your Ronwar, Clemente, my dear, is connected with ours. It seems to be so. And so far, it has been a happy connection for all of us. I think that your presence helps us live up to the Oon Code. Without you, we might falter."

"Oh, Teddy, if anyone lives up to the Oon Code it is you," cried Clemente.

"No, not always. I have my limitations. Tonight, for instance — I questioned Hat's judgment. That was a violation."

"Perhaps Hat is not living up to it; perhaps you were questioning that," said Loren. "If you want my opinion, I don't think she really cares about it any more."

"I'm sure she does, deep inside of her. The Oon Code implies faith in people. But let's go find the atlas. Let's choose an inconspicuous dot that probably won't even have a name, where the boat only stops once a month, where the natives are still unspoiled, where there are no souvenir shops —"

"I have to go feed Spot," said Becky. "Then I'm going over to the Always and watch the astronauts."

"They aren't going to pre-empt the *Revenge of the Puppet People?*"

"They are broadcasting from Outer Space. Live."

"That depends on your definition of life. It's really Outbarish. The next thing they'll do is corrupt the moon."

"Perhaps it will do some good; perhaps it will help stop wars," said Clemente timidly.

"The wars are within us," Teddy said. "The engineering

minds at Mission Control will not stop them. Love and imagination are needed. 'Queen and huntress, chaste and fair.' No longer chaste, alas. I have sent away for a telescope, but I have lost interest already. Mission Control has, in the new vocabulary, 'pre-empted' me. Forget the moon — we'll find an island in the midst of the sea."

Becky rose and tiptoed from the room.

"I will be like Prospero and spread . . . enchantment . . . over all of us. You shall be my contented slaves."

Loren looked thoughtfully at her left arm.

"Yes, we are such stuff as dreams are made of, no matter what they do." Teddy lifted his glass toward the candlelight and gazed into the burnished depths. "We could not survive without dreams," he said, then he polished off the brandy with a flourish.

Clemente said, "Loren, what did you do to your arm?"

"I scratched it on a *Rubus fruticosus.*"

"Maybe I should put some disinfectant on it."

"It was a clean scratch and bled nicely," Loren said.

22

Dear Zimmy,

Before your letter arrived, I had what you call "angst" — a malaise of the spirit. I think it is something which is not afflicting me alone, but rather the entire country. Large forces we cannot control (could we ever, or was that an illusion?) speed us to destruction. The young blame it on the old, but, unless one manufactures bombs, what can one do? Have we lost the hardiness of our ancestors, or is the situation more complex? Impotence is a paralyzing state; I would gladly join the forces of freedom, but where the hell are they?

Or could it just be me? Postholiday blues, approaching old age, the fact that my oldest daughter has left the fold to work in the city. The Beginning of the End? Women, I think, understand these things better than men. Timing, cycles. (We ought to let them manage the buying of stocks.) They know when it's time to put up their hair, figuratively speaking, when it's time to marry, to have children, perhaps even to grow old and die. Does their exquisite sorrow spring from the knowledge that all things end, that even the concept of the Family, to which they devote their lives, is a fraud?

What is the Institution for these days, Zimmy? We don't need heirs for the throne or sons to till the fields; we certainly don't want sons for cannon fodder. As for the protection of helpless infants — there is the Pill. Is it a kind of desire for immortality, for reseeding the Earth? But my eldest daughter has informed me not to expect grandchildren; she has no intention of contributing to the Population Explosion. These are thoughts which have occurred to me.

But your letter has changed my morale. Women, so busy with their seasons, may not have the energy for dreams. You are fortunate that Bobsie respects yours. Make the break — dropouts are fashionable these days. I will help you in any way I can. We might consider a nonprofit foundation — I should be pleased to serve on its board in an advisory capacity. We'll also need good legal aid. I would recommend my old friend Carter Alway for this. I shall also be on the lookout for a proper piece of land — a country retreat — though this, as you have realized, will be the stickler. I'll give you a ring and we'll get together soon.

A Happy New Year to you and Bobsie.

                Teddy

P.S. We are planning a trip to Europe. Hopefully, Hat will join us. One last trip, *en famille*. Oh, my God, what then?

He reread the letter, liked it, then worried that it might sound pretentious. Who wrote letters like this nowadays? Gentlemen no longer exchanged ideas on the human condition; conversation was shallow; you didn't discuss things discursively on the phone or in business memos. If Lord Chesterfield were living, he would have written a How to Do It Manual.

Even Zimmy was a professional listener, not a reader, a Sherlock Holmes searching for clues while his patients droned on. In his own case he sometimes thought Zimmy had searched for clues in order to cover them up; if a lead looked promising Zimmy had had a way of changing the subject. He often quoted poetry at such a time:

> *What I aspired to be,*
> *And was not, comforts me . . .*

"You expect a great deal from life; you will naturally have disappointments, but it is the Quest that is important."

But what if the Quest, which Zimmerman considered so wholesome in itself, was an unholy quest? Besides Percival and Galahad, there had been Faust. Had Zimmy been a kind of Mephistopheles egging him on, knowing he was headed for disaster?

"Sometimes I think I may have failed my wife —"

"Pooh," said Zimmy, "wives are more ordinary than we think. We put them upon a pedestal in this country. In your case, perhaps you were too much in awe of Catherine's background. Don't get me wrong, but from what you say, it seems to me she needed your firm and guiding hand."

He decided to rewrite the letter, skipping the comments on the human predicament. Zimmy would just hurry through that part anyhow — stopping only when he got to the business which interested him. Like Mother Humilitia, perhaps like almost everyone, he was only basically interested in his own affairs. Why not accept this fact of life? Why bore people?

He cut the old letter ruthlessly, put the new version aside, and gazed out of the window. A pale, sunless day. A gray cloud forming overhead, casting its shadow over the empty tennis court, the deserted pool. Nearer, below the window, the black, stunted grapevines looked like evil dwarfs. He did not like evil dwarfs. He rose from his desk, poured himself a drink, and sat back down at his desk. If he was so well-adjusted, as Zimmy had pronounced, terminating the therapy, why then was he so sad? Perhaps he did expect too much. Perhaps he had expected too much of Zimmy, of the psychiatric method. Had he hoped to be graduated with a diploma declaring he had earned the right to live happily ever after? Or was he supposed to have acquired some technique for handling such moments as these, for looking into the abyss without faltering? Maturity? A word much used. Courage was more like it. He lacked courage, an old-fashioned virtue. He was afraid of dwarfs, of ghosts. He was a haunted man, and Zimmy's "pooh" had not exorcised the demon. Zimmy, for instance, could not bring back Catherine, even for one moment, in order that he might make his peace with her. The clock had struck; it was too late for that, forever. It was odd, he thought with a shudder, about clocks, about . . . Time.

After Stanford, the war. An ensign of the *U.S.S. Hawaii*. Stationed on Treasure Island. Parties. Pretty girls. Then back to civilian life. Two years in the city, editing a trade journal for the hotel trade — a grubby little job, but one of few, it seemed, that an English major without a Ph.D. and with few connections could find. (He had hoped to write short stories at the same time, but found it impossible to write all day for a living, and then return to his small flat and write again at night.) He had felt cut off, adrift from that bright world for which Stanford and the navy had given him a taste. It was not a good time.

Then his father died; a year later, his mother. The small inheritance he received, combined with the G.I. Bill, rescued him from his drudgery. He returned to Stanford to get a Ph.D. in English. A professor could also write; he would even be given sabbaticals for this purpose. Moreover, he thought he would find the life congenial.

He had met Catherine in The American Novel and Social Criticism, a course which concentrated on the social problems of the thirties as reflected in the novels of Steinbeck and Dos Passos. Since he preferred literature without an obvious message, the class bored him; but the young girl who sat at the back of the room did not.

She was tall, with a lovely, oval face and long, chestnut hair; fine-featured, with large, dark melancholy eyes. She dressed in a peculiarly uncollegiate fashion — not arty, either, lacking any flair, utterly hiding what he suspected was a magnificent figure. One might have thought she had borrowed one of her mother's dresses. She sat at the back of the room, taking notes with a painful urgency; occasionally, she asked the professor a question in a shy voice. It was this voice that gave her away; she could never disguise that rich girl's private-school articulation.

He began to wait for her after class; she seemed eager, even grateful for a chance to talk, not, apparently, because he was a man — she was curiously lacking in flirtatious ways — but because she wanted to discuss the lecture with someone. Her interests, unlike his, were not so much in the novels as the conditions which had inspired them. Over coffee in the Union, she talked of

California's farm labor problems, the plight of the migrant workers today, of Harry Bridges and the workers on the docks. She felt personally involved, she said timidly, because her great-grandfather had become wealthy by exploiting the Chinese immigrants during the Gold Rush. After several meetings, he managed to guide the conversation away from social questions and find out about other things.

She had grown up an only child in San Francisco, in a mansion on Pacific Heights. She hated what she referred to as her "life" there. Gradually, he discovered this had meant Society, a debut to please her parents, not herself, and before that a proper convent education, proper camps, proper lessons, proper friends, trips to Europe, where she had been put into Swiss schools or into the hands of a governess. Two years ago she had been orphaned; her parents had crashed in the Sierra Nevada Mountains in a private plane. She had no close relatives. "Everyone in our family dies young," she said with a kind of proud morbidity.

He had gone to the library, searched through a file of the *San Francisco Chronicle* of two years ago, and found it, a story on the front page. His eyes picked out the salient details:

> *Edward and Jane Keeble Laiken. . . . Edward, owner of a large import company. Sportsman, civic leader, contributor to many charities, member of the Board of Directors of the Peninsula Bank, the Bay Salt Company, Redwood Products, the Pacific Union Club. . . . Jane, San Francisco Opera Association, De Young Museum Board, Children's Hospital, a founder of the Los Altos Hunt. Both were members of the Burlingame Country Club. Plane crash had taken place on way to Reno for ski holiday at their chalet at Sugar Bowl. High Requiem Mass, St. Mary's Cathedral. One daughter, Catherine Holman Laiken, only heir.*

Catherine was eighteen. She had not registered as a full-time student. She could not imagine herself living in a dorm or sorority, she said, and having to participate in college social life. She had found herself a small, dingy, two-room apartment in an old house on Tennyson Avenue in Palo Alto. The rooms were utterly lacking in any personal effects — there were no photographs, pictures, knickknacks or mementos which belonged to her. It gave him a queer feeling; she was like a fugitive trying to cover up any traces of a former existence. She drove an old Ford and pretended both to him, and evidently to herself, that she lived on a "budget." But perhaps the most touching and pathetic part of her "disguise" was the part-time job she held, hashing in a hamburger joint on El Camino from five to ten at night, three times a week. But none of these efforts could hide her lack of the everyday, common experience she was trying so desperately to know. She was, as he had told Loren, the Pea Princess, who gave herself away because she tossed all night on a tiny pea placed underneath a pile of feather mattresses.

Over coffee in the Union, over cheap sherry in her apartment, she had questioned him about his life, too. When she learned he was what he wryly called a "poor boy," she had been enraptured, as if she had come across a tremendous and exciting discovery.

"Well, we weren't that poor," he said apologetically. "I'm afraid we were, well, just middle-class. Lower middle-class, maybe," he added, so as not to disappoint her. "My father had a real estate business in Siskiyou City. I won a scholarship to Stanford, but I competed with the farm boys who stayed out for the harvest."

"But you want to do something with your life; you want to write! Think of the possibilities! You can expose this rotten society we live in." Her eyes shone with admiration. "I want to do something, too," she said. "But I don't have talent." Then, wistfully, as if afraid of a rebuff, "Do you think I could be a social worker?"

She was like a child, he thought; she made him feel protective, almost fatherly, toward her.

"You have a lot of time to think about that, Catherine." To him she was not, somehow, a Cathy, or a Katie or a Kay; despite a more sophisticated social background, she seemed, in comparison to other girls, naïve and old-fashioned.

Perhaps this was why she surprised him, one evening, only a few weeks after he had met her, by going to bed with him; he was surprised more by a kind of simple directness, a lack of false modesty, which in another girl he might have called boldness. He was taken aback, even oddly disturbed, by her passion. Had she let him make love to her as part of her learning process? Did he, for her, symbolize the world she felt she had been sheltered from? Was she making love to that world? Or had her innocence, her inexperience with boys — after her debut she had refused to attend the parties — made her an easy prey? Or was it possible she had really fallen in love with him?

"What is love?" Zimmy had said, almost petulantly. "We don't know. We only know it can do a lot of damage. Young people kill themselves for love. They write beautiful suicide notes. The rest of us, who survive, must manage somehow. A and B. Adam and Eve. Eve worries that Adam doesn't love her; she meets Snake. Et cetera. Finally, with luck — a suitable domestic arrangement. That is what it comes down to in the end. And yet we worry that we don't love enough? What are we supposed to do if we don't? Your friend Shakespeare said: 'Love is in the heart, not in the mind, therefore is winged Cupid painted blind.'"

Had love been in his heart or in his mind? Teddy wondered now. Could one even separate the two?

For him, the very thing that Catherine wanted to undo was what had charmed him. He yearned to join her isolation, not rescue her from it. The poverty, the bareness of her tiny bedroom, had a seductive air of luxury about it; she didn't have to be there; she was acting out some fairy tale. And her lean, girlish body, bare upon the white sheets, seemed, even after their lovemaking, an exclusive, precious thing — to him, still virginal.

Had he loved her or this aura which seemed to surround her? Would he have loved her if it had been different? But then she would not have been Catherine, he told himself sternly. You could not separate someone from her origins, any more than you could separate mind and heart.

"Have you made love to other girls?" she asked him once shyly.
"Do you really want to know?"
She did.
"A few."

"Am I . . . different?"

He wanted to say, if you are, that's how I want you to be. "There's no way of comparing it," he said awkwardly. "I mean, the others . . . meant nothing."

"Poor things. But then perhaps you'll say that about me someday, to someone else."

"It's not . . . likely. Catherine, I love you."

She put a hand over his mouth.

"You don't want me to say that? Because you don't feel the same?"

"No, it's just that no one has ever said that to me before. It's hard to get used to."

"You never let them, probably. But I'm going to keep saying it until it doesn't sound strange. That's what you need," he added fatuously. If she had seduced him, it was into playing this kind of father-lover role.

"I need a lot of things. Oh, Teddy, you can help me!"

He wanted to ask her to marry him, but he had been afraid. He thought he knew something of rich people — the girls he had met in college who seemed so democratic on the surface but who, it turned out, when it came to marriage, always chose someone of their own set. He had been interested in this; he had made an unconscious study of it. He read the society pages; he remembered names, the places they went to, the sports and activities and charities they participated in. Even a strange rich girl like Catherine, who was troubled by her wealth, would, no doubt, due to her early training, unhappily, perhaps, follow the same route.

Then she became pregnant. The protective-father role now seemed justified. He was excited, euphoric; this new feeling overwhelmed his caution. He proposed.

She said, "It really isn't necessary. I have some money. There are things you can do, aren't there?"

"Not with my child. That's my middle-class upbringing, I'm afraid."

"You mean — we'd get married and be like other people?"

"You could never be like other people," he said.

She looked disappointed, almost frightened.

"You need someone to take care of you, Catherine. Whether you know it or not!"

They were married a month later by a justice of the peace in Reno. A shabby little wedding, he thought. But Catherine had loved it.

"Isn't there someone you want to tell?" he had said afterwards.

"I suppose you will have to meet my financial trustee someday. He's an attorney in the city, a nice old man. He won't approve of what I've done. Let's not think about it now."

Teddy continued in school until after the baby came. But she had a hard time with the birth. Though she would not admit it, he felt she was not up to living in rented rooms on his meager savings combined with what she called her "budget" — in reality, the allowance she drew from the trustee — an allowance which she herself, evidently, had specified.

He went himself to see the old man, Everett Rattigan of Brenner, Rattigan, and Mader. Their office was on Montgomery Street in the city. For this purpose, he wore his gray flannel Brooks Brothers wedding suit, with a button-down collar white shirt. He sat in the formidable outer offices, decorated with comic English prints of bewigged judges and courtroom scenes, unfashionably furnished with old oak office furniture and presided over by an ancient lady, more like somebody's maiden aunt than a secretary. He could see into another room, which was busy with typists and file girls. At last the old lady led him into a small, unassuming office, which looked as if it might have sheltered the junior partner rather than the senior one. The room smelled of cigar smoke. No books lined the shelves, no papers littered the desk. If work was done here, plainly it was done inside the large, craggy, white-haired head of the gentleman from whom he now sat uncomfortably opposite. He wore an old, black, shiny serge suit and vest and a white, starched broadcloth shirt.

There was a moment's silence, then Everett Rattigan said, "You are here on Miss Laiken's behalf?"

"On Mrs. Oliver's. I am her husband."

The old man did not blink an eyelid. "My congratulations, Mr. Oliver," was all he said.

"Thank you, sir."

"My client, Miss Laiken — you will excuse me — Mrs. Oliver — is a most charming young lady. I wish you both happiness. But I assume this is not merely a social visit. Does your wife know that you are here?"

"No, sir. I have come without her permission. For two reasons." He had rehearsed. "The more important one is Catherine's health." He paused, but, again, there was no reaction. "Aside from that, sir, I dislike the subterfuge. I honestly can't see any reason for it."

"As to the last — the 'subterfuge,' as you call it." The old man spoke slowly, weighing his thoughts. "My client is of age. Her personal life is her own business. If she chose to marry without consulting Brenner, Rattigan and Mader, then that is her decision. We merely handle her financial affairs. Naturally, I wish her the best. I knew her parents well." He paused. Teddy could almost feel the slightly amused scrutiny. Then the old man changed his tone. "As to her health — I should like to know about that — as an old friend."

"She recently — we had a baby."

Rattigan nodded. "My congratulations again."

"A girl, Harriet."

Another nod.

In a rush of words, Teddy described Catherine's frailty.

The old man listened carefully, then he leaned back in his chair, and again, a long silence ensued. Then, "What do you think should be done?"

"I think she ought at least to live more comfortably. In a decent house, with some household help."

"I quite agree, but that's up to my client. Have you discussed this with her?"

"It's very difficult. We can't afford anything much better on my savings and what she calls her 'budget.'"

"Ah, she calls it that, does she?"

"I am aware she has . . . resources. But she doesn't take an interest in them; she is vague about them."

"We are not vague about them, Mr. Oliver. You can rest assured about that. We merely send her what she asks for. She has of course been informed there is . . . more. If you would send us her permission in writing — she has never made a habit of visiting us — more will be made available. That is all I can really say. Now, tell me what you do, if you don't mind?"

Teddy told him about working toward his Ph.D.; he had counted on this to win the old man over, to impress him with the fact that, though he lacked money for Catherine's present comforts, he was heading toward an honorable career.

But Rattigan just blinked at him with his hooded eyes.

"An English professor has time to write. I want to do that, too," he added.

"I don't know anything about writing," said Rattigan. The modesty of this statement seemed, somehow, motivated by the implication that he did know about a few other things; whatever they were did not increase Teddy's comfort. "No, nothing at all," he added. He stood up, extended a spotted, gnarled hand. "I wish you luck, Mr. Oliver," he said.

It was not until Teddy had reached the street again that it occurred to him Rattigan had known about the marriage and the baby all along. From Catherine? He was convinced not. No, undoubtedly, he had his spies. Undoubtedly, he had had Teddy investigated. He had read about rich fathers doing this; wasn't Rattigan a kind of surrogate parent? Well, he would have discovered nothing except his lack of money and social background. Why then did he feel suddenly like a criminal, as if he were being shadowed?

He began to walk faster down the narrow street lined with tall, gray buildings, monuments to mysterious finance, the temples of the priests who, like Rattigan, watched over the secular affairs of rich people like his wife. What right had he had, the son of a small-town realty broker, to attempt to penetrate this world, to ask to be received as an equal? The gaucherie, the presumptuousness of what he had done made him feel hollow and ashamed.

It was noon hour; the sidewalks were crowded with soberly dressed businessmen, attorneys, stockbrokers, pretty secretaries. Was he perhaps being shadowed at this very moment? He glanced furtively over his shoulder, but the detective was invisible in the lunchtime mob.

"If you will send us her permission in writing," Rattigan had said. It was obvious that he did not believe she would do this; that she was purposely keeping her fortune a secret from her new husband, whom she did not wholly trust. This thought made his paranoia vanish; he knew suddenly how to deal with this crusty old man. It was extremely simple. He would undermine his cynicism about love and human nature by doing exactly what he intended to do anyhow: by being a good husband to Catherine, by cherishing and protecting her, by enshrining her in close family life from which she would never want to escape. All his energies, all his talents would go into this. The first step would be to have her send him that "permission in writing." He would convince her she must do this, if not for her own sake, then for the baby's. This would show the foxy Rattigan that she trusted her husband. After that — the domestic retreat, the sheltered island on which Catherine would flourish like a rare flower, while he managed her affairs, without Rattigan's help.

At the same time he came to the conclusion that he ought to get straight at the writing and forget the Ph.D. He needed to show Rattigan as soon as possible that there was more to life than his limited view of human nature. As soon as their domestic affairs were straightened out, he would begin!

But perhaps the first part of his scheme had worked out too well. Cherishing and protecting Catherine became a full-time job. First, the house, then the babies — suddenly, a menage on his hands. Catherine grew frailer, more remote. He was needed more and more to handle domestic matters, as well as her estate, to which she continued to be indifferent.

Occasionally, she would have moments of feverish excitement; she would be the girl he had first met, charged up, almost exhilarated with the problems of the world. She would send a radical political candidate money; she would open up their home for gatherings in which such people would explain the issues, clarify events. From here, she would feel her way, find out how to become more involved. But he found it easy to discourage these distasteful ideas: she was not strong enough; moreover, she was inexperienced, naïve.

"You're right, I couldn't. It isn't in me. I don't have the talent," she would say.

But except for these rare bursts of irrational energy, she remained serene, almost passive. It was he who created the microcosm which was their world. Form out of chaos? Had he succeeded or failed?

"We don't talk of failure," Zimmy had said in one of their sessions. "The chaos is there, for everyone. Most people can't manage it at all. But you are sensitive, imaginative. With me, also, this is true. I ache for more, but am trapped by the sordid, petty details of others' grubby little lives. Where is the meaning? At least you seek it. I have told Bobsie we will come down to play tennis on Sunday. Maybe we can also have a little talk about a certain secret project which I am planning."

23

Dearest Clemente,

Sorry about not having a good rap before I left. That's why I'm writing to explain all. I don't like not playing straight with you, even if we're not completely on the same trip these days — maybe the old Oon Code has stuck with me, despite other important changes.

I'm living with Arab — it's a tremendous experiment. You probably wonder why I didn't level with Teddy. I never thought, in all my life, I could be phony with him, and especially about love, because he has *tried* not to stuff conventional codes down us. So why couldn't I tell him? It's weird, but I wanted my own thing and Teddy just can't let you have it somehow. I mean, you think he does, because he says so, but he would have wanted to "talk it out" and I didn't feel up to that just at the moment. Are we communicating, Clemente? Probably not, because you're so unselfish you don't feel the need for a private experience you don't want to share.

Well, I can share a few of my feelings, sort of, in this letter. For one, not being a virgin any more isn't such a big deal as we used to think it would be. It's weird, but when I wake up in the morning, it's just like, well, being virginal all over again. Sometimes I think I waited too long, that I've already turned into an Aunt H!, that I'm not capable of sexual satisfaction. I thought even of seeing a shrink about this hang-up, but most shrinks are Freudian-oriented and put women down, so where does that get you? Arab does try to understand; he's really very beautiful, but he's hung up with the Cause. It's a heavy Scene here, right now — he wants to purge the decadent elements from the Movement. Like there's this kid, a switch-hitter, who lives in our pad, he has this rat, not a white rat from a store, but a real, black, city rat, and Arab says the rat has to go, pets are decadent, and this cat just loves his rat, and he cried, and Arab took the rat and shot him, he said it was good practice, and the poor switch-hitter freaked out. I wanted to cry, too, but I knew I couldn't. I have to work on my discipline and get over my bourgeois sentimentality. I honestly shouldn't even be taking the time to write this letter. I should be stuffing envelopes instead.

How are Becky and Loren? Did you ever finish the Monopoly game? How is Hurwulf? Is she still on diet dog food? Are people still trying to marry Teddy off?

I do miss you all — but especially you, Clemente. Sorry I can't explain things better.

Love,
Hat

P.S. The Loss of my virginity is not to be included in the Family Mural. Sorry if I sound like the pope.

P.P.S. When you write, include something about Clyde. I kind of told him the truth, but I'm afraid Loren's right, he has a caveman psychology.

P.P.P.S. On second thought, never mind about Clyde. Who cares?

H.

24

"A child of nature," said Leah Lawrence. She was looking down at Loren, who was squatting in her gypsy skirt in the soft, moist, cultivated earth of her herb garden. Her feet were bare, her long hair scraggly and uncombed, half hiding her dark eyes. She was weeding. "I hope I'm not interrupting your communion with growing things."

Loren gave her an impish smile, then rose, holding up her skirt, and, tiptoeing delicately through the furrows, joined Leah.

"It's a lovely garden. It shows tender loving care. What, for example, is that?"

"They're all herbs. That is fennel, known also as sow or hog's. The Latin name is *Peucedanum officinale*. It helps those troubled with lethargy, frenzy, giddiness of the head, the falling sickness and cramp. It also gives ease to women in childbirth and helps toothache."

"I hope I won't need it, but I shall remember you if I do. What is that one?"

"Tansy, or *Tannacetum vulgare*. It can take off freckles, sunburn, and is good for the whites in women."

"My goodness. And that one?" Leah pointed to a tall, flowering shrub.

"*Cannabis sativa*. Excellent for female weakness, gout, malaria, beriberi, and absentmindedness."

"Well, I won't take up any more of your precious time. I only wanted to ask you one question. It's about the book. You don't mind?"

Loren shook her head no.

"It turns out you're the easiest one to interview. It's a matter of temperament; some people just aren't. Could you join me on this bench for a moment?"

Loren sat beside her primly, on the edge of the warm stone bench.

"It won't bother you if I take notes?"

"Not at all."

"It's about your lovely language. What do you call it?"

"Oon."

"I want to understand it. Its structure, grammar, vocabulary. Languages have always fascinated me, though I'm not awfully good at them. I can just manage to do some research in French."

"Oon is a secret language," said Loren. "It expresses some very beautiful ideas that you can't express any other way."

"Oh, I know I'm asking a dreadful thing. But writers are dreadful people —"

"It isn't that." Loren thought. "It's just that it can't be explained, like French, for example. It's only for certain people who already understand. Teddy and I are the only ones who really know it. Hat —"

"Yes?" Leah sat with her pencil poised.

"Hat used to know it, but she has lost it."

"You mean, she forgot?"

"Forgot isn't exactly the right term. It was taken away from her when she went out into the Outbar and became involved in Outbarish things."

"The Outbar?"

"The ordinary world that most people inhabit."

"But Hat doesn't seem ordinary at all."

Loren picked up a stick from the ground and idly began to trace a pattern in the dirt.

"Cary — she is Cary in my book — is filled with fire and passion."

"For what?"

"For life, for love, for the underprivileged — the poor, the halt, the lame — I'll tell you a secret, if you promise not to tell."

Loren nodded solemnly.

"Cary marries a Black revolutionary, and they flee to Algeria or Cuba, I have not decided yet which. She sacrifices her American, middle-class comforts, even her nationality, for the man she loves."

"How long does she stay?"

"Pardon?"

"How long does Cary stay without her comforts?"

"I rather thought the book might end there — with that magnificent gesture. She writes a beautiful farewell letter to her father, explaining her decision."

"What does the father think of it?"

"He is sad, naturally, but he knows that that is how he brought her up — to be sacrificing and brave. He will be lonely, but proud. He puts the letter in a special place to be reread and treasured."

"What does he do with the stamp?"

"The stamp?"

"Teddy always saves stamps from foreign countries. He has them in a drawer. He is meaning to begin a collection one day."

"I'm not sure I would go into that. I think it would spoil the effect somehow. Well, I haven't learned much about Oon, but perhaps that is just the point. Yes, I think it is. I will sketch it in lightly. There are some places even authors should fear to tread. Thank you so much for being helpful. You won't mind my intruding again?"

"Not at all," said Loren.

25

Dearest Clemente,

Thanks for funny drawing of household. I've pinned it up on the wall. When I feel that the Outbar is too heavy, I look up at it — Leah is typing in my room, Becky is riding Spot, Loren is tending her garden, Teddy is in Fala, looking over the atlas, Hurwulf is asleep (natch!) — but where is Clemente? Missing, as usual! I can guess what you're doing, Clemente — the dishes, probably!

Clemente, you ought to split, too — you ought to come up here and learn what it's all about. Like, take women — Arab says my failure to achieve an O stems from my uptight middle-class environment. (Wouldn't Teddy die if he heard that?)

Today, some of us are going to picket the St. Francis Oak Room — a Men's Only Bar. It's for the men's good, as well as ours; we want to liberate them from the fear of their homosexuality. I mean, that heavy male thing, like Clyde when he's putting you down. It's too much, don't you agree? Even Teddy, when you analyze it, practices Male Tyranny. He may think he's modern in his outlook, but he keeps his womenfolk practically in purdah with his tricks and games. Frankly speaking, I think even Arab falls back on Male Chauvinism when it suits him. Oh, dear! Get your hands out of the sink, Clemente, and find out who you really are.

Power to the People, and that means women, too.

Love,
Hat

P.S. I've stopped shaving my legs and under my arms.

26

TEDDY worked all day in Fala. With zoning maps he searched for possible sites for Zimmy's institute; he checked ads for country property, then tried to find the general range of prices from brokers on the phone, without getting involved. Everything was highly inflated. Moreover, from his Neighborhood Association days, he knew that people who lived in residential areas didn't want even a church, much less a therapeutic institute, in their neighborhood; he himself, except for Fred's Place, felt the same way. Now zoning laws reflected these wishes. There was no "retreat" upon the mid-Peninsula for a commercial endeavor where you could also milk cows and tend chickens, such as the impractical Zimmermans had in mind.

At three o'clock, he rolled up his maps. The sky outside his window had an unwholesome pallor; a wind had come up; the trees shook beneath it, and dried leaves scudded across the tennis court and over the road. He wanted a drink, but he was pacing — it was too early for that. Then he remembered Loren's Christmas present. He had put it into an old candy tin in a drawer. He took the tin out, now, and went into his bedroom and sat down upon the bed and opened it.

The joint — a thin, twisted, chocolate-colored twig — looked distasteful. Still, he felt a kind of duty to try it. He put it in his mouth and lit it timidly. It tasted harsh; the odor was acrid. He remembered Loren's instructions and inhaled deeply, then choked. But he kept valiantly on until the nasty thing was gone. Then he sat there, waiting for a sensation. He felt nothing.

Perhaps he had not had the proper attitude. Perhaps, no matter how he tried, the right attitude could only come if one were young. He felt old and cheated — was life to be bereft of all sensual pleasures from now on? He also felt a little sheepish. He stretched out on the bed, wondering whether or not to tell Loren about his failure. He could say that he had lost the thing. He shut his eyes and took a little snooze. . . .

He was in Rome. Of course, it must be Rome because he was sitting on the Spanish Steps, among the tourists. A gladiator was coming down the steps toward him, wearing his little short skirt and carrying a shield. Only it wasn't a gladiator; it was Clyde. Clyde looked foolish in the gladiator costume, Teddy thought. But he looked ferocious, too. He was a little afraid of him. Clyde marched down the steps, through the rows of potted flowers, ignoring Teddy and the tourists, and stepped into the fountain which lay below.

The fountain was a great baroque swirl, in which naked stone naiads were sporting. Clyde took off his costume. Teddy could see now that Clyde was not an ordinary gladiator; he had a curly tail and cloven hoofs. He did an odd little dance in the fountain, then he embraced one of the naiads, clasping her about her cold waist. The naiad put her stony arms around Clyde and kissed him back. Then Clyde and the naiad, still entwined, plunged beneath the water, which seemed suddenly very black and deep. Above them, the fountain continued to dance in airy patterns. Occasionally, an arm or leg emerged, occasionally a wet white buttock. The dark water beneath the spray surged ominously. Undoubtedly, thought Teddy, Clyde and the naiad were committing an erotic act. But the tourists came and went, seemingly unaware of what was going on. Teddy awoke. The naiad, he realized, was Catherine. Catherine? But she was not the type for these primitive antics; it was after their trip to Rome, in fact, that they had stopped sleeping together. Her health. Her frailness. Separate bedrooms had seemed a sensible solution, then — a habit.

He had, in fact, in a peculiar way, fallen more in love with her; her aloofness had for him an aesthetic appeal. She had become more and more the person she had tried as a girl not to become, but the one, perhaps, to which he had been originally drawn. Had he, he wondered, encouraged this image at her expense? Did she really prefer sporting beneath the fountain in pagan abandon? Had she been waiting for him to break down her door like a caveman and ravish her, rather than respecting her ill health? (Leah Lawrence had said his Hero-Savior was not made of flesh and blood.) Had he, after all, despite Zimmerman's assurances, failed her?

He shut his eyes again. The fountain reappeared; the water surged ominously. Tourists strolled by, oblivious to the goings-on. Except for one. A twinkly-eyed satyr of an old man who sat upon the steps watching with intent amusement, his stomach shaking with mirth. It was Rattigan, Catherine's lawyer, who had long since died. The satyr-Rattigan's laughter became rhythmic, loud. Teddy sat up, drenched in sweat. Someone was knocking on the door. His first thought was that it was Leah coming to "interview" him. Who else would intrude upon him here?

He rose with an effort and went into the next room. He said, "Yes?" warily.

The door opened. It was Clemente.

"Teddy, I was worried about you. You didn't come up for lunch. I wondered if you were depressed again?"

"Depressed? No. I've been dreaming. I had a — a kind of a nightmare, I guess."

"Do you want to tell me about it?" She stood with her back to the open door in a pool of sunlight. The sun gave her face an added radiance; it made her hair more golden. He stared at her in wonder.

"You are . . . saintly," he said, scarcely knowing what he was saying. "You have a . . . halo." He took her hand, and, bending over it, kissed it lightly. Then he looked up at her face again. Her blue eyes were filled with tears.

27

"YOU are now equipped to enter the world of business, taking the skills which you have learned at Girl Friday Secretarial School with you." Miss Glover, the head of the school, transformed for the evening in a lavender chiffon formal with puffed sleeves, her hair tightly waved and tinted a lovely blue-gray, a double purple orchid corsage upon her bosom, paused, gazed solemnly at her Commencement Class.

There was a reverent hush in the room. Mary could feel her heart throbbing. She was going to enter this "world of business" on Monday morning. She had been interviewed and accepted for the stenographic pool of a large electronics plant in Sunnyvale. Though she would not earn as much money as she had at the Olivers, she would receive "fringe benefits," which her friend, Dolores Gomez, whom she had met at the school, told her were a good thing. Dolores had also invited Mary to share her apartment near the plant; her husband was in Vietnam, and she did not like living alone. Mary's bags were packed and at Dolores's apartment; she had left her farewell note to the Olivers on top of her empty dresser.

She and Mary had worked out the note together, copying it from the Typing Manual with a few appropriate changes. Then Mary had typed it on Glover Girl stationery.

January 18, 1970
Oonhall Way
Los Robles, California

Mr. Theodore Oliver and Family
Oonhall Way
Los Robles, California

Dear Sirs:

This is to terminate my position in your household. I have accepted a position connected with the electronics industry.

I have enjoyed the pleasure of your acquaintanceship, and trust that you will soon be able to fill the vacancy which I am obliged to create.

Yours very truly,
(Miss) Mary Miller

Mary was sorry she had not been able to say good-bye to little Becky, but she had not felt up to facing the rest of the family in person.

At five minutes of seven this evening, she and Dolores had entered the carpeted lobby of the El Patio Motor Cabana. Near the entrance was a large bulletin board on a stand; in plastic white letters it said, "Girl Friday Secretarial School Banquet, Moroccan Room, Second Floor."

The Moroccan Room was the grandest room Mary had ever seen, outside of television. It was filled with long tables covered with white cloths and electric candles; a bowl of white flowers was in the center of each table. Long, diamond-shaped, black metal lamps hung on cords dangling from the ceiling, casting strange, oblong shadows over the walls and white cloths. On the far wall was a large mural of a camel train wending its way across a beautiful desert. Soft, recorded music played in the background. The room was crowded and noisy, with the graduation class drinking fruit punch from a large cut-glass bowl. The girls all looked so pretty and different in their new dresses that Mary found it hard to recognize them.

After the punch, they found their place cards at the tables;

Dolores switched hers quickly, in order to sit next to Mary. There was a souvenir menu at each place. Dinner was crab cocktail, roast beef au jus, green peas, Lyonnaise potatoes, spumoni and coffee. When the coffee was served, Miss Glover, the director, stood up at the end of the first table and rapped on her glass for silence. Then she began her speech, which went on for several minutes.

"I hope," she was saying now, winding up, "that you will also take Something Else along with you. A subtle, not so easy to define Something Else, which, for lack of a better term, I shall call Spiritual Response." Miss Glover paused again, the way a minister pauses in a sermon. Then she repeated, "Spir-i-tual Res-ponse" very solemnly. She paused again. "Thank you, and God Bless," she said, and sat down. Everyone applauded. There were tears in Mary's eyes.

When the applause had at last died down, Miss Glover stood up again and began to call out each girl's name, one by one. One by one they marched across the big room, received their diplomas, shook Miss Glover's hand, and, while everyone clapped, walked back to their seats. Mary was terrified she might stumble on her new high heels and disgrace herself; when her name was called, she froze, right in her seat. But Dolores gave her a little nudge, and she found herself standing up, then walking slowly, as if she were in a dream, across the carpet, under the oblong lights, to the sound of the soft music. Miss Glover handed her her diploma and they shook hands. Mary walked back, trembling slightly, but with her head held high; the applause seemed deafening. It was like Pete's graduation, she thought. How she wished Pete and her mother could be here to see her. She sat down in her seat again, in a daze.

Dolores pressed her hand. "You looked very sophisticated," she whispered in her ear.

28

It was the night of Linda Alway's debut. Becky stood in front of the full-length mirror in her bedroom, a bewildered expression in her freckled green eyes. She looked at the pink velvet gown with its high, puckered waistline and its puffed sleeves, like pink puff pastry; she ran a hand softly over her newly arranged long hair, which Clemente had brushed until it shone like glistening straw. She stared at her naked forehead; the bangs were gone, held back by a simple barrette. She glanced timidly down at her feet in their pink satin slippers with the subdeb heels. Everything, by itself, was beautiful, and yet, somehow, on her — all wrong! She turned to Clemente, who was standing beside her, holding her black velveteen princess-style coat, her black velvet purse and her white gloves. In a grave voice, which just barely trembled, she said, "I look awful, don't I?"

"I've never seen you look so lovely or so grown-up," said Clemente, who had said the same thing, already, a number of times.

"Are you sure, Clemente? Are you positive? You're not just saying that?"

"If I say it again, you'll get so vain nobody will be able to live with you. Now, no more primping! Teddy is waiting." Clemente gave Becky a firm little push out the door.

In the living room, Teddy was adjusting his tie in an antique silver mirror. Hurwulf was asleep in front of the fire. Loren sat reclined upon the sofa, her legs crossed, her head propped languidly against cushions, her dark hair rippling over one eye. She, too, was dressed formally. She wore a slinky, silver-lamé sleeveless evening gown, cut low in a V in front and back — the only one of its kind at the Los Robles Episcopal Women's Rummage Sale. The silver was tarnished, the hemline tattered, but the dress shrieked of elegance, making a kind of mockery of the debut guests' evening attire. Over her shoulders, to keep warm, she wore a new secondhand, moth-eaten fox fur. The head of the fox, with its beady glass eyes, nestled over her bosom; she stroked it sensually as she observed Teddy.

Though she could not approve of the debut, she was forced to admit to herself that he did look dashing, like one of the suave heroes out of a Sophisticated Comedy of the thirties on the Late Late Show.

Teddy, too, seemed pleased with his reflection in the glass. "Perhaps I shall wear all of this every night for dinner. What a pity to waste it on a horde of strangers one will never see nor want to see again," he said jovially.

Becky, with Clemente in back of her, appeared doubtfully in the doorway.

Teddy stepped forward to meet them. "How ravishing you look this evening, Miss Oliver," he said. "My compliments!"

Becky gave him an uncertain look; she appeared to be on the verge of tears.

"Are you positive you won't change your mind and come?" said Teddy, turning to Clemente.

Clemente smiled. "How could I?" she said placidly. "I haven't anything to wear."

"Why couldn't she wear her kaftan?" Teddy appealed to Loren and Becky. "Her kaftan looks charming on her, don't you think?"

Becky frowned.

"She is welcome to wear my gown," Loren said, giving Becky a teasing look.

"Besides, I think I might be coming down with a little cold," said Clemente. "I feel a bit feverish."

"In that case, you must go straight to bed and get well," said

Teddy firmly. "If the Always weren't old friends and if someone didn't have to escort Miss Becky, I'd stay home myself." He gave a little sigh at the prospect of his duties. "Loren can fix you some of her herb tea," he added.

Loren quite understood Teddy's not insisting that Clemente accompany them. If she, for example, had not been so resolute in her disdain for the archaic event, she might have gone and observed it from the sidelines. Then, afterwards, she and Teddy could have happily analyzed it, seizing upon each absurdity. But the debut, from this point of view, would have been wasted on Clemente. Her unworldliness, her obliviousness to gossip, her almost irritating lack of interest in human foibles would not have provided Teddy with anyone to discuss it with later. Moreover, her shyness would have been a burden; he would have had to spend the evening watching out for her. Her illness had given him an excuse.

Teddy extended an arm to Becky. "The carriage is waiting," he said.

Becky froze. "I can't go!"

"What's this now?" said Teddy impatiently.

"Debbie called me this morning; they're going to have waltzes. I can't waltz!" Becky's voice rose to a hysterical wail.

"Ah, if that's all it is!" Teddy smiled. Without saying a word, he went over to the phonograph cabinet, selected a record, and put it on.

The lilting strains of "Tales from the Vienna Woods" filled the air. "One, two, three; one, two, three." Teddy conducted with his arm. "It's so easy, you won't believe it." He turned toward the stricken Becky and bowed. "May I have this waltz, Miss Oliver?"

Then they were whirling around the large room; Becky's skirt twirled in an undulating pink disc, revealing nylon ankles and satin pumps. They took three steps forward, then three steps backwards; they dipped, pirouetted, dipped again. Their images appeared in the silver mirror as they passed it, disappeared, then reappeared, like spirits from a vanished, magical world.

Hurwulf awoke and barked frantically; Loren gave a bored little yawn.

Then, as suddenly as it had begun, it was over. Becky was laughing; her cheeks were flushed. She had to lean against the wall for a moment to catch her breath. Clemente hurried forward with her coat and helped her on with it; she handed her her purse and gloves. The Beautiful People left.

Clemente said, "I guess I'd better go to bed."

Loren nodded. She was left alone in the quiet house. She felt a bit edgy; the recent scene had been too much! Something was needed to restore her nerves. She rose, went over to the phonograph, removed the waltz, and stuffed it carelessly into the bookshelf. She selected another record and put it on the machine. Then she returned to the sofa, took out an old-fashioned Camel cigarette tin beneath a pillow, and, from its contents, rolled herself a joint.

Jefferson Airplane began to play:

> *One pill makes you larger*
> *And one pill makes you small.*
> *And the ones that mother gives you*
> *Don't do anything at all.*
> *Go ask Alice when she's ten feet tall.*

She smoked thoughtfully. Time passed.

> *When men on the chessboard*
> *Get up and tell you when to go*
> *And you've just had some kind of mushroom*
> *And your mind is moving low*
> *Go ask Alice — I think she'll know.*

An hour? Two? Five minutes? What did it matter? Words and music blended into her consciousness; music, words, consciousness became a transcendental Whole.

She did not hear the car in the driveway nor the steps in the hall.

Yet she was not at all surprised to glance up and perceive a most curious apparition standing in the center of the room. It was that of a woman dressed in a short, black skirt, a low-cut, white blouse, black net stockings and high heels; on her head, at a rakish angle, was a fuzzy tam-o'-shanter with a red knob on its top. Around her neck she wore an assortment of colored wooden beads. Silver earrings drooped from her ears, a cigarette dangled from the corner of her mouth. The apparition sidled forward, one hand upon a thrust-out hip. She took a long drag upon the cigarette, then held it out, arm's length, in a dramatic gesture. "I have just been accepted," the apparition said merrily.

The voice brought Loren out of her reverie. She recognized Leah Lawrence.

"Accepted?" she said. She sat up. "By whom? For what?"

"By the most beautiful group of young people I have ever had the pleasure of meeting — the members of the little pad where your sister lives."

"You have been to see Hat?"

Leah flung the cigarette onto the hearth, crushed it with the toe of her pump, and lit another. "I have participated in their rites." She laughed. "Oh, it was extremely sneaky of me! We writers will do anything. I found the address on an envelope and off I went — dressed as you see me, as a hippie!"

"That *is* a far-out costume. Where did you get it?"

"I put it together out of bits and pieces. After all, I was a member of Bohemia in my own youth. I still am, at heart. I have a feeling for it. I took offerings of French bread and what we used to call Dago red wine. They accepted me at once as a sister. They didn't even ask my name. It was all so Early Christian, so antibourgeois — with due respect to your dear mother — so free from all that."

"From all what?"

"I am looking at the portrait of your venerable ancestor. The representative of material values. The antithesis of what I have just observed!"

"What *did* you observe?" said Loren curiously.

Leah shut her eyes. "A small room, barren of material possessions. Young people lying about on mattresses. A girl asleep. A mongrel dog with a litter of puppies in one corner." She opened her eyes, took another drag on her cigarette. "I am trying to keep it fresh in my mind." She shut her eyes again. "A gentle young man — leather jerkin, leather pants, barefoot, playing a zither. A pale madonna nursing her babe. Another young man, cross-legged on the floor, stringing glass beads. A delightful, fierce-eyed, bearded chap, cutting up a chicken with a hunting knife."

"Was Hat there?"

"Hat?" Leah opened her eyes. "That was what was especially beautiful. They told me Hat was out on the street somewhere, distributing pamphlets to aid the oppressed. Exactly as Cary would have done!"

"Did you happen to see a batik bedspread?"

"I'm afraid I didn't notice that. I concentrated more on the people. We broke bread together and drank the wine. I donated a small offering to their Cause — then I departed. I was afraid of making them self-conscious by taking notes so I wanted to get home and record my impressions before I forgot them."

"I'm sure Hat ripped off my bedspread. She always admired it."

"You will have to excuse me. I must dash upstairs and record my impressions. They're for Chapter Six, just before Cary meets Crown. That's the name I've chosen for her Black. It symbolizes his nobility, don't you think?"

"The spread was missing just after Cary left." Leah was gone before Loren realized she had said "Cary" instead of "Hat."

29

IT was past midnight. Loren was suddenly ravenously hungry. She went into the kitchen and ate a peanut butter sandwich with wheat germ sprinkled on it and a banana dipped in honey, and drank two glasses of milk. Then she started toward the Tower stairs. On the way, she noticed a light under the door which led to the basement Playroom. She pushed the door open. There, below, wearing a smock over her flannel nightgown, was Clemente, busily at work upon the Mural.

"I thought you were sick." Loren trotted down the stairs and settled herself upon the velvet sofa.

"I couldn't sleep so I decided to finish this panel," Clemente said, without stopping her painting.

Loren studied the addition. A wine-dark sea, a gaily colored galley, manned by Nubian slaves. In the curved prow, the passengers, waving farewell. Loren recognized Teddy, Becky and herself. Clemente was now working on another figure. Hat? No. A blur of golden hair, a pale blue kaftan — unmistakably Clemente.

"I thought you didn't approve of painting yourself into the Mural," said Loren drowsily.

"I don't, but Teddy insisted." Clemente laughed lightly. "He thinks I'm much too modest, and, since I'm evidently coming, the Mural should be accurate."

"Well, he's right. We've always said that. But you haven't included Hat, have you?"

"Teddy and I discussed that," said Clemente seriously. "We both decided we can no longer count on her. I was glad that Teddy agreed. I hate to see him disappointed."

"Well, I wish someone had consulted me. I have my own opinions on that. Hat will get bored with her Revolution, that's my prediction. I don't think she should have been dropped just yet. Clemente, what are you wearing on your arm?"

Clemente glanced down at her left wrist. "The bracelet?"

"Isn't that part of Catherine's star sapphire set?"

"Is it? I don't know one kind of jewel from another. Teddy gave it to me."

"Gave it to you?" Loren sat upright. "You must be mistaken, Clemente."

"Teddy put it on my arm himself. He said it matched the kaftan and my eyes."

"Oh, dear, Clemente, you're such an innocent." Loren shook her head in disgust. "I know you're not interested in material things, but you really ought to have realized that the bracelet isn't Teddy's to give — not morally, anyhow."

"Is it legally?"

"I'm sure I don't know. Olivers don't worry about things like that. And you don't, either. It's entirely beside the point."

Clemente put down her paintbrush, first wiping it carefully upon a rag. She turned around. Her eyes were tranquil. "I only asked because I didn't want Teddy to get into any trouble. I don't see how I can refuse his gift."

"Clemente, I shall try to be patient. You know very well that Teddy is impulsive at times; he may not have been thinking, he may even have been under the influence of drink, as he sometimes is. He couldn't have meant to give you Hat's bracelet. It's part of the Oon jewels. You remember, don't you? The necklace will go to me, the earrings to Becky." Loren stood up and went over to Clemente. "You do understand?" she said, as if she were talking to a child.

"I understand what you're saying, but . . ." Clemente stroked the bracelet lightly with her other hand. "Certainly, *you* understand that I couldn't hurt Teddy's feelings." Her voice was dreamy, faraway. There was a peculiar sweet odor upon her breath.

"Clemente, you haven't been drinking, have you?"

"Teddy gave me some sherry the other day. I liked it, so he said I could keep the bottle. I had a little before I came downstairs. Teddy says it helps you to sleep."

"Teddy," said Loren, "is being very naughty. He shouldn't try to encourage others to share his bad habits. Especially you, Clemente. I can't imagine you drinking anymore than I can imagine you smoking pot. It just isn't your thing, somehow. I'm going to have to have a talk with Teddy, I can see that now." She looked at Clemente and pondered. "Yes, we shall have to be stricter with him," she said. Then her voice became severe. "You go to bed, Clemente. It's damp down here. You haven't any sense."

"I thought I'd surprise him and finish the panel," Clemente said stubbornly.

"You're just wasting your time. When Hat comes back, the panel will have to be redone, anyhow. I think the sherry has made your brain fuzzy. I'm extremely cross with Teddy, and I'm beginning to be cross with you. You let everyone take advantage of your good nature. Now, put your paints away."

Clemente sighed gently and began to collect her brushes.

"Things," said Loren, "are getting out of hand around here."

30

"THERE will be no one to prepare your breakfast," said Loren to Becky, when Becky appeared for breakfast at noon, after the debut.

Becky blinked at her sister with drowsy eyes. She was still in her nightgown; around her neck she wore a brown, limp, gardenia lei.

"Mary's split. She has gone into industry. There is no more servant class; somebody will have to learn to cook."

"Well, Clemente can," said Becky sleepily. She walked in a daze toward the refrigerator, took out a bottle of milk, then got cornflakes from a cupboard. She poured the cornflakes and milk into a bowl and sat down at the table.

"Where is Clemente? I was hoping for bacon and eggs."

"Clemente got up to work on the Mural. Now she's probably sicker; she's still in bed. It serves her right for being so dumb."

"The Always have lots of food left over. I can eat there tonight, then."

"Tell me about Miss Linda's debut." Loren sat down opposite Becky.

Becky became fully awake; her eyes sparkled. "Oh, wow, it was far out; you were crazy not to come." She put down her spoon. "It was like Shakespeare — you know, Renaissancy. All blue and wine-colored. They had footmen in livry —"

"Livery."

"— holding up these big candles. Tapers, Mrs. Alway called them. Linda looked like Juliet. Her dress was wine-colored velvet. She had one of those hairpieces on her head like a bump, with tiny seed pearls around it. Her real hair flowed down her back. There were the Gorgeous Groovies and a bar-rock band for the grown-ups."

"Baroque?"

"The Italian consul was there and the tennis coach from the Always' club and Linda's riding master and this television star Mrs. Alway knows from Los Angeles, he's going to be in a series about a famous open heart specialist, she went to school with him. There were ten private policemen and two whole wild boars from the Carmel Valley with an apple in their mouths. Debbie and I both danced with Mr. Alway and with Teddy, and then we just wandered around. We got the television star's autograph, and he kissed us both. The Italian consul kissed us, too, on our hands. We got to drink all the champagne we wanted." She giggled. "We got drunk. Debbie threw up in the bushes, then we went back and drank more. We planned Debbie's debut. It will be in the summer and she wants a Hawaiian luau. Teddy was cross you didn't come."

"Was Teddy cross Clemente didn't come?"

"I don't know. I don't think so. Clemente isn't really . . . family."

"Did Teddy 'fall' for Mrs. Collier?"

"He ate dinner with her. But she had broken her ankle and couldn't dance. She said it was a blessing in disguise, because everyone at the party autographed her cast, and she will keep it in memory of the event. The Italian consul wrote on it in Italian."

"Did Teddy dance?"

"I told you, he danced with me and Debbie, and, of course, with Linda. Everyone danced with Linda. He looked very handsome. Linda said so. Mrs. Alway said it was good for him to go to parties; she said he seemed like his old self again."

"How does Mrs. Alway know what Teddy's 'old self' is?"

"Mrs. Alway knows things. She understands people. Mr. Alway says she has a special gift. She thinks Teddy has become too ingrown since Catherine died."

"Mrs. Alway is a busybody, like Aunt Harriet."

"Teddy bet Linda she'd sleep for a week, and Linda bet Teddy she wouldn't. She can't, because she has to go into training for the May Day Hundred Mile Trail Ride. It's an old English custom, like when the king moved his court. Teddy bet Linda she couldn't ride a hundred miles. Linda bet Teddy she could. She said she'd ride over on her horse the day after she got back — it takes five days — and win her bet. Teddy said if she didn't show up, she'd have to be his slave for an afternoon. Can you imagine Linda's being anyone's slave? She'll have to clean up Fala for him."

"Fala!"

"Take down all his books and records and papers, and dust it. Wouldn't that be far out?"

"Extremely. What did he bet her?"

"A handcrafted silver Spanish buckle to wear with her Spanish riding clothes."

"That's Catherine's buckle. Was Teddy drunk?"

"Everyone was drunk," said Becky happily, and began her cornflakes.

31

CLEMENTE did not come down for dinner that night. Teddy went up to see her and returned, reporting that her fever was a bit higher, but that she refused to see a doctor. Becky had gone to the Always to eat up the remains of the debut feast. Leah did not appear. Teddy made scrambled eggs for Loren and himself, which they ate at the round kitchen table.

"I am disturbed about Mary," said Teddy, over the eggs.

"I am, too. I won't miss her cooking, but I did like having my bed changed once a week."

"I was thinking more of our moral responsibility," Teddy said.

"What is that?"

"We tried and failed. Otherwise, she would at least have confided in us."

"Perhaps she was afraid we would try to change her mind. After all, we could use a servant."

"If only she could have thought of herself as more a part of our family. I blame myself for this. I made an effort, but obviously not enough."

"It isn't easy to become an Oliver," said Loren.

"No, perhaps not. But it still seems so awful. To grow up in that beautiful northern wilderness and then to enter the electronics industry. Upward Mobility, the American Dream of Life."

Teddy sighed. "These eggs are too dry," he said. "Clemente puts something in them, doesn't she? Is it cream or milk?"

"It is unfortunate having Mary and Clemente gone at the same time. Would you say we have the right moral attitude toward Clemente? Have we integrated her?"

"Clemente is an entirely different category," said Teddy.

"Yes, I suppose. Is that why you gave her the Oon jewels?"

"The Oon jewels?" Teddy looked at Loren in amazement. "Whatever are you talking about?" he said. "I didn't give Clemente any Oon jewels. I haven't the slightest idea what you mean. No! Stop! Let me guess. I did let Clemente try the bracelet on, just for fun. She's like a child; she enjoys playing with pretty things. Is that what you mean? Is that what's making you so snappish this evening?"

"I was led to believe it was a gift — last night."

"Good heavens, did Clemente give you that idea?"

"Unmistakably."

"The poor girl must have been feverish. Oh, dear, what an awkward situation. But she will probably have forgotten all about it when she gets well."

"It is in her possession."

"I should have put it back into the safe. I left while she was wearing it — she was dusting around — I assumed she would take it off. Perhaps I should call a doctor. She looked very pale. She may be sicker than we think." Teddy pulled his chair firmly back to the table. "Look here, Loren, I'm glad, actually, you've brought this up. I've been meaning to talk to you about it anyhow. I've been worried about Clemente lately. It seems to me that, beneath her angelic nature, there is . . . a sadness. And why shouldn't there be?" He gestured upwards, toward Leah's room. "The poor girl has never had a proper homelife. We've tried to help her, but one never quite knows how to help best." He rose suddenly, went to the kitchen shelf where the liquor was kept, and fumbled about. "Would you care to try some of Aunt Harriet's apricot cordial? It seems to me we ought to give it a chance."

"Thank you, no."

He brought the bottle to the table, poured some into a glass, tasted it, made a face. Then, bravely, he continued to drink more. "You mustn't worry about the bracelet," he said after a moment. "There's no problem whatsoever. Clemente doesn't have a possessive bone in her body."

"She has never had anything to possess."

"You're right! The child never has! Only scraps from other people's tables. She knows nothing of material values — the bracelet was a mere bauble to her. That's part of her charm." There was another silence. Then: "Perhaps we should give Clemente something . . . more solid? Help her with an education? I've thought of that, but it's not her thing, is it? I'd welcome any ideas from the floor."

Loren thought. "We might set her up in a little arts and crafts shop," she said.

"Clemente doesn't have a business head. That's part of her charm."

"Her charm seems to be getting in the way of everything. Maybe she must learn not to be so charming."

"Oh, dear, I can sense you're not in a helpful mood this evening. I'm sorry, because you have a perceptive mind." Teddy finished off the coffee in a brisk gulp. "Well, we can discuss Clemente's future later, I suppose. There'll be plenty of time after our trip."

"Won't the trip be just more scraps, more dependence?"

"I hope you're not suggesting that we tell her she can't come after she's been invited! Would you rather we throw the poor child out on the street?"

Loren considered. "Why couldn't she live with Aunt Harriet?" she said brightly.

"I'm sure you're not serious, Loren."

"When you think about it, they have certain things in common," Loren said, half to herself.

"It's hard to imagine what they are." Teddy looked at Loren anxiously. "You're not coming down with the flu, are you?" he said. "You don't seem yourself, somehow."

"I feel very well."

Teddy stood up. "Well, then I must get some work done. I suppose I must write the Department of Interior about Mary. I believe there's a legal responsibility. And tomorrow I'll make a date with the travel bureau. Planning a trip of the sort we want is like drawing up a battle plan —"

"Aren't you going to get the bracelet back?"

"Now? This minute?"

"The longer Clemente has it, the easier it will be for her to assume it's hers."

"Yes, I suppose you're right." He started toward the door, then hesitated. "I hate to wake her up, though, if she's asleep."

"You don't have to wake her up, just take it. Since she has no possessive bones in her body, she won't even miss it."

"Yes, that's a good idea."

"Also, somebody will have to think about meals tomorrow."

"Oh, damn, life is complicated, isn't it?" Teddy said.

32

February 18

Dearest Teddy,

I was going to call you, but I'd have to use a pay booth, and I just couldn't see telling you what I want to tell you in a pay booth, somehow. I mean, it's complicated, but absolutely beautiful and groovy. Teddy, the city has become a Bad Scene, and a lot of us are going to split. We're dropping political activity because the Resistance is Bad Karma, too, because resisting means resisting something, and we no longer recognize that something. I mean, it just doesn't exist. How can it, like when everything is One?

If this sounds weird, try to think about it, not with your mind, but with your whole being, like this guru, this fabulously beautiful man, he studied in India and explained it to us in his talk. Well, it wasn't a talk, exactly, because he doesn't talk, he just is, you feel his vibes, and they're beautiful vibes. I had this funny feeling like I had died, sort of, and the real part of me separated from the unreal, materialistic part and was floating around in a purer form, part of the Whole. This might be hard for you to dig, because you've brought us up as Individuals, and Individuals are out. The far-out goal is Nothingness, only that's hard to achieve in one lifetime, only a few do. As you can see, this isn't like Loren's trip at all — can you imagine her willing to give up her Personality? I mean, she comes on so strong and is awfully attached to her Ego, but frankly, I'm not satisfied with mine, and I'm going to make the try.

Teddy, this is the thing. There's a place in Mendocino County. I've seen photos, it's called Enlightenment City. Anyhow, it's a commune, where you live and work with the soil and raise goats and do spiritual exercises to find out who you are. There aren't even any different words for girls or boys or men or women — everyone is just a Disciple. There are seven hundred acres this rich cat has donated, but the people up there are against communes, and so they're making us put in a better well and flush toilets to try to force us out. And then there are taxes. I gave Arab most of my savings, and he's on his way up there now, in my Porsche, to look it over. I thought you might want to help out, too. It's definitely a spiritual movement, only it isn't Baptist or Catholic or even Zen. It's just where it is. I know your opinion of present-day civilization, and you could visit us and become enlightened, too. (The only problem is — no drugs or alcohol are permitted. We only use this ancient Indian drug for religious ceremonies.)

Could you possibly send, say, something like a thousand, to help out with the toilets. (Stanford would have cost more!) I'll call you as soon as Arab is back, and we've made our plans. Incidentally, we change our names, like nuns, and it's an honor to name somebody, like being a godfather, and if you are a donor, you have that privilege and can name me.

> *The cherry tree blooms each year*
> *In the Yoshino Mountains.*
> *But split the tree and tell me*
> *Where the flowers are.*

If you say that over and over it will blow your mind, and you'll just have to send me a check.

Love and Kisses,
Hat

February 20

Dear-to-be-Enlightened,

The cherry tree blooms each year, and each year I grow older. My desk is filled with unfinished business. Not to mention that Mary has split, and we can find no help. Not to mention that I am having to deal with the ever-ubiquitous school authorities about Loren's "delinquency." (It seems there is a law you have to attend the Halls of Ignorance until you are sixteen.) Sometimes I wish I hadn't brought up my daughters to think for themselves.

    I am trying to help Zimmy find a site for his Therapy Retreat, not so easy a task in this day of inflated real estate prices. We are also, dear daughter, still playing with our plans for a trip to Europe. We cherish hopes that you will join us. Enclosed, find money for your flush toilets. Since I have not yet reached the blessed state of Nothingness, it is frankly a bribe. If you come on our trip, we will try not to corrupt you.

Love,
Your Pa

P.S. At the very least, Miss Oliver, you owe us a visit.
P.P.S. At the very very least, write something about your activities which would be suitable for Clyde's ears. He is pestering me about your loose life.

33

It was a Friday afternoon in early April. The brief winter was gone; brief spring was at its climax. Green fields and hills were sprinkled with poppies. Beneath the apricot trees which had escaped the bulldozer, mustard bloomed. Yellow acacias bordering the road were a powdery mass of pollen. Colts had appeared in the corrals next to the ranch houses, awkwardly shadowing sleek mares. Noisy birds darted and plunged through the fragrant air, mating, falling apart, remating.

Clyde, in Stetson and jeans, drove his cream-colored Cadillac up the Olivers' driveway and parked several yards from the house, across from the tennis courts. Taking a toolbox from his luggage compartment, he strolled across the weed-choked lawn to the court. There, he kneeled down, opened the box, and began to repair the gate. Anyone watching him would have thought he worked with a single-minded preoccupation, but his hands moved expertly, independent of his thoughts. He was thinking about the Olivers, and especially of Hat: how he would rescue her from her misguided way of life and return her to her family where she belonged.

Clyde had never had a real family of his own. He had been born in Arizona, the son of an itinerant farm worker, who, unable to support his family, had solved the problem by disappearing. Clyde's mother had drowned in a flash flood when Clyde was ten; her Ford had stalled in a wash, and rather than heeding a roadside sign to head for high ground, she had stayed with the car and been swept away with it. These two events had produced a peculiar mixture of fatalism and caution in Clyde. He was a gambler, but he always made sure that the odds were in his favor.

After his mother's death, his mother's sister, who had six small children of her own, took him in. Conscious of his foster-child status, he worked hard at odd jobs and attended school only enough to keep the truant officer away. At sixteen, he was almost self-supporting. At seventeen, Pearl Harbor gave him his first big opportunity.

He enlisted in the army air corps without finishing high school. He became a tail gunner, flew fifty missions, was decorated for bravery in action, worked up to top sergeant, and was one of the first men to be released after the war. He received his mustering-out pay in San Francisco, then found a job as foreman on a cattle ranch in San Benito County near Hollister.

The owner of the ranch was an old man whose closest heir was a nephew, a "city fellow" whom the old man feared would either sell the ranch or ruin it upon his demise. After supper, which he shared with Clyde, the old man dwelt upon this anxiety.

Clyde was not slow to see another opportunity here, but since he genuinely liked his employer, he suffered no pangs of conscience. He worked hard and gradually took over most of the responsibility of the ranch. At the same time, he became the old man's closest companion.

Gleefully, to thwart the nephew, and gratefully, because of Clyde's loyalty, the old man made Clyde his protégé and devised a plan.

Clyde understood cattle and land, but he was ignorant of finances. The old man sold Clyde the ranch for nothing down and the agreement that he would spend the rest of his days upon the ranch. Then, with the old man's guidance, Clyde borrowed to buy more cattle. In the early years after the war, meat prices were rising; costs were still low. The old man taught Clyde how to avoid high taxes by plowing back the profits from the cattle into more land, which was tax deductible. By the early sixties, this game was over; cattle were no longer profitable, but Clyde was now able to sell off half his land holdings for enormous cash gains, which he invested in tax-free municipal bonds.

When Clyde was thirty-four the old man died. The nephew settled out of court for a reasonable sum; Clyde was a millionaire, and the original ranch, which he still owned, was almost a hobby. Clyde was now alone. But he had been alone much of his life; it was a condition he accepted without question, until, seven years ago, Catherine and Teddy had driven up to his ranch house in Teddy's Mercedes, looking for land.

To Clyde, the Olivers were strange, glamorous creatures, representative of a life he had only glimpsed in the movies. But this would not have been enough. He fell, too, for their friendly manner, their air of helplessness, their naïveté about owning a ranch, their quick, instinctive dependence upon his judgment, and for the fact that they, too, had quite openly fallen in love with him.

They spent the day together; he took them on a tour of the ranch. Everything entranced them, like children. And like children, they were disappointed when he discouraged them from becoming ranchers. Wistfully, Teddy asked if he might bring his daughters to visit. They had been brought up in the suburbs, he wanted them to see a working ranch. In return, Clyde must visit them. This was the beginning of the love affair between Clyde and the Oliver family.

Clyde knew he had been re-created out of this love; the Olivers became both his children and parents. They represented all he had never had — beauty, stability, and family life. But even more important was the fact that they, too, seemed to need him. Though he knew he was not intelligent in the same way that they were, that he lacked their education and culture, he had other gifts which he could offer and which they valued. Besides fixing fences and swimming pools, teaching the Oliver girls to shoot and fly, he had a more practical knowledge of the world outside theirs, which they respected; he guarded their innocence jealously, like a fierce watchdog. Like a watchdog, he had an innate distrust of anyone who came close to them. Aunt Harriet was all right, because she, too, was innocent, and "family," but he had never cottoned to Mad Fred, the Zimmermans, Leah Lawrence, or even Clemente. Innocence, he knew, was always in danger; it was his job to remain alert to this.

And then, one day four years ago, this new, happy world into which he had been so wholeheartedly received was shattered for him. It happened in the early autumn, in Rome, where Clyde had gone because both Teddy and Catherine had begged him to join them there. Except for the pleasure of their company, such a trip was the last thing which would have appealed to him; the more Teddy talked of what they would do there — of the churches, museums, and antiquities they would see — the more he was convinced it was not for him. But they had cajoled, pleaded. If he didn't like Teddy's plans, then he could entertain Catherine, who had seen all those things as a girl with governesses and chaperons. Either way, he must not disappoint them.

Clyde, against his better judgment, had finally agreed, but he had made one firm stipulation. If he did not like Rome as much as they promised he would, he would come home after four days. Both Teddy and Catherine found this especially amusing and charming. How could he not like it when they would devote themselves utterly to his entertainment — he had only to wait and see!

The moment Clyde drove into the city from the airport in his Stetson and boots (he had worn them because he had sensed this would please the Olivers), he knew that they had been wrong and he, right. Later, he blamed everything that happened on the Eternal City, which he had felt immediately and instinctively to be evil and corrupt.

In the U.S.A. you knew where you were; you could separate good from bad. You could go to a cathouse, as he often had in his youth, and you could go to church, if you had a mind to, and know the difference. But here, the churches were too opulent for his taste, the fountains too showy, the statues too brazen. There was a kind of heavy languor in the autumn air. Even the whores on the street were hard to distinguish from nice girls — to him they looked exactly like the other smartly dressed women on the Via Veneto.

When Clyde joined the Olivers in their suite at their hotel, Teddy was jumping with excitement like a child. Guidebook in hand he was ready to plunge into the city and explore everything from B.C. to A.D. Catherine, in a negligee, lay on the bed; there were dark shadows under her eyes. She was smoking one cigarette after another and turning the pages of an Italian version of *Life* magazine. She refused, she said, in a petulant voice, to look at one more church or palace. Clyde, relieved, offered to stay with her. Teddy, delighted with this arrangement, had rushed off.

While he was gone, Catherine had declared her love for Clyde.

The scene of this declaration was fixed forever in Clyde's memory. The big, fancy room; the damasked walls; the plaster frieze of fat, bare-assed Cupids prancing about in abandoned poses; the large bed with an apricot-colored spread, a ridiculous satin love seat facing it; the heavy, pale-green draperies which when pulled revealed a tiny, useless balcony like the kind in the movie houses of his youth.

Standing in the center of this room was Catherine, whom he had always assumed to be different from other women — her pale face flushed, a mysterious half smile upon her lips, her dark eyes, usually so serene, alive with a shocking coquetry. Clyde was a Puritan, and Rome for him at that moment was a nightmare from which he thought he would never recover.

But Clyde was tough. He sat down on the edge of that silly sofa and lit a cigarette and puffed on it and considered. Old instincts of self-preservation, long dormant, rose up and began to act for him. It was this way, he decided: Catherine did, after all, belong to the frailer sex. This frailer sex had always made Clyde edgy; there was something dark and scary about them, a kind of unpredictable frivolity, a tendency to hysteria, perhaps even an innate corruption. One had to pity them in a way, but you couldn't let them get out of hand. If Teddy had a weakness, it was this: he had been so devoted to his wife that he had neglected to keep her under control.

This was, alas, what Clyde must do now for Teddy. In order to do it, he must stay cool, play his cards close to his chest, bluff for time. Yes, the worst thing he could do right now at this moment, he thought, was to do anything at all. There was no knowing what Catherine might have up her sleeve in her present condition; he would kind of let her talk it out, steady her, let her feel his own calm and mastery.

"Now, Katie," he said in his most sensible tone, "I believe you're having a sort of crazy spell, I really do. You're all tuckered out; the trip's been too much for you. Don't you think that's what your problem is?"

"Life has been too much for me," she said. "No, I don't mean that — it hasn't been . . . enough."

"You're forgetting all about Teddy," he said severely.

"What about Teddy?" she gave a shameless little laugh. "You don't imagine he'd care!"

"Yes, I do, Katie. I think he would care a whole lot."

"Teddy's a dear, but I assure you, he won't."

"Well, I think he would, Katie. I think that's what we need to talk about."

"Talk! I thought I could count on you not to talk — I thought I could at least count on that. Don't you see, I'm sick of talking. Especially . . . in Oon." Her voice became wistful; her expression changed from boldness to a childlike appeal. "Don't you understand?" she said sadly. "I want something . . . real."

Clyde felt himself suddenly dazzled by her sorrow — this sorrow of a woman who had, he thought, everything. It was as if her misery was the most extreme of luxuries, like a rare and precious jewel which only she could afford to wear.

"That's why I married Teddy, Clyde. I thought he was more real than all those people I was brought up with. I thought we would . . . do things together. Important things. I was young, naïve. I couldn't judge people. In some ways Teddy's a worse snob than the Pacific Heights crowd."

"Teddy hasn't snubbed me," Clyde said.

"No. He finds you . . . colorful. Like Mad Fred."

Clyde was hurt by this, but he did not show it. He said, "You're worn out, Katie. You don't know what you're saying. You've got an excellent husband and three lovely girls."

"The girls are Teddy's," she said plaintively. "They adore him, not me."

Although Clyde had always taken chances, they had been calculated ones. He had never been reckless just out of caprice. Now he was thunderstruck by Catherine's blatant insincerity, by her nerve, her daring. He wondered if perhaps she was tougher than he thought — tougher even than he.

"I don't think we should stay here while you make up a lot of nonsense," he said. "I'll tell you what. You get something on and we'll go out and get some air."

"There's nowhere I want to go. There's nothing I want to do. Oh, Clyde, I used to have such marvelous ideas. I was going to help the poor, the disadvantaged. I was going to be a social worker, or a journalist who exposed things, or —"

"Well, I'm glad you didn't," Clyde said.

She wasn't listening; she seemed to be just listening to herself. "And what have I done? Nothing. Even my parents did more. At least they sponsored charity balls and were on boards and committees. I opted out for something better and got . . . what?" She came closer; he could smell her perfume. "And got what?" she said again mournfully.

He was made dizzy by her anguish, her peculiar needs.

"Well, if you ask me, Katie, you got a lot," he managed to say. "Come on. Be a good girl. Get something on and show me the sights. Isn't that what you wanted to do?"

"I told you, I don't know what I want."

"We'll get a cab and go somewhere."

"Where?" she said sulkily.

"Well, we'll ask the driver, Katie."

The driver, a man with a large trunk and short legs, said, "In Rome, many churches. That's why so many Romans in Paradise."

"No chiesas," said Catherine.

"You speek Italian. Very good. I speek English. We see a lot. Campidoglio? Very famous, very historic?"

"No."

"Foro Romano? Foro Traiano? Castel a Sant' Angelo? Villa Borghese? You like pictures? Statues? Moses? Santa Teresa in Ecstasy? The Pietà!"

"No statuas."

"You like mummies? Church of Santa Maria de Concezione? Very beautiful. Decorated with bones and skulls."

"No."

"We drive out of noisy city? Too hot? Villa Adriana? Tivoli Gardens? Very peaceful."

"No."

"We drive by villa of Gina Lollobrigida. You look."

"Trattoria," said Catherine. "Piccolo."

The driver threw up his hands. He took them the long route to the Tre Scalini.

It was warm and humid, and everyone was sitting at tables upon the sidewalk. Clyde could remember some fountain in the center of the piazza — languid, lounging stone gods, dolphins with puffed up cheeks spouting water from their mouths. The monsterlike creatures made him uncomfortable, and he was glad when Catherine led him indoors.

They sat down at a tiny round table; he had trouble finding room for his legs. Catherine giggled at this, and took his hand. A waiter appeared, smiled discreetly down upon them, and took their order. Catherine asked for a campari; Clyde, a Coke.

"Imagine my coming all this way to tell a cowboy who drinks Cokes that I love him," she said, overcome with amusement. She cocked her head strangely, brushed her long hair back with her hand, and looked into his eyes. "You have such fantastic eyes," she said. "They always make me wonder what you're really thinking. Do you think I'm a bad woman?" She giggled again.

"Katie, you're attracting attention," Clyde said.

For the rest of the four days of Clyde's self-imposed probation he went out with Teddy — trudged dutifully through museums, churches, castles; listened with a polite, studied interest while Teddy, standing in front of a statue or painting or altarpiece, read to him from the guidebook.

"I showed Clyde the Vatican today," he told Catherine proudly when they returned to the hotel.

"How was the Vatican, Clyde?"

"Well, it was something all right. Teddy pointed everything out. He's done his homework."

"I showed Clyde the Forum. We hired a guide."

"Did you like the Forum, Clyde?"

"It was great, all those old buildings."

"Clyde and I did the catacombs this morning."

"Was it fun?"

"They sure buried a lot of folks down there. I'd hate to get lost in those alleys."

Catherine joined them for dinner, but retired early, while Teddy took Clyde on a tour of Roman night life. The names and places were all a blur to Clyde. He did not care for the food, the music, the sissy-looking men and their stylishly dressed women; he could not imagine what Teddy, a family man, saw in the lewd floor shows. When whores approached them, Clyde bristled inwardly as Teddy said, "No, thank you just the same," as politely and apologetically as if he were speaking to a well-brought-up young lady. If this was travel, Clyde preferred home. But his four days were almost up; he could leave gracefully, making up some excuse about the ranch. When the Olivers got back, their madness would, he thought hopefully, have passed, and all would be the same again.

On the fourth night, after they had returned from their rounds, and Clyde had gone to bed, Catherine knocked upon his door. She was wearing a coat and high heels. When he let her in, she sat down on the edge of his bed and kicked off her shoes; then she removed her coat. She was naked and in high spirits.

"Katie, put your coat back on," said Clyde.

"I don't want to." She cavorted about his room like a naughty little girl, showing off. He watched helplessly. Then she rushed up to him and threw her arms around his shoulders and began to sob.

"Oh, hell," said Clyde, giving up.

"So, we've persuaded Clyde to stay on," said Teddy the next morning, over their breakfast. Catherine and Teddy were eating what they called a Continental breakfast — hard rolls and black, bitter coffee. Clyde was having ham and eggs and Nescafé.

"I think so. Haven't we, Clyde?"

Clyde nodded. Rome had got to him, too, he thought. He was as loony as the Olivers by now. If he lived through his nightmare, he would stay down on the ranch for a good, long time, until he was sure they were all sane again.

"I thought we'd change his mind," said Teddy gleefully. "Today, we'll do the Etruscans."

But, on their return from Europe, Catherine had turned up at the ranch.

"Where does Teddy think you are?" Clyde said sternly.

"There's absolutely no problem, darling Clyde. I'm on Retreat!"

"You're on what?"

"Retreat. Rome has revived my feelings for Catholicism."

"We can't go on like this, Katie. Maybe you ought to go see what's his name. Zimmerman."

"He sucks Teddy's ass."

"Ladies don't talk like that."

"By now, haven't I convinced you I'm not a lady? You're so old-fashioned and quaint, I think that's why I love you. I adore the way you furnish your house, by the way. Did you use the Sears Roebuck catalog?"

What a god-awful, crummy mess, thought Clyde.

She had come three times. Each time she seemed to grow more restless. After they made love, she would lie upon the bed, watching him as he dressed, with a faraway melancholy smile. He had not driven away her melancholy; it was like a curse which resisted all cure. It was contagious, too. It infected him, and he knew, now, it had infected Teddy. He felt a deeper tenderness toward this friend whom he had betrayed. They were in the same boat together, and it was rocking dangerously.

The last time she came, he left her lying on the bed like that. He went outside and got into his pickup and drove around the ranch erratically. His head was confused; he knew it had to end. But how? When he returned, she was gone, but she had left a note.

> Dearest Clyde,
> Do please forgive me. It was all so silly, wasn't it? Middle-aged boredom, I suppose. I'm sure, though, you'll agree that it will be best for us not to see each other again. You can make up some excuse, can't you? I shall miss you.
> All my love,
> Katie

No more Teddy, he thought. No more Becky, Loren, Hat. No more Katie. It were as if she had purposely seduced him in order to destroy him. It had not even been a fair game; the cards had been loaded in her favor from the beginning. At the same time, he was stunned by his loss, and despised himself for not being able to prevent it.

Katie was killed that night on her way home. She ran into a telephone pole, oddly (but fortunately, for Teddy's sake) across from the Convent of the Precious Blood. If Teddy suspected she had not been on her Retreat, he had never once betrayed it. Still, Clyde had never been sure how much Teddy had known. Together, the two men mourned; together, they consoled the children. A stronger affection seemed to grow up between them. Katie was gone; they had both adored her and had both, somehow, failed her.

What in hell had happened, Clyde often wondered. The mystery haunted him. He only knew that he and Teddy were both sadder but no wiser. Not unless wisdom came from knowing there were things you couldn't ever understand. He knew, too, where his duty now lay more than ever — it was to Teddy and the girls. His protectiveness toward them increased. If he had been so easily outwitted, what perils were perhaps lurking for the even more innocent Olivers?

Clyde swung the gate back and forth several times, testing its action. Then he collected his tools and put them back into the car. He had not come just to fix the gate. He had come for another reason. He left the car where it was and walked around the house to the stable. Through the open doorway, he saw Becky, currying Spot. Hurwulf lay on the stable floor in a spray of sunshine which came from a hole in the roof, watching Becky; she stood up, walked stiffly over to Clyde, and nuzzled against his legs. Clyde took off his Stetson and scratched Hurwulf's back absentmindedly.

"Hi," said Becky.

"Hi," said Clyde. Then, "Where is everyone?"

"Teddy's gone to talk to the travel agent. I've told him I'm not going on any long trip, but he doesn't pay any attention. I'm not going to leave all my friends, especially Debbie, and I'm certainly not going to leave Spot, am I Spot? I could never leave Spot for longer than a few days."

"What's Loren doing?"

"Don't know, don't care. Reading in her room, I guess. Why?"

"Just wondering."

"Well, why wonder about her? She doesn't like you, anyhow. She says you cut down trees and they hurt. She says you slaughter animals and eat their flesh."

"Loren's just mad at me because I told her she ought to damn well go back to school. Where's Clemente and Mrs. Lawrence?"

"Clemente's cooking one of Teddy's favorite dinners. Something a la something. Mrs. Lawrence shuts herself up in her room and types all day. She's writing a book about us." Becky giggled. "She's kind of buggy, if you ask me."

"Well, she's one of those intellectual women," said Clyde. He leaned lazily against the doorpost and lit a cigarette. "What do you hear from Hat?"

"We don't. She's probably in jail or something."

"I kind of wondered, because yesterday I was up in the city, and I dropped in on that pad she's supposed to be living in. Nobody seemed to know where she was. So I asked for that fellow — Arab. Somebody thought he'd gone to the Big Sur, somebody else thought he'd hitchhiked to Mendocino. So I got kind of tough. I said, I want to know where that young lady is, and if somebody doesn't come up with the information fast, today, I'm calling the cops."

"Neat. What did they say?"

"One of 'em, a gal, said she'd try to find out for me. She gave me the phone number there. I said I'd call her this morning. So I did. The number's been disconnected. I think maybe I'll just mosey up there again. No point in bothering Teddy about this, though — not until I do a little more detective work, anyhow. Okay? Mum's the word?"

"Mum's the word. Spot has a tick on her rump."

"I'll smoke it out with my cigarette for you. Whoa there, Spot, there's a good girl. Here's your tick," said Clyde, presenting the black, swollen, wriggly insect to Becky.

"Squish it, please, Clyde."

He threw it on the floor and stamped on it with his boot.

"Why don't you forget about Hat and go riding with Debbie and me?" said Becky, in her most winning, coquettish way.

"I'll take a rain check on that, sweetheart."

"Hat can take care of herself."

Clyde put on his hat. "Maybe she can and maybe she can't," he said.

34

It was the middle of April. Clemente had finished the panel of the Olivers' Sea Voyage and had invited Loren to inspect it.

"The color of the sea bothers me a little," Clemente said, standing beside the Mural. "I'd like your opinion."

"It's groovy, all of it." Loren threw herself down upon the sofa, her bracelets jangling. "Really far out, Clemente." She took an apple out of her skirt pocket and began to polish it on her crushed velvet, wine-colored blouse. "I just hope your beautiful work isn't going to be wasted, that's all."

"Wasted?"

"Well, you know what so often happens to Teddy's plans. We were supposed to go in spring, and it's almost May now. Our trip seems to get more vague every day."

"Teddy was looking over travel folders last night."

"Looking at travel folders isn't the same thing as actually going on a trip, is it? Oh, I don't mean he's said we're not going; it's just something I sense. In the first place, Becky's terribly turned off by the whole thing. She can't bear to leave her precious Debbie and her precious Spot. And then Hat's gone. I do believe, despite what Teddy says, he's worried about Hat. She calls once in a while from mysterious places, but there's no way to reach her. She says she can't see people she has close ties with for a time, because she has to renounce old relationships. It's a purifying stage on the way to Spiritual Awareness. When she's all purified and we can no longer corrupt her, she'll let us know. On top of everything, the school establishment is becoming stuffy about my prolonged absence." Loren sighed. "It's an old story. You're as familiar with it as we are." She took a bite of her apple. "It's just that I wouldn't count on any trip in the near future, if I were you," she said with her mouth full.

"I've never counted on a trip for me," Clemente said. "I don't matter. But I thought we agreed it would be good for Teddy."

"That was when I was worried about a Wicked Stepmother, Clemente. But, if you recall, I decided long ago that Teddy won't get himself into a mess like that. In the long run, he watches out for himself. I'm even more convinced of it now."

"Still, I think he needs a change, don't you?"

"A change from what?"

"I think he's been a bit depressed lately, Loren."

"Why should Teddy be depressed?" Loren put her apple down upon the sofa with an absentminded gesture. Her voice was curious.

"Well, for some of the reasons you've just mentioned. And . . . for others, too."

"Others?"

"Perhaps there's a side you don't see, Loren. Children often don't see their parents as other people do. As *people,* with problems."

"It seems to me I've just mentioned a few problems Teddy has."

Clemente smiled demurely. "Of course you have, and you're right. But there are certain things you don't talk about — with your own children." Clemente sat down beside Loren. Her blue eyes had an earnest gaze; her voice was gentle. "One's own children can't be expected to see their father as a human being. And, after all, why should they? As you said, Hat's gone. She wants to be independent. Becky is busy being a healthy little girl. And you're all wrapped up with your books and your ideas. I don't read and I don't have ideas. I can be more sensitive to Teddy's needs."

Shock replaced curiosity. Clemente's voice began to sound to Loren as if it were coming from the far end of a tunnel.

"What you haven't realized, Loren, is that Teddy is lonely," the voice in the tunnel was saying. "For example, he has bad dreams."

A peculiar dizziness came over Loren; she groped for the apple, fumbled; the apple rolled off on the floor. Clemente bent down and picked it up; she rubbed it meticulously on the back of her smock and laid it on Loren's lap. "He dreams about Clyde and Catherine," she said softly.

"Clyde and Catherine!"

"He dreams that . . . Clyde betrayed him with Catherine. Of course, they're just dreams. He thinks he has them because he didn't do enough for Catherine. Naturally, we know that's not true. But I try to cheer him up. It's the least I can do for him after all he's done for me." Clemente's face became luminous with joy. "It's my duty," she said.

Loren's dizziness grew; the room began to rock. To fight the feeling, she stared straight ahead at the wall. The Oliver Family Mural became alive; the figures whirled, danced, turned topsy-turvy; the colors shrieked. She looked quickly away at the empty space which would contain the next panel. But this void was even more frightening. Its blankness stared back, like the hollow eyes of a skull. It was the unknown future, that future which she suddenly knew had always terrified her and which she had tried so energetically to control. I still must try, she said to herself. I still must try. With a great effort of will, she turned and looked steadily at Clemente.

"Yes, well, I'm sure we're all very grateful to you for helping Teddy," she said.

Clemente's voice was elated. "Thank you, Loren! I was sure you'd understand." She covered Loren's hand with her own; it was soft and strangely cold.

Loren shivered.

"I knew if I could just explain things to you . . ." Clemente began to laugh; her laughter was tremulous, as if she were on the verge of tears.

Loren sat stiffly, forcing herself not to draw away her hand.

35

It was a drizzling Monday afternoon, two days later. The night before there had been a heavy rain. Loren, dressed in a long, black-beaded gown, her fur piece over her shoulders, boots on her feet, and a wide-brimmed, floppy purple hat from the Goodwill upon her head, walked down the road from Oonwald toward the Convent of the Precious Blood. She was pleasantly stoned.

The road shimmered, gutters roared, the leaves of the eucalyptus bordering the road shone like silver in the fine mist. Silhouetted against the brow of a distant hill stood four horses, as if rooted there in stolid resignation. Horses! It was as if she had never seen a horse before. Anyway, not a *horse*. Horse. What a strange word. It blew her mind.

A man in a black Mercedes Benz drove past her, staring straight ahead; the man and the car were like together, their existence, at this moment, joined, the way a toy man in a toy car is made out of one piece of plastic. Like everything was joined. She was part of the shimmering road; it rolled beneath her, carrying her, like an escalator, to her destination. Everything was joined, everything was changing at the same time. Air, smells, sounds, objects, creatures, man and car were being created, like now, just for her. The hum of creation buzzed in her ears like an electric generator; she herself was charged with its energy.

The road vanished; she had turned into the convent gate. A path propelled her forward, between beds of storm-battered flowers. Ahead was the convent — an old, Spanish-style, two-story villa with delicious little balconies and archways. Now, a door — heavy, nail-studded. Next to the door a little window guarded by wrought-iron bars; from within a blue terra-cotta statuette of the Virgin looked out at her. Then an iron bell appeared; she pulled its rope. A young nun, dressed in a short black skirt and short black veil, stood on the threshold.

She said, "Good afternoon."

"I have come to see Mother Humilitia," Loren said.

"Does she expect you?"

"Yes. Please tell her Loren Oliver is here."

Loren waited in the visitor's parlor. The young nun had led her there through an open, arched doorway. She walked about, curiously examining the room. The walls were tan jazz plaster. There was a mixture of interesting furniture. There were overstuffed sofas and chairs, their plump arms covered with lace tidies. There was a color TV set on top of which sat a cut-glass bowl of dusty, cinnamon-striped candies. There was an old German straight piano and a piano stool with claw feet, each foot holding a glass ball. There was a metal dictionary stand with a *Webster's Unabridged* open upon it. There was a tile-topped coffee table, with two neat stacks of newspapers — one was called *The Pilot,* the other *Waif's Messenger.*

Loren ran her hands over the jazz plaster, twirled the piano stool, then helped herself to a candy from the cut-glass bowl on the TV set. On the wall above the set was a large picture. It was a pastel Jesus in a fumed oak frame. His heart was exposed; it was bleeding: beautiful red drops of blood fell from His heart in a straight line. Oh, wow, she thought. Far out! She was staring at this in fascination when Mother Humilitia's voice in back of her caused her to jump.

"That's a dreadful picture, isn't it?" Mother Humilitia said. "I'd love to give it to a rummage sale, but Sister Jenine would never understand."

"I think it's terrific," said Loren dreamily.

Now Loren was sitting upon one of the overstuffed chairs; Mother Humilitia sat opposite her on a high, straight-backed, carved wooden chair, which resembled a throne. Beneath her long, black serge skirt, Loren could see elastic stockings and heavy, orthopedic black shoes. A yellowing ivory cross, the color of Mother Humilitia's skin, dangled over her black bosom. Light from the casement windows fell upon her rimless spectacles, producing a glitter which hid her eyes. Her voice was crisp but genial. Loren thought she was far out too, and wondered why she had waited so long to come.

"It was nice of you to call on us," Mother Humilitia was saying.

Loren smiled.

"Is there anything special we can do for you?"

Was there? Idly, she traced the pattern of one of the lace tidies with her finger. She had come for a reason, but for the moment, she seemed to have forgotten it.

"Perhaps it is a purely social visit," Mother Humilitia suggested.

Loren suddenly remembered. She said, "I wanted to talk to you about Catherine."

Mother Humilitia shifted slightly in her chair; the glitter left her spectacles, exposing her dark, hollow eyes. They were nice, mournful eyes, like Hurwulf's, Loren thought.

"What would you like to know?" said Mother Humilitia.

"Sometimes I can't recall her very well."

Mother Humilitia nodded.

"It's been three years since her Oonwald."

"Pardon?"

"That's our Oon language for when a person disappears."

"Disappears? You do not believe in death?"

"Do you?"

"Yes."

"I thought that Catholics didn't."

"If you are referring to the Resurrection of the Body — yes, many of us believe in that. I am not sure that I do, that is, not in any literal sense. I find the word 'dead' a useful word, with a great deal of meaning. Certainly, unless you can convince me differently, better than 'disappear' or 'Oonwald.' "

"That's what Clyde O'Mahoney thinks, too."

"I don't know the gentleman, but I would agree with him about that."

"He's not a gentleman, but I didn't come here to talk about him. I wanted you to tell me what you remember about Catherine. I was only twelve when she had her accident. And you saw her last."

"I have sometimes wondered why no one has asked me before," said Mother Humilitia. "Your father, for example —"

"Yes, I didn't think he had. But he has his memories. Perhaps he doesn't care to . . . tamper with them. But I was just a little girl. You know how little girls are, so busy with their own lives." Loren gave an ingratiating little laugh.

Mother Humilitia looked at her skeptically.

"This is a very attractive room," said Loren. She had begun to tremble slightly. Perhaps the pot was wearing off.

"What would you like to know?" said Mother Humilitia again.

"I'm not exactly sure, now that I think about it. Perhaps you really don't remember much. You see so many people, I suppose. If you like, you could think about it, and I could come again, when you aren't busy."

"This is as good a time as any," Mother Humilitia said firmly.

Loren looked about at the room. It really wasn't nice at all; it was actually extremely ugly. It was so ugly she wanted to escape from it at once. But she could feel Mother Humilitia's dark, sad eyes fixed upon her, imprisoning her in her chair.

There was a silence. Then, "It's a mortal sin for you to tell a lie, isn't it?" Loren burst out.

"A lie is sometimes hard to define," said Mother Humilitia rather loftily. "Or, rather, perhaps, its opposite — the truth."

"I only want a simple answer."

"Very well, but I must warn you, simple answers can sometimes be lies in that they obscure the truth."

"Catherine never came here for Retreats, did she?"

"No."

There was another silence. "Then you have lied all these years," Loren said savagely.

"I told you, no one has ever asked me."

"You let Teddy assume she came; you let him give you money in her name."

"You have touched on a delicate problem. There is such a thing as a sin of omission; it is possible that I am guilty of that, that I encouraged your father in his make-believe. I told myself if giving money made him happy, why should I prevent it? Nevertheless, I have been troubled — until today. God moves in mysterious ways. Here *you* are."

"I am not Teddy."

"No. I suspect you may be tougher than he. Truth can be painful, and you have sought it out. May I ask what you intend to do with your information?"

"Expose Clyde O'Mahoney."

"The gentleman you just mentioned, I believe."

"He was her seducer. I am now convinced."

" 'Seducer' is one of those simple words that are often used incorrectly. Aside from that, what makes you think he was?"

"I have reason to think that Teddy suspects it, that he believes, somehow, he was at fault. He is not himself lately. I should like to reassure him."

"In what way would it reassure him to know this?"

"He needs someone to talk to about it, someone he can trust."

"And you have appointed yourself this person?"

"I have always been the closest to him."

"Perhaps for that reason you are disqualified."

"We have always been open with each other," said Loren with sudden vehemence.

"May I offer you some advice? I knew your mother slightly, though she never came here for Retreats. We were, after all, neighbors for years, and though she was a backslider, she was extremely generous to the convent." Mother Humilitia paused, then continued. "We had a few occasions to talk on that account. She was a very beautiful woman, and I think a troubled woman, too. She wanted to make a greater contribution to life than perhaps God had intended for her to do. Things are sometimes more complicated than they seem. Even, if I may suggest, your own motives. You may have to learn to grow up more before you see that. You might even have to learn compassion."

"Compassion?"

"Charity, understanding — call it what you like."

"I am more interested in the facts. Not in a religion based on myths."

"Ah, but it seems to me you have your own mythology. Your private language, your perhaps limited notions of life and death, good and evil, love and betrayal. Facts have different interpretations — people used to fear eclipses. It seems to me you are as busy interpreting as anyone else. What is that thing you are wearing around your neck, for example?"

"I am Scorpio. It is my sign."

"Moreover, you reek of *Cannabis,* which is often used in mystic rites."

Loren shifted uncomfortably in her chair.

"But if you like, let's return to these facts you claim you are so interested in. The only fact we know for sure is that your mother did not join our Retreats. Why don't you stick to that for the time being and let other things alone and see what happens. Though perhaps something *has* happened — perhaps that is why you have chosen to come at this particular time?" Mother Humilitia's dark eyes looked piercingly at Loren; Loren felt she was being swallowed up by her gaze. "Is that a possibility?"

"No."

"Then let's leave it at that. If something comes up which disturbs you, you're welcome to come and talk to me at any time."

"How do I know you aren't just saying that because you want Teddy to go on giving you money?"

"You don't. I was only noticing this morning that we have a serious erosion problem in the back garden after the winter rains. It will be costly to repair it." Mother Humilitia smiled. "You don't know, that's just the thing. Perhaps I don't even know myself. Nothing in this vale of tears is black or white. But that's what can make life so fascinating, don't you agree?"

Loren looked up at her, startled.

"You do agree, don't you? I can tell that you do. Life interests you more than you think. It would be a pity to spoil the drama by preconceived notions, as so many unimaginative people do. Why not wait instead, and see it evolve. Dear me, what a clumsy metaphor! What I mean is, if you'll forgive me if I employ the idiom of my own mythology again — God moves in mysterious ways."

36

LOREN said, "Clyde?"

"Yes," said Leah. "I can't seem to fit him in. I mean, he's always around; he must play a role. But what, exactly, is it?"

It was late afternoon, in early May. Teddy had gone to Fala, Becky was in school, and Clemente was cleaning up the kitchen. Loren was lying on the sofa in the living room when Leah had unexpectedly appeared. Loren put down her book and gazed thoughtfully at the ceiling. "I suppose you want an honest book," she said.

"You're very understanding. Most people don't appreciate artistic integrity." She began to pull a chair up to the sofa, but Loren stopped her. "Let's go out on the porch," she said. She rose and Leah followed her; Loren closed the door. They sat down opposite each other on wicker chairs.

"The thing is, there have to be others beside just the family. I have put Clyde in — the old family friend. But he can't just be there, he has to have a part in what happens. As I have so often told my students at Writers' Conferences, you simply cannot describe a gun over the fireplace without having someone murdered with it later on. Everything must have its purpose. Do you see what I mean?"

Loren nodded thoughtfully. Then, "Would you like a villain?"

"A villain? Oh, my dear, what wouldn't I give for one? Of course, it can't be a member of the family. And it can't be Cary's Black. No one would stand for that."

"Clyde is ostensibly an old family friend." Loren looked down at her feet.

"Yes? You say 'ostensibly'?"

Loren looked up with a sad little sigh. "I'm not sure he can be trusted," she said simply.

"Oh, my dear. But why?"

"He does not, for example, like our Oon language. He wants to stamp it out."

"Stamp it out? Why should he want to stamp out Oon?"

"I'm not completely sure."

"I need motives," said Leah. "My characters must have motives."

"Perhaps he feels left out, somehow. Perhaps he is jealous."

"Jealous of what?"

"Of our happiness, perhaps."

Leah was silent for a moment; she seemed stunned. Then she brightened. "Why, that's absolutely marvelous. It's marvelous. Say no more. I mustn't confuse myself with details. Happiness frightens people, doesn't it? It frightens Jamie O'Keefe."

"Who?" said Loren.

"Jamie O'Keefe. That's the name I've given to Clyde. He can't bear to watch it and yet — it has a horrible fascination for him. It is something precious and intangible which he cannot possess, the way he possesses his . . . possessions. In the long run, he finds it necessary to try to destroy what he cannot have himself. There is the conflict — you have resolved it. Of course, there must be details. A story line."

"Like what?" said Loren in an interested voice.

"Like, well, supposing he were to run off with one of the girls?"

"Which one?"

"I was thinking of Cary."

"I thought she marries the Black."

"She still can, at the end. But something must make her a revolutionary, and what better thing than if a trusted friend of the family, a member of the Establishment, shows his true colors? Yes, that would work in nicely. He loathes her innocence; he wants to corrupt it. Oh, how it preys upon him — this happy family!"

"What does he do with Hat?"

"With Cary. He ravishes her, of course. But . . ."

"Yes?"

"But that's purely a physical act; her basic innocence, being of a spiritual quality, remains untouched. In the long run, it overpowers him."

"What does Cary's father think of all this?"

"Craig Simmons? I don't think Cary would tell him. She would wish to spare his feelings."

"Is Craig Simmons a sensitive man?"

"Oh, my, yes."

"Then perhaps he suspects. Perhaps he tries to ignore his suspicions, but he has a dream —"

"A dream? About what has happened?"

Loren nodded.

"I used to have my characters dream. The hero falls asleep, in the dream there is a strange noise which disturbs him, he awakens, sits up, someone is knocking at the door." Leah laughed. "No, I've stopped doing dreams. They are a cheap technique, a cliché."

"I don't know anything about writing," Loren said humbly. "I was only thinking that Craig Simmons might be disturbed; he may think that it is, somehow, all his fault. He might be brooding about it when someone enters his room — a young girl, for example, who is under his protection. Might he not seek solace in her arms?"

"A young girl who is under his protection? I'm afraid that would make him as bad as our villain. We can't have that."

"What if the young girl were also a villain? A villainess? What if she has been waiting for the right moment to seduce . . . her protector?"

Leah thought. "A moment ago I had no villain at all, and now you are trying to give me two. In the first place, it's confusing. The reader likes to know where he is — everyone can't turn into a villain. Moreover, Cary is young and inexperienced; for her to be seduced by Jamie O'Keefe is understandable. But we can't have Craig messing around with young girls — it would spoil his whole image. He is faithful to his departed wife and lives only through his children. That's the whole thing. That's what makes him heroic. Thank you, but the wicked Jamie is quite enough. He is the gun over the mantel. Poor Cary! I'm so glad she will be able to escape to Algeria. I wonder if she becomes pregnant first? Well, if she does, her Black lover will offer to help bring up the child. I rather like that. And I think I'll change the Jamie to Jim. It's a bit more sinister. I shall go to work on him at once!"

Leah had gone back upstairs. Loren returned to her place on the living room sofa. Her book lay on the floor. She was reviewing her conversation with Leah. At first, she decided she had been very clever; then she thought, what good was it to be clever when Leah was so dense? Then she thought, perhaps she had not really been clever at all; then — reluctantly — perhaps it was Leah who had been clever and she who was dense? Finally — was it a matter of cleverness versus denseness at all?

Leah, after all, was only writing a book; in a book, the characters must behave, the plot make sense. But from the point of view of Real Life, something seemed to have gone wrong. If only she could say, the plot has thickened! But it was more as if there were no plot at all. Just as she was about to grasp what appeared to be a theme, it slipped away or changed elusively. In Leah's book, the gun over the fireplace would have a purpose; for Loren, the gun was ominously there and yet remained . . . merely a gun. Leah had heroes and villains; it was not at all obvious any more to Loren who the Real Life heroes and villains were.

"Things may be more complicated than they seem," Mother Humilitia had said. She had not cared for this remark; she did not care for it now. It made her uncomfortable. She was relieved, therefore, to be diverted by a noise — the sound of horses' hoofs upon the road. She got up and went to the porch and peered out from behind the curtain.

There, upon the driveway, was a striking sight — Linda Alway, like a goddess, astride her Irish hunter! She was dressed in her English riding habit — hat, coat, breeches and polished boots; her long, toffee-colored hair was tied back with a black velvet ribbon. She had a long, bony face, an aristocratic nose; on her thin mouth was a slight but unmistakably triumphant smile. Around her, like a terrier, danced Becky, who had just arrived home from school.

"Linda won the bet! She went on the May Day Hundred Mile Trail Ride! Linda won the bet!" she was screeching.

Then Teddy came hurrying across the meadow from Fala. At breakfast, he had worn a dressing robe; now he was strangely transformed. He had on a pink-checked sport shirt, wide-wale corduroys and — a new note — a silk paisley scarf knotted about his neck. He fairly scampered across the high grass to reach Linda's side; in contrast to the large mare and its rider he looked like a pygmy. This gallant pygmy took the reins and assisted Linda down; upon the ground she became less of a goddess, more of a large, slightly awkward girl.

"Linda won the bet, now you owe her the silver belt," Becky yelped.

Teddy handed Becky the reins; then he and Linda strolled together, back across the meadow. They were going toward Fala. There was something pathetic and faintly distasteful about Teddy's demeanor — the foppish scarf; the way he guided Linda with his hand upon her elbow, as if the great, tall girl were not capable of walking by herself; his laughter, which, even at this distance, seemed childish and conspiratorial to Loren.

"It would be a pity to spoil the drama," Mother Humilitia had said. "Why not wait, watch it evolve?"

Like a movie?

Very well, she would. She had no choice, anyhow. But it was too bad she didn't have a bag of popcorn; the little attack of giddiness she was experiencing might vanish sooner if she had something salty to munch upon.

"Who is it?" said a foggy voice. Clemente, wearing an apron, a dishrag in her hand, stood in back of Loren.

"The Deb upon her Irish mount. She has come to call upon Teddy and claim her prize."

"Oh," said Clemente oddly.

Loren turned around. Clemente's face was ashen.

"They're rather an attractive couple, don't you think?"

Clemente gripped the back of a wicker chair; she poised there for a moment with a startled, stupid expression.

"Don't you think so, Clemente?"

"I'm sorry. I wasn't listening, I guess."

How ugly she looks, thought Loren. "I said, don't you think they're an attractive couple?"

Clemente rushed from the room.

Loren returned to the drama outside the window. Becky was patting the nose of Linda's horse; Teddy held the door of Fala open for Linda, then they both disappeared inside.

A villain? Oh, my dear, what wouldn't I give for one!

How ugly Clemente had looked! But how pitiful, too, somehow.

Then a sudden illumination, like the light bulb that appears over the head of a comic strip character, provided Loren with an instant insight. She felt certain she knew what was wrong with Leah's book. The certainty made her strong; the giddiness left her. How stupid I've been, she thought, almost as stupid as Clemente!

37

CLEMENTE did not come down for dinner that evening. Teddy went up to see her, and remained a long time. Loren, passing Clemente's closed door, paused, and heard the sound of weeping. God moves in mysterious ways? Not so mysterious after all, she thought smugly. Then she tiptoed away. She went to her room and arranged herself comfortably on a pillow on the floor and began to make notes upon a lined tablet. At ten o'clock she smoked a joint and fell fast asleep.

She was awakened the next morning by the sound of a car in the driveway. Looking out, she saw Teddy and Clemente standing beside Teddy's Rover. Clemente was all bundled up in one of Teddy's old coats; her face was red and swollen; she seemed groggy. Teddy assisted her in, then he returned to the house and brought out Clemente's two suitcases and put them in the luggage compartment. They drove off.

Loren went down to the kitchen and prepared and ate a good and wholesome breakfast.

Shortly after noon, as she lay on the living room sofa, she heard Teddy's car in the driveway again. She rose and went out to the porch and peered out; Teddy was going directly to Fala. Loren reviewed the notes she had written the night before.

"You took an innocent, young girl under your protection and then destroyed and abandoned her." She crossed out "innocent."

Then she crossed out the whole sentence and wrote, "You have swept her under the rug like so much dust!" She crossed out that sentence and wrote, "You have tossed her into the rubbish pile like a cast-off garment."

She worked at her composition for an hour, memorized it, tore the notes into pieces, and burned them in the fireplace. Then she left the house and marched resolutely across the meadow to Fala and entered the door without knocking.

Teddy was sitting at his desk, a half-empty bottle of Scotch on the floor beside him. He inclined his head in a courtly little bow.

"Are you very drunk?" she said coldly.

"*Comme ci, comme ça.*"

"Your faculties are mostly intact?"

"Unfortunately, they are."

She began her speech. "What," she said, "have you done with Clemente?"

"Clemente?" He half raised his head; he seemed to be trying to remember. Then he sat up. "Oh, yes, poor thing. She's sicker than we thought. I did what you suggested: I took her to Aunt Harriet's. We can't stop her from working here, and there was no point in discussing the problem with Leah. I had to be very firm, but it's all in her best interests. Harriet was delighted to help out. It was a brilliant idea. I must thank you."

"I don't want your thanks. You have seduced an innocent, defenseless girl. Then you have tossed her away like a cast-off garment!"

"Pardon?"

"You have swept her under the rug like so much dust!"

There was a silence during which Teddy seemed to be undergoing some violent inner turmoil; she watched with pleasure. But it was as brief as it was violent; within a moment he appeared to have conquered his emotions and achieved, if not peace, a kind of drowsy detachment.

"Your similes," he said mildly, "are not especially apt."

Was her style getting in the way of the message she wished to deliver? "Similes don't matter," she said, furious at her own failure. "What matters is that you have also betrayed Catherine, your family, and the Oon Code." She took a deep breath. "Unless you see fit to be honest with me, as you once were, I shall not be able to accompany you on your trip."

She waited for the response; he pulled down the lid of one eye by its lash; the other eye continued to look at her with a steady gaze.

"You are a bastard!"

Teddy let go of his eyelid and both eyes suddenly filled with tears. She had got through to him at last! Vanity made her reckless; she improvised. "And stop sniffling, please. It's degrading to see your father sniffle!"

"I'm not sniffling; there was something in my eye!"

Lies could not stop her; she stepped backwards and hurled her finest line at him. "I can see now why Leah had trouble with her book. It was because the hero was really the villain and she never recognized this, as I never did — until now!"

Teddy took out his pocket handkerchief and dabbed at his tears. "What did you say?" he said.

"Which time?"

"About a book?"

"I said I can see why Leah had trouble. It was because the hero was really the villain and she never recognized this, as I never did until now!"

"Ah." He yawned. "I thought that was what you said."

What did the yawn mean? Surely not boredom? He had never been bored in her presence! He could not possibly be bored now. She said, "Why?" The "why" came from a genuine bewilderment. She was conscious of losing control over the situation.

"Life," he said, "is not a book." His voice was blurred and somewhat disdainful. "It is not a work of art. I am not a hero, but I am not a villain, either."

She had been prepared for lies, but not for truth — especially for truth delivered in such an undramatic way. It took her unawares; she felt its power, but was powerless to deal with it. All she could do was to continue in the role she had created for herself. She forced herself to stare sternly at the drunken man in the chair. To her satisfaction, he slumped and closed his eyes.

"And now, I shall help you to bed," she said, in the firmest tone she could muster.

He opened one eye and cocked it at her. "That sounds like the last line in a bad play," he said with a sudden grin. 'Exit Teddy.' Thank you, but I am not ready to exit quite yet. I believe I shall decline your thoughtful offer!"

Loren stamped out, slamming the door behind her.

She started back toward the house, then suddenly changed her direction and marched resolutely down the road in the opposite direction. Hurwulf appeared and began to trot after her; Loren picked up a pebble and hurled it at the dog, who, tail between her legs and head down, shuffled sadly away.

38

LEAH Lawrence, wearing an old corduroy jumper, her spectacles attached to a cord around her neck, her coat over her arm, scurried across the meadow. She had just searched the silent, empty house. Why was the house so silent and so empty? Was her watch wrong? Was it early afternoon, as she had thought, or was it later? But there had been no bustle in the kitchen, no music on the phonograph; no Becky, Loren or Clemente. Had they all gone on some interesting expedition she had forgotten about? She trampled through the vineyard and peered into the window of Fala. Ah, there was Teddy, sitting at his desk!

Dear Teddy, she thought, pressing her face against the glass. Such a handsome man! His hair had grown longer lately, shaggier; the gray lock tumbled over his forehead in Byronic style. He was, she decided wistfully, just the sort of man she would be happy to go to bed with to enjoy a Passionate Interlude, with, as they used to say, "no strings attached." But, alas, Teddy was not that kind of person. He was a family man; he would feel responsibility, a tiresome emotional attachment. For this she had no time nor inclination. She tapped on the window; he looked up, startled. She blew him a friendly little kiss. Then she ran around the little house and burst through the door.

"No, no, please don't stand up. I have come for a reason. I shall only detain you briefly!"

Teddy remained standing; he stood so stiffly that he swayed a bit back and forth. Such dreamy manners, Leah thought. Still, sometimes his insistence on gallantry could be a bit trying when one had other things on one's mind.

She glanced about the room, spotted a small stool embroidered with cupids and flowers — she vaguely remembered Clemente working upon it. She drew it over and sat down. Her coat fell to the floor and her jumper crawled up, exposing her silk thighs. She hugged her knees and smiled. "Well, here you are! But where is everyone else?"

"Everyone else?" Teddy sat down again cautiously.

"Your delicious family. There is no one about."

"Yes, I believe they are all out. As my dear sister foretold, I have been forsaken. Becky — the Always have captivated Becky. I think they have taken her to something or other after school. Loren?" He paused. Then, "I seem to recall seeing her walking down the road. As for Clemente . . ." He shifted awkwardly in his chair. "I was under the impression that Clemente had written you a note."

"A note? I don't think I've seen a note. I can't imagine why Clemente would write me a note."

There was a silence. Then Teddy said, "Would you care for a drink?"

"As a matter of fact, that would be lovely. I have an announcement. You must prepare yourself. A drink is needed."

He reached down to the floor and picked up a bottle of Scotch.

What a funny place to keep a bottle, thought Leah. But then, the Olivers were always original.

"You will forgive the lack of ceremony — and ice."

"I got used to warm Scotch in England. I always had a tumbler after a bout with Strongbow."

"I'm afraid I have only one glass. You can have mine. I can use the bottle cap!" He seemed delighted with his ingenuity.

"No, no, we can use the same glass, Teddy dear! A loving cup!"

Teddy poured some Scotch into an empty used glass on his desk, then handed it to Leah. She raised it, toasted him, sipped, then handed it to Teddy. He raised it to her, bowed, drank. He returned the glass. She sipped again and gave it back.

Leah sighed happily. "As I was hinting," she said, "I have news."

He nodded and continued to drink.

"I had hoped to make a more general announcement. But you are the most important person, after all."

He nodded.

"Very well, this is it. I am not capable of writing *The Happy Family!* I have . . . failed!"

"I hope it is not we who have failed you."

"In a way, you have."

"You did not find us 'happy'?"

"*Au contraire!* That was the problem. It isn't easy to write about Paradise. One needs conflicts, crises, intrigues. You forgot to return the glass to me, Teddy dear."

"Oh, so sorry. I think we'll have to fill it up again." He poured.

"I thought I had worked it all out. Your clever little Loren tried to help me. She gave me a villain. Jim O'Keefe. He seduces Cary. But one knows when one is on the wrong track. The scene didn't come off at all. Cary isn't an old-fashioned, ignorant girl. She was brought up to be independent and is quite capable of taking care of herself. Moreover, she wanted more out of life than even to bother with Jim O'Keefe. Her Black lover? Algeria? Yes! But that's hardly a conflict when her own father encourages her and is proud of her decision. I believe it's my turn with the loving cup. Thank you. Cheers! Oh, I tried for weeks, as you know. I buried myself in my room. But it just isn't there. Your lovely children never even had a serious quarrel."

"You forgot to return the loving cup to me. Thank you. Cheers!"

"So it's back to Strongbow again. Back to battles, illicit relationships, murder, rapine. I'm a pro at that." She giggled. "I'm leaving at once for the city, and then to the British Museum to do more research on medieval weaponry. My readers get very cross with me if there's a technical error."

Teddy handed her the loving cup.

"Yes, well," — she raised the glass — "to Strongbow! But I did want to say good-bye to the children. If your family were a book, you would win the Nobel Prize."

"Perhaps we should freshen our loving cup a bit more," he said.

"Not for me, thanks. I must keep my head clear. That's all I have — it's my only asset." She fished about in the pocket of her jumper and came up with a pack of cigarettes and a crumpled piece of paper. "How silly of me! This must be the note you were referring to. I found it under my door this morning. I've trained everyone not to bother me, you know. Then, my mind has been so occupied I just stuffed it into my pocket and forgot it." She attached her spectacles and began to read aloud.

> Dear Mother,
> I'm going off for a little while. I need some time for myself. I want to do some thinking.

Leah glanced up at Teddy. "I can always tell Clemente's writing because it isn't writing; she prints.

> Perhaps I'll find a job. I'll let you know where I am as soon as I'm settled. Good luck with your book.
>
> Love,
> Clemente
>
> P.S. You mustn't worry. I'll be all right.

"Well, of course I won't worry," Leah said. "I have never worried about Clemente. I brought her up to be self-sufficient. I had to, in my line of work. But I can't imagine why she wants to leave your lovely home. I've always enjoyed thinking of her here. So safe, surrounded by warmth and love. But perhaps she thought she had presumed on you too long. If she has a fault, it is overconscientiousness. No, I won't worry. Clemente could walk down a dark and dangerous street and never be accosted. She is protected by her incredible innocence, wouldn't you say?"

Teddy gave her a blank look, then poured more Scotch.

"I really don't know where she got it. Her innocence. I made a dutiful effort to teach her the facts of life. I got books about the birds and bees from the library, but I don't think she ever connected birds and bees with *people*. Besides, she was never much of a reader, not like your Loren. It was my only disappointment." She took out a cigarette from the package and put it into her mouth.

Teddy rose to light it.

She gave him the long look it was her habit to give when gentlemen lit her cigarette. "Now that your house is so quiet, perhaps you'll be able to think about yourself more," she said impulsively.

"About myself?"

"Your children are growing up; you have fulfilled your obligations. A little frivolity, now and then, might be therapeutic."

"Frivolity?" He stood there, looking down at her with a strange new expression. How would one describe it, she wondered? A kind of reckless abandon? An interesting romantic despair? Had it always been there, beneath the paterfamilias image? Had she, so occupied with her notion of Craig Simmons, failed to see it? Or had her suggestion produced a new Teddy?

"But now I must go." She sighed wistfully. "I must leave your attractive home. I must leave it because it is so attractive. My bags are packed; they are in the car. I'll dash off a bread and butter letter one of these days. If I don't, you'll understand, won't you?" She stood up, almost bumping into him. "Kiss your dear girls for me." He had not moved. It seemed heartless just to push him aside in order to make her exit. Friendship required something more. She took off her glasses. "And here is a little good-bye kiss for you, too." She put her arms on his shoulders and kissed him affectionately upon his cheek.

Teddy said, "Stay."

"Dear Teddy, how I should like to. But Strongbow is waiting."

"Stay and teach me to think more about myself."

"I only meant that you take your responsibilities so seriously — now you can take the time for some recreation."

"I should need guidance."

Really, I must go, she thought. I must arrange for tickets, passports, shots. I must write that little hotel — what's its name? — across from the British Museum. Still . . . one night? One didn't find handsome men like Teddy Oliver growing on every bush. Certainly, it was unlikely she would find one in the weaponry archives.

"You are a bad influence, Teddy, dear."

"I have recently come to that conclusion myself."

"I only meant that you are too nice."

"I am a wolf in sheep's clothing?" He smiled at her.

"Hardly a wolf. But you are naughty. To think that all these years I left my little girl in your charge." She giggled. "I'm not at all sure you are to be trusted!"

Teddy stumbled into her arms and buried his face in her bosom, almost crushing her spectacles.

She disentangled herself and twirled the spectacle chain around so that the spectacles dangled down her back. Teddy groped, found her again, and wrapped himself around her in a clumsy embrace.

Strongbow could wait, thought Leah, as Teddy nibbled at her ear. It had been too long since she had allowed herself a Passionate Interlude. But she must discipline herself! She had discovered from experience that such "interludes" had a way of dissolving into domestic boredom if they lasted much longer.

The nibbling was producing a delicious little shiver that ran right through her, down to her toes. She broke away once more, removed the spectacles, and flung them in a gesture of romantic surrender upon the desk.

39

"I feel like a kept woman," said Hat dreamily. She lay in a king-sized bed in a large, sunny, top-floor suite of the Clift Hotel. There were roses on the dressing table, a box of Blum's chocolates on the bedside table; she was wearing a frilly, sprigged muslin bedjacket which Clyde had just bought her at I. Magnin's. In her hand she held a large orange.

Clyde, who was extremely moved by Hat's condition (though not so moved that he could not also be pleasantly conscious of the fact that he had rescued her), paced the floor smoking a cigarette. He was wearing, for this rescue mission, an expensive, hand-tailored tweed suit and a yellow checked shirt with a button-down collar. Lean and dapper and sunburned, he might have been taken for a wealthy sportsman (who had inherited, not earned his wealth) just returned from a safari.

"You *are* a kept woman," he said dryly. "And you're damn well going to stay kept until you get some meat on your bones. I can't stand skinny females."

"You make me sound like one of your fucking cows."

"Ladies don't talk that way."

Hat laughed. "I was going to say it isn't too unpleasant being kept, even though I don't believe in it, theoretically."

"Never mind your theories, either. Which reminds me, when you're stronger, kindly shave under your arms."

She grinned, then lay back suddenly with that exhausted look which undid him. He came to her bedside and put a firm hand upon her forehead. "You're feeling better now, aren't you?"

"Every day. I just get tired."

"Well, you've had a nasty experience. My God, Hat, why didn't you call one of us? You could have died if you had kept your date with that butcher. Dr. Sorensen told me so."

"Dr. Sorensen is a typical Establishment M.D. He doesn't know a thing about the Underground. This abortionist is a far-out cat; he's a medical technician, and he just wants to help. He's very hygienic. Several of the girls have gone to him. The thing is, I got flu, so he said I'd better wait. And then you came along — on your big, white steed." She bounced the orange in her hand.

"It will be all over in a few days, Hat. As soon as that psychiatrist fills out the papers and we get Teddy to sign for permission. Then you can have a good rest and forget all about it." He knew he would never forget, himself, but then he did not have Hat's theories to bolster him.

"Clyde?" Hat sat up.

"Yes."

"That flu I got. I think it was psychosomatic. The shrink agreed with me."

"He agreed with what?"

"You see, I told him I didn't think I wanted it done, subconsciously, that is. Well, consciously, of course, I do. Having the baby would go against all my principles. Population explosion, women being tied down, and all that." She nibbled at the orange rind thoughtfully. "But, then, I've been going over all that in my mind and . . . well, what's *one* baby when it's already started and you have enough money to take care of it? So he isn't going to fill out the papers yet. He doesn't think I know my own mind." She grinned again, mischievously.

Clyde felt bewildered. He had found Hat three days ago, in a rundown rooming house on Polk Street; she had been feverish and listless and had wept when she saw him. She had gone with him docilely to see Dr. Sorensen, and then to the psychiatrist to whom Dr. Sorensen had referred them. Now, she seemed to have oddly revived; the docility was gone; it had been replaced by a peculiar euphoria.

"I've already become fond of it in a funny way. I've even been thinking of names." She patted her stomach comically. "Of course, I realize it's an anachronism. I mean, it's just the way I've been programmed to feel. But I wouldn't be changing the whole world with one abortion, would I?"

Clyde couldn't argue this. The very word "abortion" made him shudder; when applied to Hat, sick. Rescuing her had been one thing; this other was out of his depth. He wished she would let him call Teddy now; he could take his credit and bow out gracefully. But she had refused to permit it.

"I think it's ridiculous that he even has to sign for permission for what I do with my own body," she had said. "Anyway, I'm going to wait until the last minute. He'll sign, that's not the point. But, in the meantime, why upset him? What I really mean, I guess, is there's no point in upsetting me. Teddy's a dear but, well, he never did like Arab."

"I would say that showed excellent judgment."

"Maybe. But I think it was really because Arab made him feel old and unwanted. He wasn't interested in Teddy's decadent, softheaded liberalism."

"Well, I don't know about that. I just feel funny not letting Teddy know."

"If you call him before it's time to sign I'll jump out of the window," she had told him.

Hat's tone of voice was not serious. Still, women did peculiar things in her condition. He had acquiesced. He had even been, perhaps, a little flattered. But now this talk of not having what he referred to as the "operation" was an even heavier responsibility, one which he suddenly realized Teddy would not have to legally share.

"Well, you can't just keep a baby, Hat. Babies have to have fathers."

"I don't see why."

"I do. I grew up without one."

"And you've turned out very nicely. Lots of girls keep their babies nowadays. Just because I don't want to marry Arab, or even ever see him again, for that matter, is no reason why I should be forced by society to —"

"I'd like to get my hands on that Arab," said Clyde.

"I don't like Arab for personal reasons, but it really wasn't his fault. I got mixed up with the Pill."

"Holy mackerel, Hat, he has some responsibility! He's the father!"

"Biologically, I suppose he is. But as far as I'm concerned, that's all. The baby's my trip. Being a father just isn't Arab's thing." She rolled the orange between her hands, then dropped it into the bedclothes. "But I do wish he'd return my Porsche. He's probably smashed it up or sold it for drugs or bail or something —"

"I'd like to smash him up," said Clyde fiercely. He lit another cigarette and stared down at her with a puzzled expression.

"Give me one, please."

"No. Not until you're stronger. You ought to quit, anyhow. I don't like to see women smoke."

Hat sighed. "You're so bossy, Clyde. But you're pretty in your store-bought clothes. Come here." She reached for a chocolate on the bedside table and held it up teasingly. "Come on, open your mouth like a good boy."

He approached the bed; she dangled the chocolate higher.

"Closer, Clyde."

He held out his hand, and she pulled him down toward her. Warm arms were flung about his neck; a warm, soft mouth was pressed against his cheek.

"There!" she said, releasing him and handing him the chocolate. "That's for my being such a hassle for you."

Clyde looked at her solemnly, to hide his shakiness. He had to keep cool. Women were frail, inclined to get out of hand. There was something scary and unpredictable about them. Moons and tides. Dark, primal forces. She was, after all, her mother's daughter. All he knew was that women needed to be protected, especially from themselves.

"What's the matter?" Hat was saying. "Isn't that what kept women are supposed to do for their keep?"

"Don't talk that way, please, Hat."

"Why not?" Her eyes gleamed; she smiled at him in an uncomfortably seductive way. "Why not?" she said again, like a petulant child.

Oh, Christ, thought Clyde. Her recklessness, her frivolity, her pale, elegant beauty clutched at his heart. She was like Catherine and Teddy both, he thought. She was both Olivers in one. He said, "It's not . . . becoming."

"Oh, pooh!" She patted her pillows into shape, then curled up on the bed in a touching childlike posture. "I was thinking, if it's a boy, I might name it after you," she said with a yawn.

40

It was seven-thirty on a May morning. Teddy and Becky were eating breakfast in the kitchen. They were alone in Oonhall.

Hat was recovering from her bout of "flu" at Clyde's ranch. Both to Teddy's and to Hat's amusement, Clyde had insisted upon a chaperone; Mimi Alway had produced her old friend Mrs. Collier for this role. Mrs. Collier had had a little "breakdown" following the debut; she had no money but was in need of fresh air and country life. She had been introduced to Clyde and captivated by what she called his "western courtliness." Perhaps, she had told Mimi, her temporary lapse in health would be a "blessing in disguise."

Loren was living at the convent, learning French and Spanish and Latin from the nuns. Mother Humilitia had agreed to this as a favor because of Teddy's generosity; also, because, it turned out, Loren had a special gift for languages. But there was to be no nonsense: Loren was to study hard. Therefore, she was seldom seen at Oonhall.

The kitchen was not what it had been when Clemente had been in charge of it. Dirty pots filled the sink; the counters were cluttered with groceries which had not been put away; a parade of ants marched under the back door and bivouacked about spilled marmalade. The cleaning service men came three times a week; they did the heavy work, but did not attend to details such as these.

Teddy was having coffee and an egg sprinkled with wheat germ. An assortment of vitamin bottles were arranged before his place; he was no longer certain of getting balanced meals. Becky was eating her cornflakes out of a mixing bowl and reading the *San Francisco Chronicle*. Since it was a school day she had "first rights" to the paper. She had finished the comics, Dear Abby, the Animal Column and the Society page. She was now glancing over the front section for anything which might attract her attention.

She said, "What was Mary's last name?"

"Mary who?"

"Mary, our maid."

"Mary Miller."

"Was her brother's name Peter?"

"I believe so, yes. Why?"

"He was murdered. Listen." She read aloud:

> The body of the American Indian youth found stabbed to death in the fourth-floor community shower room of a Tenderloin hotel Thursday night has been identified as that of Peter Miller, 19-year-old unemployed Hoopa, originally from the Hoopa Valley Reservation near Eureka.

"Oh, my God," said Teddy.

> Police said Miller had been arrested on a charge of possessing illegal drugs two weeks ago. The charge was awaiting court action. Sergeant T. R. O'Conner of the Narcotics Squad believes it may have been a racketeer "revenge job," that someone may have believed Miller had turned police informant. Police are questioning several suspects in the

area. It was the city's 49th homicide of the year, according to police records.

"Oh, my God, poor Mary! Are you sure?"
Becky handed him the paper; he read the story. "Oh, my God. It must be her brother." He put the paper down. "She must know by now, I suppose. She probably had to identify the . . . remains. What should we do?"
"Well, what is there to do, Teddy?"
"I don't know. I don't see how we can ignore it."
"She has ignored us. She didn't even bother to say good-bye."
"We must send her a note, at least. I can send it through the Indian Affairs office. We could add a little offering, in memory of her brother. I'm sure she'd find some extra money useful at this point. I'll do it at once — this morning. I'll sign all of our names." Teddy pushed his coffee cup away. "If you don't do those things immediately, sometimes they don't get done."
"I still think she might have said good-bye to me."
"Becky, we have to put ourselves in other people's situations. It's true, she should have given us notice, but she came from a very disadvantaged background. We thought we did our best to make her feel at home, but perhaps it wasn't our best. Yes, I can see now that we might have done more. I can see that we were to blame."
"I don't see how we were to blame that her brother was murdered."
"When the bell tolls, it tolls for all of us, Becky. Mary has suffered a great tragedy and we must suffer with her; we must share the responsibility. We are both victim and murderer, because we are part of the System. The System from which we benefit killed Pete."
"Clemente did the same thing, too, if you think about it."
"Clemente did the same what?" said Teddy sharply.
"Left without saying good-bye."
"Clemente never had a happy, normal homelife, either," said Teddy with a sigh.

"Then why leave ours for Aunt Harriet's? How could she be happier there?"

"I was under the impression I had explained that to everyone. Aunt Harriet needed her more than we did. Clemente needs to be needed."

"We needed her cooking and her cleaning. We haven't had a decent meal since she left. And the house is a mess. I'm embarrassed to have Debbie see it. Teddy, I have to go, but please save the paper. I want to show Debbie the story about Pete." Becky took a last swallow of milk, then rose from the table. She came around to Teddy and stood in back of him and put her arms around his neck and gave him a kiss on the top of his head.

"An unaccustomed gesture of affection. You want something. Let me see if I can guess. A new saddle? A new dress?"

"Teddy, Debbie's going to Miss Potter's School for Girls in the fall. That's near Pasadena; you've heard of it. It's a groovy place. You can keep a horse and you take trips to Mexico and it's right next to two private boys' schools, they have parties together. Oh, yes, and you have to study very hard and wear uniforms on weekdays. Mrs. Alway has looked into it. Debbie told me all about it while we were riding yesterday."

"I see. I thought we were planning a trip, but our plans seem to have bogged down."

"Teddy, I can't go off and leave Spot all summer and I have to go to school in the fall and I can't go back to school without Debbie. I'd just die."

"Well, we'll discuss it later, Becky. This morning has been too much of a shock. It's hard to concentrate. Still, I suppose I shall have to get used to the pleasure of my own company."

"There'll be lots of holidays and there's a special Fathers' Day when the fathers come down and you have Hurwulf and Mad Fred and the Zimmermans and Clyde and Mrs. Alway has promised to see you won't be lonely. She thinks you should marry again, Teddy."

"Yes. I have failed her by spurning Mrs. Collier."

"She isn't cross about that. When she saw Mrs. Collier again, after all these years, she agreed she wasn't your type. Mrs. Alway thinks somebody younger would be more suitable. She says you're good with young people and can bridge the Generation Gap. She's going to call you this afternoon about Miss Potter's."

"It sounds as if it's a *fait accompli*."

"What's that?"

"That's French for my being all alone."

"I have to run or I'll miss the bus, Teddy. Please don't forget to save the paper. Okay?"

41

A small celebration was taking place in the parlor of the Lexington Arms. It was the first time, after three weeks of illness, that Miss Oliver's guest, Miss Lawrence, had come down for tea. Clemente sat in an armchair, and everyone was crowding about her making delicate inquiries about her health. In return, she thanked them all for their kindness. She had so enjoyed Winnie's pound cake, which the Misses Spencers had sent up; Mrs. Everett's African violet was still blooming nicely; she had gorged on Mr. Carlyle's peppermint creams; Mr. Dobbs's yogurt and brewers' yeast from the Health Food Store had appreciably contributed to her recovery.

Harriet sat next to her, on a straight chair, gazing at Clemente with wonder and pride. It all still seemed like a dream. It was such a nice dream that she sometimes felt a little guilty. It was as if, feeling lonely and desperate, she had gone out and kidnapped a sweet young person just to keep her company. She had to keep telling herself it had not been that way at all.

But how had it been? She had gone over and over it in her mind, reconstructing the events of that strange morning. She had been dressing to go out to hunt for an apartment; yes, that was right. Then the phone had rung.

It was Teddy. "We have a little problem down here," he had said.

Harriet's heart had beat wildly in her breast, then it seemed to sink, still fluttering, into the pit of her stomach. A problem? Teddy had never called her about a problem before. He had not even called her the night Catherine had died, but had waited thoughtfully until the following afternoon. What problem could he have that could prompt such a call now? Her first thought, naturally, was that something dreadful had happened to one of her nieces. But it was not this at all. The "problem" had to do with that Lawrence girl who had just settled herself down in the Oliver household. Harriet was ashamed now to remember her relief.

"Clemente?" she had asked, puzzled.

Yes, it seemed that Clemente was not well. The Indian girl had left, and she was working too hard. She was overconscientious, and it was impossible to make her rest at Oonhall. But she had no place to go. Her mother was in London and hopeless at this sort of thing, anyhow. Clemente was not a hospital case; she simply needed some time in bed and a bit of waiting on. Would it be possible, would it be asking too much, for Harriet to take her for a few weeks? A house without a mother was not the place for a young girl who needed special care.

Teddy was actually asking her for help! Harriet had been almost overcome by the honor. She had said yes, by all means, you must bring her here at once. Teddy had thanked her and hung up. Harriet had remained dazzled. For a few moments she could not remember why she had dressed to go out. When she did, it seemed like the most unimportant matter in the world. Even if she were forced out upon the streets, her duty to her brother would come first!

Her next memory was more confused. Teddy had appeared with a pale, haggard Clemente, who had barely managed to totter to the sofa and sit down. Teddy had deposited Clemente's luggage in the guest bedroom, then he had signaled to Harriet to accompany him out into the hall.

"I'm going to leave at once," he had whispered to her. "I had a terrible time convincing her to come up here. If I hang around, she'll begin to fret again about our not being able to manage without her." He had begun to edge away toward the elevator, as if the weak, sick girl might rush out at any moment and attack him. "I'll keep in touch by phone," he said, pressing the elevator button. The door of the ancient cage opened creakily; Teddy stepped into it. "Needless to say, I'm extremely grateful," he added hastily, as the door closed upon him.

Bewildered, but made happy by his words, Harriet had returned to her apartment. Clemente stared at her oddly, then burst into sobs. Harriet had helped the poor child into the guest room, had undressed her, and got her into a nightgown from a suitcase. Clemente, still sobbing, had let her do everything for her as if she were a helpless infant.

For three weeks Clemente had stayed in bed. Harriet had brought her trays of wholesome food; she had picked flowers from her pot garden on the windowsill to decorate the trays; she had given her back rubs and stuffed her with vitamins. Teddy called every few days, and Harriet had reported on the progress. He would not speak to Clemente, he said, for fear of reactivating her conscience and causing a relapse. "Needless to say," he would add, "I'm extremely grateful . . ."

It was funny how these words had less and less effect on Harriet. Almost without realizing it, she had transferred her loyalties and affections to her patient. It was suddenly Clemente, not Teddy, who needed her, whom she was helping. Sometimes she felt a strange twinge of guilt at this defection. This was why she often had to remind herself that she had not stolen Clemente; she had been *asked* to take her by Teddy.

Slowly Clemente gained in strength; she no longer had her disturbing little spells of weeping; she grew cheerful and companionable. Harriet bought her a drawing pad and pencils, and she sat up in bed and did sketches of the furniture and articles in the room. And, now, here she was, miraculously sipping her tea and chatting pleasantly with everyone, quite as if she had lived at the Lexington for years.

It was true that she was not the same Clemente whom Harriet had seen at Christmastime. The golden girl with the ethereal air whom Harriet had not quite trusted was gone; in her place was a faded, slightly old-maidish young lady who had grown plump from her stay in bed. Clemente's youth had been brief, but she did not seem to mourn for it. If anything, thought Harriet as she watched her, she was perhaps too much lacking in vanity. A little rouge, for example, might improve the sickroom pallor; Harriet had suggested this before they came down. But Clemente could not be bothered; she seemed to have no interest in her appearance at all. This, no doubt, was what Teddy had meant when he had called her saintly.

"Miss Oliver," said Mr. Dobbs, with a courtly bow in Harriet's direction.

"Yes, Mr. Dobbs?"

"I should like to offer my congratulations. You have done an excellent job with this young lady."

"She was an excellent patient," said Harriet.

"Perhaps," Mrs. Everett suggested, "Miss Lawrence will even feel up to helping you apartment-hunt before long."

"Oh, I'm sure I will. I want to do anything I can to repay Aunt Harriet for all she's done for me," said Clemente.

Everyone was very moved by this remark.

"Young people are not too apt to feel gratitude these days," said Mr. Dobbs. "They are more inclined to think only of themselves. In general, I would pronounce them a selfish, self-indulged generation. Our little girl, here, is a rare jewel."

"Hear, hear," cried Mr. Carlyle, clapping her hands.

Clemente blushed modestly.

42

"CLYDE, do you like my new maternity jeans?"
"They're mighty nice, ma'am. You don't exactly need them yet, though, do you?"

"I know, but it's fun." Hat, suntanned and sleeker, her face filled out, the shadows gone, paraded in front of Clyde like a styleshow mannequin. "I've soaked them in bleach to get that extraspecial superfaded look." She sat down on the sofa beside him. "You know what? I'd like to be a decorator. I'd start with this house first. Get rid of your crummy old mail-order catalog furniture."

"I like my furniture," said Clyde. "It suits me."

"You'd like what I'd do better. I have a flair! A touch! You wouldn't recognize this room. I would transform it — magically! By the way, where's Colly?"

"She went into town to get her hair fixed."

"You mean she left us alone?" Hat grinned. "How shocking! Especially when Colly's got the hots for you, Clyde."

Clyde grimaced.

"No, I mean, honestly. She freaked out after she failed with Teddy, but a millionaire cowboy! Far out! Are you a millionaire, Clyde?"

Clyde nodded solemnly.

"You know, that's really gross." Hat giggled. Then she yawned.

"I wish I didn't get so sleepy. It's such a drag. If I take a nap, can we drive up on the ridge and see those Indian hieroglyphics you told me about?"

"I'm not taking you in the jeep in your condition, Miss Oliver."

"We can walk, then. I feel really terrific."

"I was thinking: tomorrow maybe we ought to drive into the city and call on Clemente and Aunt Harriet."

"You're always so correct, Clyde. But they're such bores. I mean, I'm glad and all about Clemente finding a home, especially if you're right about her having a crush on Teddy. Imagine Clemente being my mother!"

"That never would have happened," Clyde said firmly. "Clemente isn't up to Catherine. But it wasn't a proper situation, her living at Oonhall with you girls gone. She might have got some crazy ideas, which could have been hard for Teddy to handle."

"She could have become his mistress. Like in the old days. The Lord of the Manor and the servant girl. Teddy would drink more and more, and the trees would grow up, hiding the house, and there would be all these little illegitimate kids running around — you know, the bastards. I think we used to have to read garbage like that in English class —"

"Well, that's what it is. Garbage, Hat."

"And you thought I ought to go on and finish college!"

"I guess I didn't know that's the kind of stuff they made you read."

"There was something about a scarlet letter. I don't remember it very well. But this girl got knocked up by the minister and had a baby without getting married and they put this big A on her, which stood for Adultery, and she just walked around wearing this A, like a nitwit, because she had sinned or something. Big deal."

"There must be nicer books," Clyde said. "That's the trouble with those professors. Most of them are Communists, anyhow."

"Maybe *I* should get an A to wear, Clyde."

"Well, that's not going to be necessary, and you know it. I don't like to even hear you joke that way."

"A nice, big, scarlet A —" said Hat dreamily.

The phone rang. Clyde got up to answer it. Hat stretched out full length on the sofa and listened idly to the conversation.

"Hello. Well, howdy there, Sheriff," Clyde said jovially. There was a pause, then his voice grew more serious. "Yes, Hank, Miss Oliver is here. Yes, I can speak for her. We heard all about it from her dad. The boy was obviously no good, I met him once, but we were all sorry for the sister. She was a nice little hardworking girl. Yes, that's correct, Hank. Miss Oliver only saw him once in her life, when he stopped in to visit his sister. He was after money to support his drug habit, I guess. Miss Oliver gave him the check for a charitable cause. I suppose he couldn't cash it. . . . Sure you have to check things out, don't apologize. . . . Yes, you can tell them that. Just say you know me and that the Olivers are a fine, upstanding family. It was a kind of mistaken generosity, you might say. . . . Thanks, Hank. We'll have to get together one of these evenings and have a little poker game. Sure. . . . Goodbye."

"Was that about that check?" said Hat lazily.

"Yes, it was. If it weren't for your condition, I'd give you a good lecture." Clyde lit a cigarette and gazed sternly and affectionately down at Hat. "Fortunately, the local sheriff and I are old buddies. He had a call from the city; the police up there asked him to find out about your check that was found in that kid's room. The next time you have a charitable urge, Miss Oliver, go through an established agency, will you please? There's plenty of them who will be happy to grab your money."

"Are we going up on the ridge, Clyde?"

"No."

"Well, what are we going to do, for Pete's sake?"

"I was thinking we might go into San Juan Batista for lunch."

"What about Colly?"

"Well, I don't approve of lying, exactly, but maybe we could tell her we are going to the ridge."

"What makes you think she wouldn't want to come along?"

"I happened to mention I saw a rattler up there the other day. She doesn't think much of rattlers."

"I guess a rattler is a 'blessing in disguise.' "

"You mustn't make fun of Colly, Hat. It was my idea to invite her down."

"I know. Colly's keeping my honor intact."

"After you've had the baby, you'll be glad you did things the right way," Clyde said.

"I . . . I guess," said Hat humbly.

43

THE telephone rang in Harriet's apartment. She hurried to answer it, so as not to disturb Clemente's nap.
"Hello."
"Harriet, it's Hazel."
"Yes, Hazel."
"Is that girl still with you, or can you talk?"

Harriet sighed gently. She had been rather brusque with poor Hazel Henderson when she had called during Clemente's illness, as Hazel's somewhat hostile tone now indicated.

"She's asleep. I was just making her some nice split-pea soup."

"Well, I hope you're not wearing yourself out, Harriet. How long do you expect her to stay?"

"We have no definite plans as yet, Hazel. She is just getting her strength back."

"I've been wanting to come over and discuss your paper for the Study Group. As you know, I'm program chairman this year and I've been trying to work up a theme, instead of having everyone just going off on their own."

"Hazel, dear, I'm awfully sorry, but —"

"Coordination is what I'm aiming for. It's really too stupid to have one person doing Wildflowers of California and somebody else the Letters of Robert and Elizabeth Browning. We could also do with something more *au courant*. What would you think of The Problems of the Single Woman in Today's Society?"

"Hazel, dear, I think the soup's boiling over. I'll just have to hang up. I'm sorry."

"Did you have a nice nap?"

"Very nice. Before I slept, I sketched the view from the window. I thought I might do a series of water colors for the walls of your new apartment."

"What a lovely idea. Would you care for a little sherry before supper?"

"Yes, please."

"How would you like me to brush your hair first?"

"If you'd like to. . . ."

Harriet got the brush and tenderly began to smooth the matted, tangled hair. There were still streaks of some horrid dye Clemente had used before she came.

"We might get you an appointment at the beauty parlor in a few days," she said. "Would you like that?"

Clemente smiled vaguely.

Harriet put down the brush. She drew a chair up in front of Clemente's bed. "I have something to talk to you about," she said nervously.

A month had passed, and though Teddy still called occasionally, the spaces in between had grown longer. That he had not called for a whole week had escaped Harriet's attention until a letter from him arrived this morning. At first she had not had the courage even to open it. Clemente was well? Why burden Harriet any longer? Why should she not return to Oonhall? She had invented several versions, but all had the same theme — she was to lose Clemente. Well . . . there was no point in postponing the inevitable; she cut open the envelope with her letter knife.

What an amazing letter it was! She had read it over and over and had even memorized part of it:

I've been thinking over your plight and that of Clemente
. . . hardly suitable for her to live here with the girls gone.
. . . At your age, you, too, might prefer not to live alone. Have heard there are good values in condominiums in East Bay, which you could consider . . .

The only string attached is that you invest the money and live on the income . . .

There had seemed to be no point in reading it any more. She would never, she realized, understand her extravagant, aloof brother. The mysteries which lay beneath those phrases were not to be revealed to her. No doubt, to him she was not worthy.

Then, abruptly, almost impatiently, she wondered why it mattered to understand? Why worry over hidden meanings? Why be concerned that they might imply some dark secret, some disease of the spirit? Why not, instead, accept the gift in the terms in which it was offered? If she were not to be allowed to repay Teddy in the only way she could ever repay him, by a closer relationship, then she would be, at least, in the position to help someone else.

"Cast your bread upon the waters." Wasn't this what the Bible said to do? And if she, too, gained something from it, was that, after all, so wrong? Her only problem was to convince dear, unselfish Clemente that she, too, must accept this lavish offering.

Harriet cleared her throat anxiously. "I have just received a letter from my brother," she began.

Clemente waited with polite interest.

"I may as well be blunt. Yes, I shall come right out with it. He has sent me some money, an extremely large sum. It is for me to do with whatever I choose, but the implication is that he would be happy if I shared it with you."

Clemente's tranquil gaze did not alter.

"I don't know how to say this delicately. I shall just say it. Naturally, you are free to refuse. I would not insist. But the money — it is enough for you and me to find a nice home together."

Clemente nodded pleasantly.

"Perhaps find a condominium in the East Bay somewhere? After I am gone, it would all belong to you. My nieces, as you know, are cared for handsomely. Would your scruples interfere with this plan?"

Clemente looked puzzled. "My scruples?"

"It would not bother your conscience to accept this gift?"

"Oh." Clemente seemed to be thinking. Then, "Teddy has a lot of money, doesn't he?"

"Oh, yes. A great deal."

"Then I don't see why it would bother me."

"Oh, my dear! I was so afraid! My dear, you would be making me so happy!" Tears arose in Harriet's eyes; she removed her glasses and wiped them away with her pocket handkerchief.

Clemente smiled dreamily. She appeared to have lost all interest in the discussion. Her sweet innocence clutched at Harriet's heart.

"So happy," said Harriet again.

Clemente held up her sketch pad. "Do you think I've caught the view at all?" she said.

44

It was a morning in mid-August. In the kitchen garden of the Convent of the Precious Blood, the air was spicy with herbs, which Sister Jenine, the old kitchen nun, had planted along the gravel paths. Sister Jenine's vegetable plot was also flourishing. There were giant gray artichokes with spiky stems, spreading vines of squash and cucumbers, poles of climbing beans and staked tomatoes and neat rows of lettuce, onions and carrots. Yellow and orange striped gourds, shaped like bottles, balls and Turks' hats, hung upon the white adobe wall of Sister Jenine's potting shed. In the fall, she would pick and dry them, meticulously lacquer them, string them together, and rehang them as ornaments in the refectory.

Loren sat upon a stone bench beneath the shade of a lime tree, reviewing the imperfect subjunctive in her book of French verbs. Her long, rippling hair was coiled tightly into a tidy bun at the nape of her neck; upon her nose were thin-rimmed gold "granny" spectacles; she wore a long, straight, light-blue denim skirt and a long-sleeved white shirt with a high neckline.

"*Bonjour, mademoiselle,*" said Mother Humilitia, as she approached Loren, her black skirt sweeping the gravel path.

Loren stood up until Mother Humilitia had sat down and motioned her to join her.

"Sister Michelle almost refuses to believe you never studied a language before or did not grow up in a multilingual household."

"I knew a language once."

"Oh, yes, I forgot. What was it called?"

"Oon."

"And how does Oon compare with French or Latin?"

"Oon was a more impoverished tongue. It lacked preciseness and clarity and verbs of action. It contained too many vague abstractions, like love and loyalty, without modifiers. Sister Michelle has introduced me to Anglo-Saxon, and I would compare it to that, except that Anglo-Saxon is stronger and more rugged. My grandfather belonged to a fraternal lodge which had its own ritual language; I think Oon may have been similar to that in that it provided a sense of security to those of the Inner Circle. Oon could not express complicated ideas, but, then, in those days, I had no complicated ideas to express. Worst of all, perhaps, Oon lacked style."

"That is nicely thought out, though rather like a recitation. I hope we have not turned you into a pedant."

"I think I may have tendencies in that direction."

"Oh, dear, young people always seem to want to go to extremes."

"Please don't worry. It's probably just a temporary safety measure. Until I know how and where to redirect my passion. The past year has been confusing." Loren smiled brightly.

"I hope you don't think other years will be any less confusing," Mother Humilitia said.

"Oh, I don't intend to remain forever — in Retreat!"

"Good, because I wanted to talk to you about your plans."

"My plans?" Loren looked uneasy. "Must I have some so soon?"

Her question was ignored. "You could, if you like, go to college. To a good university. Your academic career is unorthodox, but we would provide you with recommendations. You have gifts; it would be a pity not to employ them."

"I like it here."

"We should love to keep you. But, as you said, you don't intend to remain here forever. You must eventually get out into the world. It was this I thought we might discuss."

"You want to push me out of the nest, then?" said Loren whimsically.

"I am famous for that. My sisters are everywhere these days. In the ghettos, in the universities, in government. The nest, as you call it, has become an anachronism, and an expensive one at that." Her voice grew sharper; there was a note of exasperation. "Take Sister Jenine's garden, for example." She turned her mournful eyes toward the vegetables. "She is so proud of it, poor thing. But the fact is, she couldn't manage it without the gardener to do the heavy spading and weeding. The gardener costs more than buying our vegetables in the supermarket. The orchard is a luxury, too. It scarcely pays the man we lease it to. His labor costs are too high. I am spending all my time trying to raise money to keep up this large and expensive establishment, and for what? A few rich women on Retreat. Easter and Christmas chorals to please the old Catholics in the parish. Sister Michelle, who would like to work with Chicanos, is burdened down with bookkeeping. I am not pushing you out of the nest; it is the nest that must go. I have been talking to the archbishop for a year, and I believe I have at last won my argument. There will be resistance in the parish, but I have already rounded up a sensible, forward-looking, understanding group on my side. But the problem is, how do I sell it? The archbishop will not let it go for a song. Fifteen acres, zoned agricultural."

"Couldn't you have the zoning changed?" said Loren.

"Yes, I have considered that. The county master plan shows us as residential. Rezoned, we would then of course be able to sell for much more. But it would mean endless planning commission meetings, and there will be strong objections in the neighborhood. They have come to think of us as their own private greenbelt. They will fight to keep it from being broken up into parcels, and I think it would be a pity myself. It will arouse anti-Catholic feeling, too, just when some of us are beginning to have a reputation for being enlightened."

"What you would like is to keep it intact and still sell it for a high price," said Loren thoughtfully.

"You have put it succinctly. If I receive a good price, it will also give me leverage with the diocese to do what I wish with some of the money. I should like to join Sister Michelle in opening a school and a settlement house for the Mexican-Americans in the valley. I don't have too many years of activity left, and, although I'm a good businesswoman, I pray every day that I may be relieved of that role."

Loren considered. Then, "I think I have an idea."

Mother Humilitia smiled encouragingly.

"Teddy must help you."

"He has always been most sympathetic. He understands the neighborhood and the value of land. But perhaps I have used up my credit with him?"

"I don't think so. You have taken me off his hands. I was, as you know, beginning to be troublesome. Perhaps you had some idea, yourself, like that, when you invited me here?" Her face remained modestly composed, except for her eyes, which sparkled mischievously.

"Oh, dear, you have always had a way of questioning my motives. Perhaps I did. Who knows? It's hard for me to say myself. Motives are seldom utterly pure, any more than they are utterly wicked. I think it is dangerous to try to believe that they are. But this is what makes life so fascinating."

"Teddy is coming to take me out to dinner tomorrow night. It's my birthday. I'll be sixteen years old. I feel twenty-five." Loren laughed. "I'll talk to him then. It will give him a project and make him feel useful."

"Sixteen is an important birthday. I must tell Sister Jenine to bake you a cake. That's all she's good for nowadays. Her sponge cakes are especially tasty. Do you prefer chocolate or white?"

"Chocolate, please," said Loren.

45

FIVE miles down the road from Oonhall, Becky and Debbie Alway sat on the corral fence of the Los Robles Riding Stables, waiting for Mrs. Alway to pick them up. Their lesson had ended at four; at four-fifteen, impatient with waiting, they decided to hitchhike home.

"My mother will kill me if she finds out," Debbie said.

"That's simple. We won't tell her."

It was a hot, late August afternoon. The girls began their hike, stopping self-consciously to thumb whenever a car passed. Several cars drove by; they stuck out their tongues at them. Then a battered pickup slowed down, a mottled face peered out, the truck stopped. "Lift, ladies?" It was Mad Fred. They scrambled up on the high seat gleefully.

"Miss Becky Oliver, I do believe. And — let me guess — an Alway of some sort?"

They giggled. "Debbie," said Debbie.

"Of course. It couldn't be Miss Linda. Miss Linda must drive some magnificent vehicle of her own when she's not on her galloping charger. Where to, O Fair Ones?"

"We're going to Debbie's house."

"Alway Mansion, Jeeves. A stately home. Uuurrrum. Urrruuum." Mad Fred made funny car-starting noises.

The girls glanced at each other, trying to stifle snickers. They drove bumpily down the road. Then Becky got an idea. In a prim, grown-up voice, she said, "I've often told Debbie about Lulu, Mad Fred. I wonder if you would show Lulu to Debbie, please?"

Mad Fred turned to Becky, who sat next to him; the whites of his eyes widened with feigned horror. "You've told this — this child about Lulu!"

Snickers erupted into more giggles.

Mad Fred slowed the pickup down; his face became stolid as he seemed to be considering Becky's outrageous request. "I don't know. I just don't know," he said at last.

"Debbie and I are going away to a girls' school next fall. It might be Debbie's last chance."

"So you're flying the coop, too," said Mad Fred.

"It's an extremely fine school. It's very highly rated."

"I went to some extremely fine schools, myself," he said. "Very highly rated, super-dooper, A-Plus, the Cat's Pajamas!"

"Debbie would just love Lulu, wouldn't you, Deb?"

"It's all right if he doesn't want to," said Debbie politely.

Mad Fred, without changing his expression, applied the brakes so abruptly that the girls were almost thrown against the windshield; then he drove off on to a shoulder and parked beneath a eucalyptus tree. He said gravely, "I have reached my decision. Lulu is a treat reserved for few eyes. But Miss Debbie seems like a good sort. Lulu shall perform for her."

He turned in his seat and faced them. There was a dramatic pause. Then he slowly pulled up the sleazy Hawaiian shirt as if he were lifting the curtain of a theater.

The girls gave little gasps. There, upon the white, flabby, hairless trunk was Lulu: flowing, dark locks, a pretty, comic-strip face, a full-formed body dressed modestly in a grass skirt and grass brassiere — an innocent, ageless vamp, whose beauty would never fade as long as Mad Fred lived.

Mad Fred began to hum a little tune, "Lovely Hula Hands," and, simultaneously, manipulated the muscles of his belly. The white flesh heaved; Lulu commenced her dance. She wiggled and undulated; her hips swayed coquettishly.

More gasps of pleasure. Laughter. Applause. Then, bending forward, Mad Fred urged Lulu into an awkward bow.

No one had seen the Rover speed by, stop, back up, and come to another stop beside the shoulder of the road. Mad Fred dropped his shirt; then raised it, briefly, for a curtain call.

"Lulu's grateful for her kind reception, but she must rest now. Her public appearances are rare; she is delicate."

He turned back to the wheel; a stony face was peering into the window of the driver's side; a stony voice said, "Is that you, Debbie? Is that Becky, too?"

It was Linda.

"You're supposed to be at the stable. Mother's having her hair done and sent me to pick you up. Please come at once!"

"Mad Fred was just giving us a lift," said Debbie.

"You know you're not supposed to hitchhike."

The girls sighed, climbed out of the pickup, waved good-bye, then got into Linda's Rover. They sped off.

Mad Fred took a cigarette out of his shirt pocket and put it, unlit, into his mouth. He patted his stomach gently, as if to cheer Lulu up. The Oliver girls were growing up, going away. Today had perhaps been Lulu's Final Performance. Nothing lasts, he thought mournfully. Well, that was the way life was. He backed off the shoulder and drove leisurely down the road toward Fred's Place.

PART THREE

46

IT was three years later. Teddy, sitting in the grape arbor of the small, whitewashed stone Hotel Splendid, the only lodging on the Greek Island of T——, gazed down upon the sea, flat and shimmering in the noon December sunshine.

The Hotel Splendid was neither splendid nor a hotel; it was the clean, simple home of a widow and her daughter, set upon a rocky promontory above the Aegean. It had only three rooms for rent, and Teddy had taken all three of them. One was his study, where he wrote letters home; kept his daily journal; worked a bit, now and then, revising his novel; and, having developed a recent interest in primitive icons, read books on this subject. The second room contained his equipment — his snorkel and face mask, his cameras and slide projectors and screen, and his digging tools. (A French archaeological expedition was camped a mile away, on the eastern side of the island; limbs, noseless heads, even an intact lekythos urn had been recovered. Once a week or so, he volunteered to help out; it was excellent exercise, now that the sea had turned cold.) The third room was his bedroom, which contained a double bed with an iron bedstead, a washstand with bowl and pitcher, one straight chair, and, over the bed, a cheap wooden icon. The icon, a Byzantine-type virgin, distressed him; it was the work of a modern artist who obviously turned them out in wholesale quantities and who lacked the true religious feeling of the primitive artist.

Apart from this lapse in taste, his living arrangements pleased him. They suited his purposes, which, though vague, had to do with spiritual cleansing — a kind of rebirth — so that he might concentrate on the good, basic things of life. Here, on T——, unencumbered by the accouterments of modern civilization — possessions, responsibilities, personal entanglements (which included, he had discovered to his surprise, even family), he felt the way one feels after one has tidied up one's desk or has fired an employee and found it not to have been as painful as one had imagined. On this island in the wine-dark sea he would begin anew.

In the spirit of this venture he was dressed in humble clothes — faded blue denims, a faded crew-necked shirt and sandals; his face was bronzed; his graying hair was long in back. He had a bushy, shapeless beard and his sideburns were shaggy. At the moment, his right arm was held in a haphazard sling made out of one of his silk scarves; he had stirred up the old "tennis elbow" on the last dig.

Below, on the water, the steamer which came twice a week was on its way out — a tiny toy upon the horizon. The mail it had brought him lay unopened on the wooden table. Kalliope, the landlady's daughter who had set it there, leaned against one of the thick, gnarled branches of the old vine. Her dark, lustrous hair was caught up in a loose bun at the nape of her sturdy neck; she watched with curious black eyes as the rich "Amerikano," who looked like an aging hippie, carefully removed the stamps from the envelopes and tucked them into his wallet.

"Wine?" she said, when he had finished.

"Parakalo, Kalliope. Just a glass." He spoke slowly; he was helping the girl with her English.

She left to fetch the wine.

Teddy glanced at the letters. One was from the Zimmermans, one from Mother Humilitia, one — mysteriously — on airmail stationery from the Shelbourne Hotel, Dublin.

With a kind of hopeful anticipation, he opened Mother Humilitia's first. Inside was a card, a prosaic etching of some saint offering half his cloak to a beggar. "To give is to receive" was printed upon it; at the bottom of the card, in smaller print — "The Little Sisters of the Street will welcome your donations in the spirit of our patron, St. Martin."

Mother Humilitia had added a short note. "I thought perhaps you might be interested in our new project. Trust you are well and happy and as proud of Loren as we are. Go with God."

Would the woman never be satisfied, he thought with a sense of disappointment. A year of his life spent at planning commissions, obtaining a special-use permit for her convent land; six months spent setting up Zimmy's institute, which combined Oonhall and the convent property in a way which would not offend the community, and, at the same time, would serve Zimmy's needs; another six months buying the convent land, which, owing to his own efforts, had risen in price. But, now, instead of a word of gratitude, she had the nerve to point out *his* debt to her. Even here, in this pagan atmosphere, she was able to make him feel guilty, to reawaken that ghost of conventional morality he had come to T—— to escape. Damn the woman, he thought crossly. If I send her a check, it will be a modest one.

He opened Zimmy's letter. A brochure fell out: its coy, amateurish design — two naked lovers holding hands — obviously Bobsie's handiwork. Beneath it, more nonsense.

Rolling Hills Farm — An Adventure in Fundamental Living
Rolling Hills Farm — An Environment
Rolling Hills Farm — An Experience in Intimacy
Rolling Hills Farm — A New Kind of Therapy
Psychodrama
Sensory Awareness
Nonverbal Communication
Et cetera, et cetera

He turned the brochure over. On the back was a collage of photographs. A group, sitting around the pool, labeled "Recreation"; The Convent of the Precious Blood, labeled "Extensive, comfortable facilities for group conferences, churches, lodges, corporations"; Oonhall, labeled "Guest Chalet." (Already, he noted with shock, it had an institutional look.)

He scanned the written message. "Tidings of comfort and joy . . . we are thriving. . . . Bobsie manages the domestic affairs, relieving me to . . . A reporter from the *San Francisco Chronicle* is coming down to . . . Your friends, the Always, sent us a Mrs. Collier, who is having emotional difficulties. . . . Wish you were here to sit on the board in person."

Kalliope returned with a carafe of retsina, which her mother made herself and which he had disciplined himself to drink in the daytime, saving his limited supply of Scotch for evening. She poured him a glassful; he took a sip and opened the letter from Dublin. The writing was in a precise, cramped, girlish hand. Puzzled, he glanced at the signature. It was from Linda Alway!

> Dear Teddy,
> I'm here on a crummy old art tour. Our director, Mademoiselle, calls us "Jeunes Filles" and does a bed check at night. When we finish with ruins and crumbling monasteries, we're coming to see Greek antiquities. We'll be at the Athens Hilton over Christmas — from December 22 to 28. Would you like to rescue me for an evening? (I'm going to call home and have Daddy rush a letter to the Hilton saying you are an old, trusted friend of the family.) Christmas Eve would be an especially nice time, because Mademoiselle has some awful thing planned for us at the American Embassy. I've just washed my hair, so forgive water spots on stationery.
> Love and all that,
Linda

Christmas Eve? Athens?
Kalliope said, "More wine?"
"No, thank you, not at the moment. Sit down, Kalliope."
She sat down shyly opposite him.
Linda Alway? She would be twenty-one now, he remembered. It might be fun to show a young lady around the night spots in the Plaka. The younger generation didn't have much fun these days. Not like in his time. They were all sad kids. You saw it in

their faces. They lived sad, lonely, isolated lives. The things that had made life jolly and exciting for his generation — college, travel, love affairs, parties, even war — seemed to make them sadder. Of course, one couldn't fight a whole generation's malaise — he had seen that with his own children. Still, here was an opportunity; he might see what could be done for Linda. At twenty-one she would have grown up — just enough. There would still be a great deal he could teach her, but her new maturity might make her more receptive. At the very least, it would be a pleasant change. If he sent a note out by the next boat, it would arrive at the Hilton in time . . .

"Shall we have a quick English lesson before I go upstairs?" he said to Kalliope.

She nodded eagerly.

He looked into her dark eyes. "Let's start like this. You remind me — you understand what that means — you are like a girl I once knew. She lived in Mexico, far away from here. Her name was Felicita. That means happiness."

"Happiness," she repeated.

"She was killed in an earthquake. An earthquake —?" He shook the table, making the glass and carafe rattle. "It is when the gods shake the earth."

"Ah, *sesmos?*" Her eyes grew larger. "You were sad, yes?"

"To me, she still lives. You are her reincarnation. You don't understand that, do you?"

She shook her head and frowned.

"It means another life, a fresh start, a new beginning. Well, never mind. Tell me, do you have a boyfriend, Kalliope?"

She dropped her head shyly.

"I'll have just a drop more wine. *Efcharisto.*"

Kalliope poured it; he sipped. "Do you know your old myths? Do you know the stories of the gods who came down from Olympus and made love to mortal girls?"

She looked puzzled, then she giggled.

> "But with the favorite of the gods they live
> A life where there are no more tears.

Around those blessed isles soft sea winds breathe,
And golden flowers blaze upon the trees,
Upon the waters, too."

He knew she could no longer follow him, but he was enjoying himself, and wasn't that what mattered, wasn't that why he had come?

He stood up. "I must go now." He laid a hand upon her smooth, glossy head, thinking of Linda's blond one. "Wonderful things used to happen, Kalliope," he said softly, half to himself. "Perhaps, who knows, they still do . . ."

47

LEAH Lawrence walked up the stony path from the boat landing; the boy called Dino, who carried her bags, led the way. She had picked him out of the crowd of boys at the dock who had petitioned her for the job. Handsome; hard, black eyes that shone with an amoral brilliance; a foppish, elegant manner; a magnificent, sunbrowned body. They said that the modern Greeks were no relation to their ancestors, but surely Dino could be, she thought.

The boy rounded a curve in the path; above them was the small white hotel with the green door. A donkey, tethered to a stake, grazed beneath a fig tree in front. How delightful, how picturesque, how like Teddy! What fun it would be to surprise him! She might spend a week or two here; she would work in the daytime, of course, but at night — at night she might permit herself a little holiday, partake of the grape with Teddy, perhaps reactivate their too brief affair.

Dino had entered the hotel; the door was open; she could hear him talking to a pretty girl in rapid Greek. Only two weeks at the most, though, she decided firmly. Then — Mycenae. She must wander about that doomed spot, think of Troy, of fair, faithless Helen, of the aged Menelaus, of Fates and Furies . . .

Dino, who had left her luggage in the entrance, came back to

Leah's side. "She says she is sorry there are no rooms. The American man has taken all of them," he said in his broken English.

Leah laughed. "Tell her the American man is a friend of mine. He will explain —"

There was more conversation; its tone indicated a problem. "She says the American man has gone to Athens; he will not be back until after Christmas. He will be back for New Year's."

New Year's will do very nicely, Leah thought. It would give her time to do some reading, to work out the new plot. "Just take my suitcases in," she ordered. "My friend will understand. Please be careful of the small one, it contains my typewriter." She walked briskly past him into the hotel.

Dino shrugged, picked up the luggage, and followed her.

"The Amerikano is out," the girl said in English to Leah. She looked confused.

"My dear, it doesn't matter. He is like — a brother. I shall take over his rooms while he's gone and join him for New Year's. Do you understand?"

The girl listened, frowned, then nodded and pointed toward the stairs. Leah, followed by both Dino and the girl, marched up.

I'll just settle in, she thought. When Teddy comes back, we can have a drink together. Dear Teddy. She could hardly wait to try out her new idea on him. A book about Clytemnestra from the woman's point of view. After all, Agamemnon had wronged her; she had plenty of grievances; her side had never been defended.

At the top of the stairs the girl stepped ahead and opened a bedroom door. How nice! A double bed, thought Leah.

Dino brought the luggage in and put it down. Leah looked at him. She had only been in Greece for a night and a day, and already she had one character for her book. Dino would bring the water for A's bath. She could see him now, carrying the urn gracefully upon his beautiful head, while, ignorant of his fate, perhaps toying with a gloom-ridden, moody Cassandra, Agamemnon waited to be murdered.

I'll unpack the typewriter and take a few notes at once, she thought, as she fumbled in her purse for a tip. I'll have it all straight in my head before Teddy returns. She pictured his amazement when he saw her. She would have a little bar set up on the washstand, with the bottle of Haig and Haig she had brought as a present. She would toast their reunion as he entered the room.

"Happy New Year, Teddy, dear! Surprise!"

48

THEY were gathered for Christmas dinner. On the wall above the white "antiqued" buffet, Great-Great-Grandfather Phineas gazed down from his gold frame. Only two weeks ago, Hat had produced him from the basement, where he lay among the articles which she had brought from Oonhall; the young decorator from the city had thought it just the right touch. How often he had haunted auctions for just this sort of thing! And to think that Mrs. O'Mahoney had one of her very own! The gold-leaf frame would accent the blue and green striped wallpaper and balance the bamboo birdcage filled with ivy at the opposite end of the room; the solemn face would add a "tone." He had hung Phineas, admired him, shook hands with Hat, and departed. And just in time, too, thought Hat, who, wearing the green velveteen maternity smock Clemente had made for her, now stood at the end of the long table, pausing for just a moment to admire the pretty room.

She looks like a pregnant Renaissance youth, thought Felix Steiner, the bearded young professor whom Loren had brought down in her car from Stanford for the day. That strong, handsome face, those passionate, dark eyes, the short, dark curls. She might lead an army, commission a monument, fight a duel. Not my type at all, but somehow admirable, he decided, as he hastened to hold her chair.

The long day is almost over, Hat was thinking wearily. For it had started at dawn when Cathy had awakened to see what Santa Claus had brought her. It was now four, but it seemed like midnight. Still, it had gone very well, she decided with satisfaction. Such an assortment of people, all with various needs and idiosyncrasies. All had had to be catered to in their special way. Such an effort! But, thanks to careful management on her part and Clyde's, it had worked. Thanks to careful management and attention to detail, everyone — even, at last, Becky, had risen to the occasion. It was an accomplishment she felt she had the right to be proud of.

Loren's young man was hovering over her; she waved him away with an abstracted air.

"Aunt Harriet, why don't you sit there, next to Becky," she said. "Clemente?" She pondered. "Next to me."

"I want to sit next to Clemente!" Little Cathy was pulling at Clemente's gray skirt.

Hat gave her a chiding glance, more of a formal gesture than one of real exasperation. For the child, around whom the day had centered, and for whom it would be, in the future, only a dim tribal memory, was obviously exhausted. There were dark smudges under her large eyes; her voice was shrill and whiny. "Clemente is tired," said Hat. "You haven't left her alone a moment."

"How could I ever be tired of Cathy?" cried Clemente, which was the response Hat had expected and to which she, therefore, scarcely bothered to listen.

Clemente carefully lifted the little girl up and settled her into the chair beside her.

How fat she is, thought Hat. Almost as fat as I am. And she moves like a snail.

Clemente began to smooth Cathy's hair with slow, sensual strokes; there was a dreamy, glazed expression in her blue eyes. Cathy wriggled in fatuous delight.

Moreover, she is drunk. Hat could tell from Clemente's voice, from her sluggish movements. She had reminded Clyde to mix Clemente's drinks lightly during the cocktail hour. But Clemente, who was in charge of the dinner, had been in and out of the kitchen, and had doubtless helped herself to more. Oh, well, poor thing, it's Christmas, and we're her only family. But what if she sets the house on fire with all the cooking she'll be doing? What if she stumbles, carrying Cathy?

Clemente (which meant Aunt Harriet, too, alas) was going to stay on to help out when Baby came in January. One could not trust the help around here for that; they did not have the same principles of hygiene. And Cathy did adore Clemente, which might prevent traumas while Mother devoted herself to her nursing. Still, since we *are* her only family, isn't it my duty, as much as for our own protection, to speak to her about her problem? I'll discuss it with Clyde, she decided. Clyde will know what to do.

"Loren, next to Cathy, please. Professor Steiner, will you sit between Loren and Clyde?"

"Won't you call me Felix?" begged the young man humbly.

Oh, dear, he has said this before, thought Hat. This time I really must remember his name. He was a professor of what? Linguistics, he had told her. He had even attempted to explain what this was. Something to do with helping the disadvantaged to learn to read; something to do with an institution run by radical Catholics in Mexico where Loren was going to study this summer; something to do with an article in *Playboy* which he had been asked to write. In the confusion, she had found it hard to concentrate. What she had observed was that he was enamored of Loren. He could not keep his eyes off her all day. Did Loren return his feelings? If so, why did she get herself up in such a peculiar costume? That long, dark-green, wool-fringed skirt, those ridiculous high black boots, the flowing, dark hair, half down her back — she looked like a Victorian match girl in one of Cathy's storybooks. For such a pretty girl — beautiful, really — it seemed a pity. Was this the fad at Stanford now? Probably not, for Loren had always gone her own way. Should she speak to her about it? Probably not, she decided. Still, she might talk this over with Clyde, too.

She sat down awkwardly at her place and rang the little silver bell. Maria entered, timidly bearing the turkey on its platter, and set it in front of Clyde. How handsome Clyde looked in his blue flannel blazer and the red weskit Aunt Harriet had made for him! How she enjoyed watching him as he sized up his job. He went into a kind of trance, studied the bird with narrowed eyes, analyzed its proportions. Now he picked up the knife, felt its edge, sharpened it against the steel, glanced down at the bird again as if to make sure nothing had changed, then, with deftness and assurance, attacked. It was nice when a man knew how to carve, Hat thought.

Did people prefer white meat or dark meat or some of both, Clyde wanted to know.

"I want a drumstick!" shouted Cathy.

"You must wait your turn," said Hat severely.

A drumstick on a plate was passed hastily down the table and deposited at Cathy's place. Hat sighed. If Clyde had a fault it was spoiling his daughter. But what could she do? It was impossible to stop him. It would be cruel even to try. For it had been *his* day, even more than Cathy's. How he had beamed while he took the colored movies of the little girl opening her presents (far too many) under the Tree, of Hat, of Loren and her professor, of Clemente, of Aunt Harriet picking up paper and ribbon off the floor, of Becky — he had even cajoled Becky into a smile!

To think that only last night, poor Clyde had had to put up with one of Becky's hysterical little scenes.

Those reports from Miss Potter's, where they had thought she was so safe! Failing in French and Latin, sneaking out at night, snubbing her old friend Debbie Alway, whom she now called "square." It was hoped that during the absence of Mr. Oliver Mr. O'Mahoney might have a talk with her before she returned. I suppose I was like that once, thought Hat, looking at Becky's pretty, sulky face. But that was different, that was a thousand years ago . . .

Clyde *used* to be nice, thought Becky sullenly. Hat has ruined him! She made him give up his plane, encouraged him to have Hurwulf killed. She's turned him into an uptight, plastic fink. He wants to have a "little chat" with me about school after Christmas. Well, if they think I'm going back there, they're in for a surprise. As soon as this boring day is over, I'm splitting! I'll hitchhike up to Los Robles and see Mad Fred. He'll lend me some money. I won't need much. I have Catherine's earrings, too, if I can con Clyde out of getting them out of his safe. After all, they're *my* earrings. I can say I just want to try them on. I can pawn them for the air fare to Morocco. When I get there, my friends will put me up. If I can't find my friends, if I run out of money, the American Embassy will send me home.

Where is Morocco? Is it in Europe or Africa? Mad Fred will know. I have this friend on an island, too — what's it called, Ibiza? There might be a rock concert there. Is Ibiza in Europe or Asia? Is it anywhere near Greece? If it is, I can get money from Teddy.

Poor old Hurwulf. That spoiled Cathy probably pulled her tail!

Clyde had finished the carving; now he opened the wine. He tasted it, frowned, thought, nodded, announced the name and vintage — as if anyone cares, thought Becky — then walked around the table, ceremoniously pouring.

It's nice, thought Hat, when a man starts to take an interest in wines.

"Only a drop for me, I already feel a little buzzy," Aunt Harriet said.

"And a wee drap for Cathy," said Clyde, pouring a tiny amount into the little girl's milk mug.

He returned to the head of the table and raised his glass. "I should like to make some toasts," he said genially.

All eyes turned toward him in expectation.

"First, to Aunt Harriet and Clemente, who have provided us with this sumptuous feast."

Aunt Harriet blinked modestly; Clemente blushed. The rest drank.

"Second, to the absent members of our family: to Teddy and to Clemente's mother."

They drank.

"Third, a Merry Christmas and a Happy 1971 to us all!"

They drank. Maria began to pass the other dishes as Hat had laboriously trained her to do; Hat gave her an approving nod.

How ugly the wallpaper is, thought Loren, sipping her wine. How odd it was that someone brought up in Teddy's household would have chosen it. One would think that taste, if not innate, was, at least, acquired. Apparently not. But then she must try to remember that style was not the most important thing; this was a failing she had. She had discussed this failing with Felix, who had admitted that he suffered from it, too. It was something, they had agreed, that must be watched. Take today, for example. Not her style at all. Not Felix's either, thank goodness. Yet, despite this, she could see that Felix had been taken in, was even entranced. He had no real family of his own; his parents had separated when he was very young. He saw only what was on the surface here, a traditional Christmas, which probably reminded him of some book. He had no idea how precarious the whole setup was; no way at all of judging what lay beneath. He was like Leah Lawrence with that ridiculous book of hers. "Remember when Clemente's mother was writing *The Happy Family?*" she said aloud. It was a mildly malicious question; some interesting reactions might be provoked.

"*The Happy Family,*" said Hat. "I'm not sure I remember quite. Which one was that?"

"It was about us," said Loren.

"Oh, I think I vaguely recall something," said Hat. "She didn't finish it, did she?"

"She couldn't," said Clyde. "The Olivers didn't provide enough drama for her. She wanted blood and guts. And love stuff." He grinned.

"But what made her —?" Felix began.

"It was a wonderful family," said Clyde. "Anyone could see that. But I'm glad she dropped it. I don't know much about books, but I do know I wouldn't have wanted to see the Olivers in one, I can tell you that! I would have put a stop to it at the beginning, but Teddy was too good-natured."

"How remarkable," said Felix. He paused, leaned back in his

chair as Loren had seen him do in seminars; he was obviously preparing to dig in, get at the root of the issue.

But at that moment a fuss over Cathy, who had just upset the gravy boat, erupted at the other end of the table. Clyde's attention was diverted to this; Hat was scolding; Clemente was mopping up the mess. The crisis had passed.

Loren looked gratefully at the little girl, who, unabashed, was gazing indifferently at the hovering adults, a tiny, crooked smile upon her mouth. How much she looks like Clyde, she thought in amazement! It was all too much to contemplate — no wonder Felix made her nervous! She retreated within herself: this was a way she had when things became difficult. She looked away from the people at the table and idly began to examine the room again. Inanimate objects were safer than people. If the things surrounding her were not exactly her cup of tea, well, they were just objects, after all. She stared without thinking at the wallpaper, then her eyes fell upon the portrait of Phineas. Part of the decor. But, if one cupped one's hands over the eminent ancestor's head so that only the face was exposed — as she suddenly found herself doing in her mind — the determined, dark eyes, the full, sensual mouth might be an older, masculine Hat. One couldn't escape people, after all! There was really no such thing as style without content, art for art's sake. Here was another lesson for her. It served her right!

"When will Teddy call?" asked Becky restlessly. I hope Morocco is in Africa, she was thinking. You can get good hashish in Africa. She had mentioned this to Loren, recently, which had been a mistake. Even Loren was getting stuffy; she had given her a lecture on mind-blowing drugs. Loren was very fussy about her mind these days; you'd think it was an extra-special asset of hers, like having good boobs. Well, she'd take the good boobs any day. Probably Loren's professor preferred minds, not boobs; he looked like he kept one in alcohol somewhere. But the kind of boys she liked preferred boobs.

"In Teddy's last letter, he said he would call on Christmas night," Hat said.

"I sent his packages in October. Probably I should have sent them in September. Yes, I'm afraid I should have. Foreign mails are so uncertain nowadays," Aunt Harriet was saying. "Hazel Henderson warned me; she traveled widely in her youth."

"Knowing Teddy, he'll forget the time change and call in the middle of the night," said Loren. Why did I say that, she wondered. Why don't I just shut up?

"If he does, be prepared!" said Clyde jovially. "I shall knock on every door and wake you up!"

Hat rang the little bell again for Maria to clear; Clemente hurried into the kitchen to supervise the pudding.

A flash of blue caught Loren's eye. It was Catherine's bracelet upon Hat's arm. Becky was not yet "allowed" hers. The necklace was in Loren's safe-deposit box. How strange that Catherine had never worn them, she thought. Teddy had said that their opulence embarrassed her. But, if the jewels embarrassed her, why had she not sold them and given the money to the poor? Why had she saved them to pass on to her daughters? It seemed suddenly sad and poignant to Loren that her mother, dead now for so many years, had set up such high standards for herself but had not been able to carry them out. All she had been able to do was to put the jewels in a safe and pretend they did not exist. Yet, if she were here this evening, doubtless she would have taken pleasure in seeing the bracelet on Hat's arm.

And what would she think of me, she wondered. For the necklace was in her safe-deposit box not because jewels embarrassed her, but because it made her feel secure, having it there. It was more wholesome, probably, if one owned jewels to wear them. It showed you felt secure, could enjoy the sensual pleasures of life. And that was, no doubt, a good way to feel if you were going to have a baby. If one could. She couldn't, ever. For one never knew what might happen. Lovers betrayed one another, friendships dissolved, families disintegrated, empires fell, monuments crumbled into dust. Even newly decorated ranch houses surrounded by hundreds of acres were not wholly insured against disaster.

She was experiencing one of her annoying little dizzy spells, which she had thought she had outgrown. Probably, she had had too much wine. The room around her seemed to sway dangerously; Great-Great-Grandfather Phineas lay upon the floor, ripped out of his frame; the birdcage shattered; a hole yawned in the striped wall; the table was overgrown with creepers. Even a safe-deposit box could not be counted on; someday she must really investigate Swiss banks.

Clemente entered, bearing the flaming pudding decorated with sprigs of holly.

Felix, to Loren's horror, slowly arose. He lifted his glass; Loren turned rigid.

"To Miss Lawrence's pudding," said Felix solemnly.

49

ON the roof garden of a popular Athenian restaurant, a bouzoukia played the theme song from an American movie about modern Greece. Simplicity, gaiety, joy of life was its message. Below them: *Son et Lumière*. *Son* was muffled by taxi horns and bands from neighboring roof gardens; *Lumière* flickered on the famous hill. The famous temple shone like a golden phantom astride it.

A waiter suggested something called Dionysus's Blood — a chilled muscatel — for Linda, who did not care for hard liquor. It would come in a golden goblet, the lady would like it. Linda, sitting across a tiny table from Teddy, agreed indifferently.

She looked very splendid and somehow . . . changed, Teddy thought. One forgot how girls changed. In Linda's case she seemed to have grown more solid. Angularities had been firmly rounded; a sort of impatient vitality had replaced a youthful hauteur. The long, shining, blond hair had darkened; it fell naturally and unshaped to her shoulders; clumsily cropped bangs almost hid her eyebrows. She wore a simple, dark cotton, sleeveless dress of some homespun weave; her bare, sturdy arms, emerging from the dark cloth, seemed startlingly naked. He decided he had been right in coming to meet her.

"I suppose I shall have to learn," she said. Her voice had changed, too; it was huskier and oddly abrupt.

"Learn?"

"To drink whiskey."

"I don't see why. I rather like the idea of your drinking Dionysus's Blood."

"It sounds a bit phony, doesn't it? Whiskey seems more honest."

"It depends upon what you mean by 'honest,' I suppose. A certain enigmatic quality, an air of mystery, becomes a woman, don't you think?" He knew he was talking nonsense, but then girls liked nonsense; it was a form of flirting at which he considered himself adept.

To his surprise, she pondered his question seriously. Then, "I don't know whether it does or not." He sensed a slight disappointment in her tone. "At any rate, the 'what-do-you-call-it Blood' will do for tonight. I want to keep my head clear so we can talk."

"How can anyone have a clear head with this view!"

But it was apparent that the ambiance, so carefully planned, did not seduce her. She had merely given it a glance, admired it politely. Was she, he wondered, lacking in imagination?

But her next words, in a mellower voice, reassured him. "Oh, Teddy, it was really so sweet of you to meet me here!"

"But, my dear, it's my honor. I must say you do look ravishing. Despite Mademoiselle, your tour can't have done you much harm."

"Poor Mademoiselle!" Linda smiled.

The golden goblet and the Scotch arrived. Teddy lifted his glass. "Merry Christmas," he said.

"Merry Christmas. I'd almost forgotten." She sipped dutifully.

"I'm afraid I haven't. I've put a call in to the States at the hotel. I said I'd be back about midnight. Unfortunately, the night clubs only begin to get going by then. But we can drop by on our way to the Plaka."

"Midnight!"

"You don't think Mademoiselle would approve?"

"It doesn't matter if she doesn't. I'm just not used to night clubs. They sound so artificial, somehow —"

He smiled benignly. She was not, after all, sophisticated; he could offer her a treat. "I thought you might be a bit tired of 'kultura.'"

"Oh, that," she said vaguely. Then she giggled.

He gave her a puzzled look.

"You haven't noticed!" she cried.

"I thought I was noticing a great deal."

"Teddy!" A hand was thrust forward across the table; a plain, cheap, gold ring upon her ring finger was flaunted before his eyes. "I wore it for the first time since our wedding. Just for you! And you haven't said a word!"

The bouzoukia grew louder, more fretful; the lights below, suddenly vulgar. The restaurant had a tawdry elegance; the town, in fact, was a shabby mockery of its ancient glory. Only the Scotch could be counted on. He realized that Linda was still chattering.

". . . and so Mademoiselle fired him; she called him 'cheeky.' Well, he is cheeky!" She laughed in outright pleasure. "He can't bear rich, snobby, refined people; they make him positively sick. You should hear him mimic Mademoiselle. He was only being a guide to help pay for his sister's operation, anyway . . ."

He could have had his Scotch on T——, which was still unspoiled. He could have made the Christmas phone call in the village . . .

". . . I sneaked away. She thought I was at the Abbey Theatre, actually I was in this pub, listening to him recite his poetry. He adores poetry, animals, working-class people, pubs. He won't let me sit in back in a cab; I have to sit up in front with the driver. Well, then, just before we left Dublin, we got married. His parents don't mind my being American but they do mind my not being Catholic. Not that he's so faithful, himself. Only when he's buried, he says. We're going to live in one of those darling thatched-roof cottages in County Clare and make our own butter and bake our own bread and raise our own vegetables. He has a trade, he's a carpenter, and he'll go on writing poetry. He's in County Clare right now, looking for a cottage. And so I thought I'd come on to Athens and see you, and you could help out with Mother and Daddy. You will, won't you, Teddy?"

He nodded. Then, "Sorry. Will I what?"

"Write to my parents, tell them you saw me and how fabulously happy I am. I mean, I knew you'd know just how to put it. You were always such an understanding father, so much more liberal than my own. I used to envy your girls having a father like you!"

A menu was brought. Teddy waved it away. Linda retrieved it.

"I'm starved; I haven't eaten for days. I've worried so. But now that I've told you I feel ever so much better. Do you think I should try something native? What do Greeks eat? I may as well, as I won't get back here for a thousand years, we won't have a cent, but even if we did, he wouldn't approve of the political climate here."

The waiter placed another menu in Teddy's hands. Reluctantly, he scanned it.

"I've heard they have a nice moussaka here and excellent grilled fish —"

"I could eat a horse!"

Teddy shuddered.

"Of course, I'll write home at the same time. I was hoping we could work out our letters tonight and mail them together —"

"Yes, that sounds like a good plan. You don't care for another one of those?" He was looking at her still filled golden goblet. "No? I'll have another Scotch, then, please, waiter. And you might bring the young lady a plate of hors d'oeuvres in the meantime. Then we'll order. Now —" He looked at Linda; there was a duty to be performed. He raised what was left of his drink. "To you and your young man's happiness," he said.

The words were mere form; the liquor provided substance. He would fulfill his duty with grace, he decided firmly. What else was there to do, anyhow?

"I think every girl ought to have an older man besides her own father she can turn to in an emotional crisis, don't you?"

He smiled — a paternal smile. "Yes, and I'm deeply flattered you've chosen me."

He was not unpleased with his ability to bring off what he had to bring off. What had that silly Leah Lawrence said? His life was a work of art. Well, perhaps it was — though a minor one. Still, it was gratifying to have learned to play even a minor role well.

50

ALL day long the heavy draperies of the living room doors which led to the outside deck had been drawn, so that the lights of the immense Tree — multicolored and flickering — would not be diluted by daylight. Was it daylight or dark outside now, wondered Loren, as they all returned to the living room. The room itself gave no indication. A fire burned in the large brick fireplace; it was much too warm. She felt as if she were in a kind of limbo, cut off from the outside world. Her metabolism seemed thrown off, too; she was not used to eating so early; she felt disagreeably drowsy and cross.

"Teddy has not called," said Aunt Harriet. "I do hope nothing has happened . . ."

No one bothered to answer her; nervously, she began to pick up the cluttered room. She plumped up cushions on the sofa, rolled some ribbon around her wrist, then attempted to organize the array of presents scattered on the carpet. She collected the goatskin rug, the worry beads and the Greek costume dolls, which had been Teddy's gifts to Cathy, and arranged them in tidy piles upon a coffee table.

"Please don't touch a thing!" said Hat, who had collapsed upon the sofa.

"Don't touch a thing!" said Cathy, imitating her mother's sharp voice.

Aunt Harriet stopped as if she had been struck; she was still holding one of the dolls awkwardly in midair. Cathy snatched it from her and cradled it in her arms as if she had rescued it from a wicked witch. Aunt Harriet blinked, fighting back tears. The telephone rang in the hall.

"I'll get it!" cried Becky. She leaped to her feet and rushed out of the room. In a moment she was shouting, "Transatlantic call!"

Hat rose and ran quickly to the kitchen phone; Loren went into Clyde's den; Clyde and Aunt Harriet and Clemente and Cathy joined Becky in the hall.

"This is White Plains, New York," the operator was saying. "We have an overseas call for you. Go ahead, London."

"Teddy!" cried Hat.

"This is London. Go ahead Greece," said London.

"Teddy?" said Loren.

"Hello, can you hear me, California? This is White Plains. Please speak up, California, your party is on the line."

"Teddy!" said Becky.

"London," said White Plains irritably, "can you hear California?"

"We can hear California. Go ahead Greece."

There was a faint wail in the distance, like the sound of an emergency siren heard blocks away.

"We can hear Greece," shouted Hat.

"No need to shout, California. It takes time. The radio signal builds up. No need to shout."

The wail continued, grew slightly louder.

"We can't hear what he's saying," said Hat crossly.

"London, this is White Plains. Greece isn't coming through, London."

"I can hear Greece. Would you like me to communicate?" London said.

"Yes, please," shouted Hat.

"Greece is saying Merry Christmas," said London.

"California, this is White Plains. Greece is saying Merry Christmas."

"Merry Christmas, Teddy," shouted Hat.

"Merry Christmas," shouted Becky and Loren.

"No need to shout, California."

The wail, which had continued, began to recede, then stopped.

"Your party has hung up, California," said White Plains.

"Did he hear us?" said Hat eagerly.

"I'm sure I can't say what he heard. You were all shouting at once," said White Plains.

They returned again to the living room, huddling together as if for comfort. There was a letdown, a slightly funeral air.

"Did he say he received my packages?" Aunt Harriet said anxiously.

"The connection was bad," said Hat. "We really should complain." Then, "Long distance is always unsatisfactory," she added as if to explain something which no one had asked. Then, "He made the call, so everything must be all right."

"I wanted to talk," said Cathy.

"Hush!" said Hat irritably.

"Time for Cathy to go to bed," said Clyde gently. "It's been a busy day for a little girl."

"I don't want to go to bed!"

"Come," said Hat, "I'll read you a story."

"I don't want you to read me a story. I want Clemente to."

"Of course Clemente will read you a story, darling!" cried Clemente. She took the child's hand and led her toward the stairs.

"Mother and Daddy will be in to give you a good-night kiss," said Clyde.

"I want Clemente to give me a good-night kiss!"

"Clemente will, too, dear," said Clemente.

"And it's time for Mother to get her rest, too," said Clyde firmly.

His tone suddenly irritated Hat. He thinks pregnant women are invalids. Her irritation made her feel depressed. She had worked all day — and for what? For a group of silly people, when you came right down to it!

She looks like Catherine, Clyde thought with a start. For a kind of listlessness, an odd melancholy, had replaced her positive, energetic manner. But Catherine could never have organized such a day; Teddy had done all that. Really, she's a delightful mixture of both. But I must take care of her, she's overdone. I probably shouldn't have let her do all this in her condition. He swung an arm around Hat's neck affectionately, trying to guide her away.

Hat broke away. For what, she thought again! Why should she have felt the need to gather this ungrateful family around her when all she had got out of it was fatigue? Why was it up to her? Becky didn't care; Loren only came to be dutiful; Clemente and Aunt Harriet were here because they had no place else to go! A simpler, quieter Christmas would certainly have been better for Cathy. As for Clyde — his movies, his ostentatious carving, his fuss with the wine! All men were babies, she decided. Even Teddy on his island. That awful phone call, like a voice from the grave! Why did I marry? Why did I trap myself like this? she wondered with a shudder.

"I have to check things in the kitchen," she said coldly. She started toward the door, then stopped. An elfin thump, like a tiny electric shock, pulsated in her belly. She stood still, amazed. No one but she had felt it; it was a private communication between her and the mysterious new life to be. The depression vanished; once more she felt important, needed, in command. She smiled at Clyde. "But I do think things went extremely well, don't you?" she said a bit smugly.

"You did a great job, Mother," said Clyde. "Why don't you say good night to everyone and go upstairs and lie down? I'll check the kitchen."

She agreed. Voices cried after her, "Good night, Hat. Such a lovely Christmas."

"Thank you, I thought so, too," she called back.

By seven o'clock, Felix and Loren were left alone in the living room. It had grown dark; only the lights of the Tree flashed on and off.

Such vulgar lights, thought Loren. They're like a neon sign. Not my style, thank God. Still, what did Style have to do with it? It had been a satisfactory Christmas, not half as bad as she had feared. Certainly, if it had been up to her, nothing would have happened at all. She could not have made it come off, she would not have even known how to try. Probably she and Felix would have had a dreary dinner in some Chinese restaurant.

Felix lit his pipe, then took her hand.

I suppose it's important there are people like Hat, who bother, she thought. It was like being President or volunteering for committees. Somebody had to, she supposed. But what for? Still, perhaps for something. Who could tell?

She herself was saving her energies and time for something much bigger, something creative and exciting. She had been told she had "talent," but even if she had not been told, she would have known it herself. But . . . what if, like Teddy, nothing happened? What if, like Catherine, she gave up, took the easy way out? Could she bear it, she wondered. Could she survive? Wasn't it safer, perhaps even nobler, not to have ambitions, to be satisfied by life's everyday moments and little rituals? But what could you do if you weren't constituted that way?

"That book," Felix was saying. His voice was eager, curious. "The one Clemente's mother was writing?"

"Hmm?" She could hear the wheels whirling in his head. It was unbecoming, really. Such a nice, sleepy time — why couldn't he just relax and enjoy it? Why did he always have to figure things out?

"*The Happy Family!*" he persisted.

Why does he want to analyze us, she thought in exasperation. He considered analyzing things his duty, his vocation. Probably she was annoyed more than she should have been because she recognized this failing in herself. But how dreary he was! Lacking any real insight, he would, no doubt, attempt some shallow psychological interpretation, as he had tried earlier in the day when they were briefly alone.

"Hat is so different from you, and yet —?"

"And yet what?" she had answered cruelly.

"Clyde is much older than she, isn't he?"

"Yes."

"Tell me about Clemente?"

"What is there to tell? She's twenty-three, and she nips at the cooking sherry. She's turning into a pathetic, premature old maid."

"Your little sister has a twinkle in her eye. I can imagine she will have to be watched!"

"Becky will be all right," she had answered, her voice cool.

Now, she wanted to say wickedly, "Curiosity killed the cat!" Instead, she removed her hand from his and began to search the room for an ashtray for him. Since Hat and Clyde had quit smoking, ashtrays had disappeared. Failing to find one, she said, "Shall we get some air outside?"

She reached through the draperies and slid open the door; he followed her eagerly on to the deck. The cold air revived them. They stood by the wooden balustrade and looked out at the ranch. Beyond the huge barns and outbuildings were the silhouettes of hills, black humps against a dark gray sky. It was funny, thought Loren, how people who lived surrounded by all of this drew their curtains and shut themselves up in their houses more than city people did.

"Nice layout," said Felix. His ironic tone could not hide his appreciation.

Embarrassed, she turned around and faced the living room. The flickering Tree cast shadows upon the closed draperies. Above them, upstairs, lights were being turned off in the bedrooms. Undaunted, Felix changed his position, leaned against the balustrade, and smoked his pipe.

"But you didn't answer my question." he said after a moment.

"Oh, sorry. What was it again?"

"About *The Happy Family*. Were you really that happy?"

He's in love with my family, she thought with a bored little sigh. He's taken in by the ambiance, the charm. He senses a mystery he wants to understand. But I'm not going to help him, she decided stubbornly. How could I, anyhow? I don't even understand it myself. Why can't he see that? Why doesn't he shut up?

"I suppose we were as happy as most families, probably happier than most," she said impatiently. Oh, dear, I am sounding pompous, but it isn't my fault, he is pushing me into it, putting me on the spot. But there were ways of evading people when they became too insistent. In this case — she slipped her hand back into his and gave it a little squeeze. Because he was nice, when he stuck with things he understood; he was really a very nice man.

Felix laid his pipe carefully down upon the balustrade and put his arms around her and kissed her. Is he kissing me, or some phantom in his head, she wondered as she stood there stiffly. She could sense his disappointment. She was inclined toward priggishness. It was a failing she had, something to be overcome. Well, why not now? With a conscious effort, she drew his face down toward her again, and this time kissed him with affection. No bells rang; there was no resounding crescendo. Yet, on the whole, it was a pleasant sensation. Efforts were often worthwhile, she decided, if one could only learn not to expect too much.

The lights flickered off and on against the curtains. They walked back into the living room, hand in hand.